KIT DAVENPORT #1

THE VIXEN'S LEAD

TATE JAMES

Tate James

The Vixen's Lead: Kit Davenport #1

Copyright © Tate James 2017

All rights reserved

First published in 2017

James, Tate

The Vixen's Lead: Kit Davenport #1

No part of this book may be reproduced, stored in a retrieval system or transmitted in any form or by any means, without the prior permission in writing of the publisher, nor be otherwise circulated in any form of binding or cover other than that in which it is published and without a similar condition, including this condition, being imposed on the subsequent purchaser. All characters in this publication other than those clearly in the public domain are fictitious, and any resemblance to real persons, living or dead, is purely coincidental.

Cover design: Tamara Kokic

Photographer: Michelle Lancaster www.michellelancaster.com

Model: Darcie Hamilton

Editing: Heather Long (content) and Jax Garren (line).

To Cat Amongst The Pigeons Cabernet Sauvignon, Barossa Valley. You, my friend, are an inspiration. Here's to many more late nights of nonsense together

xxx

Chapter One

In the background, the shadowy outline of a naked woman haunted a painting of lilies. The rich imagery held me captive. Reportedly the work was worth a few hundred thousand dollars, but I couldn't decide if it was because of the image or the person who painted it. Maybe both. Whatever the reason, the Beverly Hills gallery had it on its walls, which meant it was without a doubt expensive.

"Nine minutes and thirty-four seconds until security systems are back online. Stop gawking at the paintings and hurry the fuck up!"

How the hell had Lucy known what I was doing? Our

comms were audio only. Still, Lucy had a point. I left the painting and crept down the corridor on silent feet. At the end a large, open room held several ostentatious pieces of jewelry displayed in glass cases on pedestals. They were part of a colored diamond showcase in which the wealthy allowed their prized possessions to be displayed for the common folk to drool over. It was a clear night, and the full moon streamed light through the windows. The moonlight refracted against the jewels and created a rainbow of Christmas lights in the darkness.

Pausing at the entrance to the room, I fished my phone out of the pocket in my black jeans and ran an application labeled "You Never Know," which Lucy had designed to scan areas for hidden security features we might have missed in our mission planning. It took a minute to fully probe the room, and while waiting, I snaked a finger under the short, black wig I wore and scratched at my scalp. Using a disguise was just sensible thieving, but seriously, wigs itched something awful! Maybe next time I would try a hat. The image of myself pulling a job while wearing a top hat or a Stetson made me chuckle.

Seconds later, my screen flashed red with an alert and surprised the hell out of me. It was the first time the app had actually caught something.

"Are you seeing this?" It was a pointless question. She had a mirror image on her computer screen.

"Huh. That definitely wasn't there a week ago when I did a walk through," she muttered, and her furious tapping at her keyboard echoed over the comms. "Okay, it's a laser beam grid linked to a silent alarm that will trigger the security shutters on all external access points. I don't have time to hack into it and shut it down, so…"

I could picture her shrug and sighed. "So, don't trip the lasers, yes? Got it. Send me the map." An intricate web of red lines appeared on my phone, overlaying the camera's view of the room. If I watched the screen and not my feet, it would be possible to avoid the beams.

Conscious of the ticking clock, I carefully started stepping across the floor. All seemed to go well until I got within ten feet of my intended loot. Suddenly my nose started twitching with a sneeze. "Dammit," I hissed, then fought to hold my breath.

"What's going on in there, Kit?" Lucy asked, worry tight in her tone.

I wriggled my nose a few times to shake off the itch before replying, "You know how I often get pretty awesome hay fever in Autumn…?"

Lucy groaned like I was doing this to deliberately test her nerves, but I wasn't trying to tease her. I might actually sneeze.

"I think it's gone," I said, relaxing minutely, and raised my foot for the next step. Of course, Murphy's Law prevailed, and the second I shifted my weight, the urge to sneeze returned full force. I clamped my mouth and nose shut, but I lost my balance even as I tried to swallow my sneeze. My leg rocked into one of the laser beams.

"Shit!"

"Fucking hell, Kit! You have thirty seconds until you are trapped. Get the hell out, now!" Lucy yelled in my earpiece.

Already screwed, I lunged the remaining distance to the display case. The current tenant was a ring with an obnoxiously large, canary yellow diamond surrounded by smaller chartreuse colored diamonds, all inset in a band with pink sapphires. The overall effect was a bit sickening, but who was I to tell the wealthy how bad their tastes were? I often wondered how many of them deliberately wasted their money on tasteless items with obscene price tags simply because they could.

Aware of the ticking clock, I whipped my arm back and smashed my gloved fist straight through the toughened glass. It shattered under the force I exerted. After snatching up the ugly bauble, I dropped a little plastic fox—my signature calling card—in its place.

"Kit, quit dicking around and get out!" Lucy screeched over the line at me. "Twenty-two seconds remaining, don't you dare get caught, or I swear to God I won't let you live this down!"

Satisfied at having grabbed my target, I raced out of the

room and down the corridor, not hesitating before crashing straight through a tall picture window and plummeting thirty-odd feet onto the rooftop of the next building. I tried to break my fall by rolling as I hit. Instead, landed awkwardly on my left shoulder. It popped out of its socket. Hissing with pain, I glanced up at the gallery just in time to see the steel shutters slam closed on all the windows simultaneously.

"Kit," Lucy snapped, barely masking the tension in her voice. "Give me an update; are you clear?"

The evil little devil on my shoulder wanted me to mess with her, but my conscience prevailed. "All clear," I said, then added with a laugh. "Plenty of time to spare; not sure why you were so worried!"

"Any injuries?" A growl underscored her words.

"Nope, I'm totally fine. I mean, if you don't include my shoulder, which is for sure dislocated, then all I have are a few scratches from the glass and a tiny bit of swelling in my knuckles. I got the God-awful ring, though!" I was rather proud of completing the job we had come there for.

"That was too close this time, Kit," Lucy admonished me. "You're bloody lucky you heal so fast, but it's still going to hurt like a bitch getting that shoulder back into place. Get sorted then drop the ring to the courier, and call me if anything goes wrong. Otherwise, I'll see you when you get back. Stay out of trouble."

My best friend occasionally cursed like an Australian ever since she developed a Heath Ledger movie crush. "You know, most people would say 'good luck.' You say, 'stay out of trouble.' Should I be offended?" Teasing her was fun, even if my track record wasn't the cleanest. In my defense, I always got myself out of trouble without too much hassle. Lucy didn't dignify me with a verbal response and left the dial tone as she hung up to serve as her answer.

Tucking my earpiece into a zippered pocket of my leather jacket, I headed over to the A/C unit on the far side of the roof. Using it to leverage my shoulder back into place, I kept my cursing to a minimum. It slid back in with a sickening pop, and the relief had me wavering on my feet. After catching my breath, I brushed some glass out of my wig then swung over the fire escape and descended to the street below. Stripping off my gloves, I blended into the crowd. Even though it was autumn, it was still nowhere near cold enough to be wearing gloves unless committing a crime. I nervously checked the time on my watch. I had a *very* long drive ahead of me to get back to school and still needed to drop the stolen ring off with our middleman.

Chapter Two

Almost an entire day of driving later, I pulled up to the towering, ivy-covered gates of the Cascade Falls Academy, or CFA as it was affectionately known. I yawned heavily and cracked my neck a few times. After clicking the gate opener tucked into my sun visor, I waited for the gates to swing inward so I could crawl up the long driveway to the student parking lot.

My little gray Prius stuck out like a sore thumb in a lot full of Range Rovers, BMWs, and Mercedes. Having spent most of my life in abject poverty in an illegally full foster home, I'd never found spending my adopted father's wealth comfortable. The only reason I allowed him to buy me the car at all was that CFA was in the middle of Nowheresville, Washington. I needed transport to make speedy getaways from my moonlit mischief-making. Not to mention it was the most perfectly unassuming vehicle for an internationally wanted thief to be driving. The best part, though, were the heated seats. A blessing in the winter.

I unfolded myself from the driver's seat and took a minute to stretch my cramped muscles out before unloading my suitcase from the trunk and hauling it through the main dorm to my room. The school itself was a beautiful thing, modeled entirely on the King's College of London, all red brick exteriors with creeping ivy and the inside decked out with polished wood as far as the eye could see. My room was the same one I had lived in for five years, after my adopted father, Jonathan, had first enrolled me here as a gawky thirteen year old.

He must have given the school a serious donation because not only had I kept the same room all this time, but I also enjoyed the luxury of no roommate. He'd told me at the time that privacy would make me feel safer, but I suspect he'd been feeling a healthy dose of guilt at sending me off to boarding school only a scarce six months after adopting me. Not that I blamed him; he was a very important man and the father/daughter routine didn't work well for either of us. Eventually we settled on more of a friendship, or at the very least a loving uncle type relationship. He had circumvented the red tape of the adoption process by providing "evidence" that we were related. His unique position of authority afforded him little leniencies like that, but it was because of his position that I knew I was safe in his care.

Looking longingly at my bed, I debated whether Lucy could wait until after I napped. If I kept her waiting, she'd likely punish me with something awful, like a glass of cold water splashed in my face or a foghorn in my ear. Both of which she'd done in the past. As much as I loved to wind her up, I wanted to see her as we had only managed to catch up via phone all of summer break. Lucifer Jones was the closest thing I had to family. We grew up in the same foster home together, so I'd been over the moon when Jonathan set her up a scholarship to join me at CFA a few years ago.

Leaving my suitcase to be unpacked later, I forced my tired feet to climb the stairs to Lucy's room on the third floor.

Since it was always good to keep my skills sharp, I pulled a couple of bobby pins out of my hair. After picking the lock on Lucy's bedroom door, I burst in without warning. Lucy's shriek as she toppled off the chair she'd been standing on, stacking books on the top shelf above her desk, proved a reward all its own.

Laughing, I didn't avoid the book Lucy flung at me as

she screamed. "Jesus fucking Christ, Kit! I could have really hurt myself, you bloody psycho bitch! Not everyone has your nifty healing trick, you know!" I quickly tugged her bedroom door shut just in case anyone overheard her talking about my somewhat, for lack of a better word, magical ability.

Since I'd turned eleven, I had been able to heal myself from any injury. The catch was that I couldn't make it happen at will. It only seemed to work when I was experiencing a rush of emotion like fear or excitement, which was available in spades on our thieving jobs.

Unluckily, if I got the same rush with no injuries to heal, I would often find myself going into almost an adrenaline overload unless I could burn it off by exhausting myself. In addition to my "nifty healing trick" as Lucy referred to it, I also had some seriously unusual strength and speed.

As far as I could tell, while my talents weren't superhuman, they were far disproportionate to my size and stature. At the time that they had manifested, I'd been a scrawny, malnourished beanpole of a kid, and I packed a punch like a full-grown man. Even now, as a five foot eight girl with just a normal, healthy muscle tone, my strength was equivalent to a serious bodybuilder or martial artist.

Maybe more.

I can't remember the last time I tested the range of my strength, so it was just a guess. As for my speed, again it wasn't something I tested often for fear of attracting unwanted attention, but I'm definitely a lot quicker than the average eighteen-year-old. My *extra abilities* had been a major contributing factor in the degree of difficulty we were able to pull off while thieving.

She attempted a glower, but it came off as adorable on her pixie-like face. She'd changed her hair again over summer break. It was now a bright turquoise blue and cropped very close to her head. She'd even added an eyebrow and nose ring in yet another attempt to look tougher than her 5 foot nothing frame suggested.

"Oh, shush. You missed me and you know it," I teased, the usual rush of love for my pseudo-sister flooding me. She grumbled a bit under her breath as I flopped on her bed and pulled a pillow over my face.

"All right, let's hear it." She recovered her composure swiftly, getting down to business while also yanking the pillow off my face. "Did everything go okay with the drop off to Marius? Also, I assume you had no troubles on the drive back, as you're here in plenty of time for school tomorrow and seem to be in one piece... that I can see..."

"You say that as though I'm reckless." I was somewhat offended by her lack of faith in me, and she raised an eyebrow. "But you are correct; no dramas at all on the drive, if you don't count extreme fatigue from driving nineteen hours straight with nothing better than gas station snacks in my belly."

Lucy rolled her eyes; she'd never been a fan of my melodrama. She knew I wouldn't turn down any food if hungry, no matter how subpar it might be. She was the same. A carryover from our childhood in the foster home where we'd starved between meager meals and savored every little morsel.

"Drop off with Marius didn't happen, though," I admitted reluctantly, bracing for the scolding she was undoubtedly going to give me. "He called right before I got to our rendezvous point and said the client couldn't collect from him until Thursday and he 'isn't comfortable holding *the goods* for that long.'" The middleman was a slimy bastard, but he was a necessary layer of security to keep our less than legitimate transactions from biting us in the ass later.

Lucy stared at me and sat forward, disbelief sharp on her pixie face. "Please tell me you did the sensible thing and stored the ring in a safe location and didn't bring it back to school with you..."

Well, since she told me to tell her the sensible thing, I said nothing and studied the new poster she'd pinned on the wall. Her screech threatened my hearing. "Ugh, you are unbe-*fucking*-lievable sometimes! Give it to me."

I fished the stolen jewelry out of my bra, where I kept it tucked safe in a little velvet pouch, and handed it over to her.

She snatched it out of my hand and spun back to her computer desk, digging around in the drawers until she pulled out one of those little metal detection wands.

"I'm fairly sure we already know it's made of metal, Luce." What was the big deal? She made a dismissive noise in her throat and didn't answer me. A few seconds later, the little wand changed from a steady, slow beep to a high-pitched whine, and Lucy flung it aside in exchange for a magnifying glass.

"Kit, you flaming idiot, this has a tracking device embedded in between these ugly green stones." Before she even finished her sentence, I swiped the ring off her palm and tossed it into the glass of soda sitting beside the computer monitor.

We both sat silent for a moment, watching the brown carbonation bubbles form and reform on the priceless ring in the bottom of her glass.

Finally, Lucy said, "Not... the smartest course of action. I would have suggested leaving the tracker active until you could lead the trail *away* from Cascade Falls, but what's done is done; there's definitely no rescuing a delicate piece of technology like that from the sugary depths of my soda."

"Oh." Once again, I'd acted without thinking. "Shit. Yeah, fair point; that would have been smarter."

Lucy shrugged and waved her hand as if to brush the problem off for another day and changed the subject. "So, I have lined up our class schedules so that we have our lunches together every day. I figure, seeing as you no longer have Ryan to keep you entertained, you're going to have a whole lot of time for hanging out with little old me." She grinned, knowing how annoyed I was that my friend with benefits from the previous year had graduated and left me rather bereft in the romance department.

Due to our negligent upbringing at Mother Suzette's, neither Lucy nor I had really attended school until after we were rescued from her foster home. Sure, she had us enrolled but a few measly bribes had the right people looking the wrong way. When we were first admitted to CFA, we had both been drastically behind in our classwork. We'd worked our butts off to catch up, but the lack left us almost a year older than the rest of our senior class. I'd never had a taste for younger men, and Lucy seemed to take almost perverse pleasure in what was looking like a very dry year ahead of me.

I pouted and pretended to cry. "Lucy, how will I survive with only you to entertain me? And no, do not even think about suggesting I start batting for the other team. That pool is all yours to swim in, thank you very much. Maybe fate will be kind and give us a really hot TA for Mr. Crowley's math class." I perked up at the idea; it could happen. Mr. Crowley was well overdue for retirement at the tender age of eighty-seven, but I suspected he wouldn't take a break until the day he died.

Lucy rolled her eyes as she fished the ring out of her glass. "You look like crap. Go to bed."

"You're so complimentary sometimes, Luce." I laughed, leaving her room. "But you have a point. I'll see you tomorrow, and hopefully that tracker isn't going to cause us too much trouble!"

Chapter Three

The first two days of the school year passed uneventfully, other than finding out that Mr. Crowley hadn't added a sexy TA to assist in his classes. Instead, he'd had a heart attack over the break, which really sucked. Although we had all joked about him teaching until he died, he was also one of our favorites, and his extra tutorials were the only reason I had caught up so fast in his classes. In his place, the school had hired a younger and far too attractive for his own good teacher named Mr. Gregoric. When we'd walked into his class the morning before, Lucy had shot me a look of warning, but it was unnecessary. There were some lines I wouldn't cross, and jeopardizing a man's career was one of them. A girl has to have some standards, right?

During lunch on Tuesday, Lucy and I soaked up the last of the summer sun on the grass in front of the cafeteria. More than forty-eight hours had passed since I'd stupidly drowned the tracking chip, but so far, no black-clad SWAT agents had kicked down my door, so things were looking good. Admittedly, we were less concerned given the fact that even if they did follow the tracker to Cascade Falls, they were hardly going to look twice at a lithe, five foot eight red-headed senior and her minuscule, blue-haired best friend. Thanks to my best friend's cunning forethought back when we'd started our thieving game, we had dropped several false witness statements that would hopefully keep suspicion firmly away from us.

Lucy cast a casual glance around us, her manner relaxed. But I knew her; she was always cautious and never shared anything if others could overhear. "How did the drop go with Marius yesterday?"

"Bit weird," I admitted, frowning and rubbing my forehead to try and ease the brewing headache. "He was super jumpy, but it all went textbook smooth, so God knows what his deal is. We should probably look at using someone new though, just in case?"

"Okay, I will sort someone out. On that subject, we've got a potential job contract."

Propping myself up on my elbows, I studied her expression. "How do we feel about taking another job so soon after trackergate?"

Lucy shrugged. "We've already covered our asses, remember? Besides," she continued, "it looks like an easy, in-and-out data retrieval job with basic security. Some CEO of a rival company wants evidence of tax evasion to shut his competition down, and apparently the files are stored on a secured server in the basement of their office block. It fits our criteria."

I chewed my lip, thinking it over. Our thieving was for more than fun and definitely wasn't for the money. Everything we earned illegally was donated to several children's charities, which we routinely visited to check the funds were being used well.

No, it was entirely a personal vendetta for both of us, and if Lucy said a job "fit our criteria," then it meant the people we were stealing from were on our list. Jobs for the men on our list didn't come up every day, so I just couldn't let the opportunity slide.

"Go ahead and accept; it sounds easy enough."

Closing my eyes and laying back on the grass to soak up a little more of the weak sunlight, I was annoyed when a shadow fell over me and didn't move. Squinting, I found a pair of well-polished Oxfords near my head. Shading my eyes with a hand, I found a handsome man in his mid-twenties with hipster black-framed glasses and floppy brown hair.

"Hi, Mr. Gregoric," I greeted him, curious what had brought him over to us during lunch. "Did you need something?"

"Christina Davenport, right? And Lucifer Jones?" He cocked his head to the side as though unsure, but his gaze was confident.

"Kit," I corrected, "and Lucy."

He smiled smoothly and nodded acknowledgement. "Of course. You two seem to be a bit secluded from the rest of your senior class. I noticed in class you don't ever seem to interact with them beyond what is required."

Lucy and I both stared at him. What point was he trying to make?

"Do you think that has anything to do with your upbringing?" He inquired, rather rudely.

I decided not to respond. How dare he suggest Lucy and I were socially inept due to our abusive childhoods? Lucy seemed to feel the same, and we let the silence sit, allowing it to grow heavier.

"Was there something you needed, Mr. Gregoric?" I said coolly, ending the oppressive quiet and suddenly no longer feeling so friendly. He peered at me for a moment more, and

I could have sworn his eyes briefly filled with the red-brown color of his iris, totally obliterating the whites and stretching the pupils like you'd see on an animal. I gasped in surprise and tried to get a closer look, but the second I blinked he had turned on a charming smile and his eyes were totally normal again, like flipping a switch.

"Yes, sorry, I came over to let you know that Headmaster Spotswood wants to see you after lunch, Kit." The sun must have been making me delirious because his teeth looked awfully sharp when he smiled.

I shook my head to clear what *must* have been light spots on my vision, then nodded in acknowledgement and waited to see if he had anything else to say. He stood there for a few moments more as if debating what to say, but eventually he just nodded awkwardly back at me and left.

"Well, that was fucking weird," Lucy muttered, and I wholeheartedly agreed with her.

"Did you see anything weird with his eyes?" I chewed my lip as I asked the question, not wanting to sound like I was losing my mind.

"No..." she replied slowly. "You've been asking that a lot lately. Is everything okay with you?"

I snorted a laugh. *Where did I even begin? I was literally seeing things.* Ever since my eighteenth birthday, I had been seeing and experiencing all sorts of strange things. Considering I could quite literally heal myself and I had way out-of-proportion speed and strength, if I thought things were strange then they were seriously strange. Still, I didn't need to dump my possible mental breakdown on Lucy's lap, so I just shrugged and gave her a forced smile.

"Yup, all good. Just need to get more sleep."

The bell chimed, signaling the end of our lunch period, so Lucy and I packed up our things and headed back inside. She left me at the door to our next class, and I continued on towards the Headmaster's office. My low heels made a hollow clicking sound against the marble floors as I took my time wandering down the corridor.

Our school uniform code was fairly relaxed about adding your own personal touches, and while I wasn't comfortable spending Jonathan's money on most things, I definitely made an exception for shoes. Maybe I was making up for lost time, having lived in holey hand-me-downs for so long. Either way, my shoe collection was something to be envied. Today I had on my classic pair of low, closed-toe, black leather Louboutin's with a cute ankle strap over my white knee-high uniform socks.

Our Headmaster's office was at the end of a long corridor lined with class photos from the past hundred-odd years as well as oil paintings of the school's founders. Presenting myself to the secretary, I wondered again what he needed to speak with me about so early into the school year. Surely it was too soon to have gotten myself into any trouble. Anything was possible, though. Ancient Ms. Flowers, who looked like she may be fossilized to her office chair, gave me a terse nod and waved towards the closed office door with her perpetually displeased expression.

I tapped lightly on the office door before letting myself in. The office was a lovely room, filled with light from the huge bay window and smelling of old books, thanks to the obligatory collection of encyclopedias stacked on the bookshelf. A short, rotund man with a meticulously trimmed white beard, Headmaster Spotswood looked up as I entered, and smiled warmly. "Kit, I see Nicholas found you!"

I assumed he meant Mr. Gregoric, so I smiled politely and nodded. There were two boys sitting in the chairs in front of the Headmaster's desk, but all I could see from where I stood was that they had very similar haircuts and broad shoulders.

"This is Christina Davenport; she is also a senior and shares some of your classes. She will be taking you on a quick tour of the school this afternoon and will be your go-to for any questions you might have about Cascade Falls Academy while you get settled in." He continued, looking at the two in front of him. I raised an eyebrow at the headmaster, seeing as I wasn't known to be the most responsible student on campus. On the other hand, if it got me out of classes for the afternoon, who was I to question his decisions?

"Kit, I'd like you to meet Caleb and Austin King. They are new students here this year, and as they're already a few days late starting, I would like them to get their bearings this afternoon so they can catch up on classes tomorrow. I trust you will show them everything they need to know." This last sentence was delivered with a stern note of warning in his voice that told me not to fuck around.

I gave him my best butter-wouldn't-melt smile, then my jaw almost hit the goddamn floor when the new students in question stood, then turned to face me. Identical twins in every way I could currently see, Caleb and Austin King were easily the most mouth-wateringly handsome men I had seen in a long time. Actually, ever. Who was I kidding? Cascade Falls was a very small town, and they definitely did not grow them like this around here. Over six feet tall with dark hair, longer on top and shaved up the sides, and builds more suited to firefighters or Navy Seals or other equally sexy occupations.

They definitely did not look at all like high school seniors. I fought my way back from my perusal and cleared my throat a couple of times before I felt confident enough to speak.

In the meanwhile, one of them watched me with an amused, emerald green gaze, and the other just looked bored and a bit pissed off. Giving myself a minute to gather my scattered thoughts, I instead turned back to the portly administrator with a bright smile in place.

"Sure thing, Mr. Spotswood. Do you have a copy of their schedules so I can point out the right classrooms?" Spotswood raised his eyebrows, looking surprised at my helpful suggestion, but held out a slip of paper to me that made me lean past the twins to accept. Being in such close proximity to two such good-looking guys was making my skin tingle, so I politely nodded to the Headmaster and gave the new students a small, tight smile before leading them out of the office.

As we passed the pursed face of the Headmaster's secretary, I attempted to break the ice and clarify their names, as I was likely to get them mixed up if I left it any longer.

"So, Austin," I said to the twin who looked less bored and annoyed, hoping I had remembered who was who. "Where did you guys move from?"

"Caleb," he corrected, giving me a lopsided grin, and I made a quick mental note that Caleb was the friendly one. "And we come from all over. Here and there, you might say."

My face flushed with heat under his intense gaze and I broke eye contact, starting swiftly down the hallway and hoping they followed. One of the twins released an appreciative hum. Walking ahead of them was giving them a prime view of my ass, and all of a sudden my skirt seemed way too short. Or not short enough. I was undecided. Either way, my imagination could feel their gazes on my derrière like laser beams. Taking a deep breath, I straightened and pasted on my most polite and welcoming mask as we approached the first set of classrooms.

"So, in this wing we have all of our math and science classes, and you will be in…" I consulted their class lists in my hand. *Shit, they were both in Trigonometry with me and Lucy; different Anatomy class though.* I stopped briefly outside the door to my usual Trig class and could see Lucy making faces at me through the glass. "Room 309, right here and room 311 for Anatomy, which is two doors down. You'll find CFA is pretty relaxed with seniors, which is cool. We are allowed to take lunch and study periods off campus and can come and go as we like on weekends and before curfew. You just need to sign in and out with the gate security."

Caleb made a polite noise of acknowledgement, but Austin didn't look like he was even listening, which got under my skin just a little. I continued rattling off dry facts about the school as I lead them through an ivy covered outdoor walkway and towards the adjoining Arts building where they would have English and History classes.

"Do you have a lot of wildlife around the school?" Caleb's question made me jump a little, as neither twin had actually spoken since I'd started my rambling commentary about the school, and I stopped to look around for what wildlife he was talking about. Across the grass from us, a large red fox sat placidly under a tree, like he was watching us while his bushy tail flicked up and down rhythmically.

"That's weird," I murmured, frowning, "Foxes are primarily nocturnal animals; it's pretty rare to see them outside during the day and even rarer when there are people around. I hope he's okay..." *Maybe I should see if I could get him some food or something. It would be rude not to, considering I was using his image for my secret identity, The Fox.* I could imagine hunger would be the main reason such a skittish animal would be out in daylight. As I was racking my brain for what a fox might like to eat, a loud, exaggerated yawn interrupted. Whipping around to face these two godlike men, I narrowed my eyes, temper flaring at the surlier of the two, whom I had no doubt was the yawner.

"I'm sorry; am I boring you?" I snapped at him.

"Oh, thank God." He rolled his eyes dramatically. "I thought you hadn't noticed!"

Before I could bite back at him, his twin stepped between us and smiled blindingly, drawing my attention back to him. "What my charming brother means to say, is that schools are fairly much the same no matter where you go. You see one, you've seen them all. Don't you think?"

"I suppose so..." I hedged—not that I would have any clue, seeing as this was my first school.

"Tell us more about the people. That's the part that

changes between schools. What are the teachers like?" Caleb fell into step with me as I resumed my path toward the next building.

"For the most part, they all seem to have one foot in the grave. Except Mr. Gregoric, but he only started here a couple of days ago, so I don't know anything about him." *Except that he gives me the creeps.* "He seems pretty young, maybe only just out of college? He has a few admirers among the students already, too."

The twins appeared to perk up with interest at the mention of our new teacher. *Maybe they're gay?* For the first time since meeting them, Austin seemed to be showing an emotion other than bored and annoyed.

"Where did he come from, do you know?" He seemed really eager to hear my answer, and when I flicked a confused glance at Caleb he looked almost… excited? *Why were the hot ones always a bit strange?*

I shrugged. "He started with this term; he didn't give me his resume."

Austin snorted derisively, muttering something. I sucked in a deep breath and fought the urge to demand he speak up so that I could continue our little scrap. I had only just met him, so his dismissive attitude shouldn't be ruffling my feathers as badly as it was.

"How about anyone else in this town?" Once again,

Caleb smoothly steered the conversation. "Anyone stand out from the ordinary? Has anyone got any particularly impressive skills?"

I was beginning to see a pattern with these brothers. Austin caused friction, and then Caleb smoothed it out. I shook my head in reply. "Cascade Falls locals are so unexceptional it's almost unbelievable. As for the school, it's one of the most expensive schools in the country, so most of the student body is made up of spoiled rich kids. Again, no one particularly out of the 'Cascade Falls ordinary' unless you count Anna Greengate's net worth." *And my own talents...* I smiled. In a sea of the rich and beautiful, I didn't stand out as being anything out of the ordinary, and I used my anonymity. I thrived being a walking contradiction.

Caleb cocked his head, as though he noticed my smile, and I briefly worried he might question me further until his brother interjected once more. "Cal, this is a waste of fucking time. Are we done here, Christina? If you don't mind, we have been travelling a lot and still need to unpack if we are actually going to attend this ridiculous school tomorrow."

"It's *Kit*," I gritted out, my temper bubbling. "And I can happily be done here. Which dorm are you in? I will point you in the right direction, and you can be off on your merry way."

"Ah, we aren't in the dorms," Caleb supplied. "We moved here with our cousin River. He's renting a house not far from town, so we decided to just stay with him rather than move into a drafty dorm." I couldn't argue with that choice; the dorms were pretty drafty.

"Great, so we're done?" Not waiting for my answer, Austin stalked off in the direction of the student parking lot without a backward glance to check if his brother was following. "See you around, Christina."

Surprisingly, Caleb didn't immediately follow and still watched me like he couldn't figure me out. Not that he would be able to, no matter how long he stared. I took pride in being an enigma.

"Can I borrow your phone to send a message?" he asked suddenly. "I left mine in one of the packing boxes a few days ago and still haven't found it."

It seemed like a pretty odd thing to do, but I would look like a bit of a bitch if I called him out for being a liar on such a trivial topic. So, I reluctantly handed my phone over. He tapped at it for a minute before thanking me and handing it back.

"I'll see you tomorrow, Kitty Kat!" He flashed me another blinding grin and winked before chasing after his crabby sibling.

I stared after them for a minute, more than a little off balance as though I'd been caught in a freak storm. Shaking it off, I headed back to my room. The headmaster had said to take the whole afternoon to show the King twins around, so I was going to make the most of my suddenly free time and take a nap.

On my way back to my room, I hunted through my phone to see what Caleb might have needed to use it for but found no unfamiliar messages in my outbox. Luckily, this phone held zero personal information on me, as Lucy ran routine data wipes and we used different phones for Fox business, so it didn't really matter what he had wanted it for... right?

Chapter Four

During Lucy's planning for our next job, she identified the easiest access point as being from the roof. In preparation, I decided to brush up on my free climbing skills because the best way up to a roof from the outside of a building was to climb.

About a half hour drive outside of Cascade Falls was a rocky cliff that was perfect for climbing, so I headed out there, parked several miles further up the mountain from my intended climbing wall, and trekked down through the rocky terrain. I followed the small, winding track zigzagging back and forth down the shallower side of the cliff and dropped my bag at the bottom. Staring up at the rocky wall, I plotted the best route up.

I'd chosen this wall in particular as it was the closest in structure to what the side of a building would be: dead vertical with only very small hand and foot ledges. Fishing out a small bag of chalk, I powdered my hands, stretched my muscles, then strapped my bag back on and got moving.

It had been a while since I last climbed, but it came back naturally. The usual rush of adrenaline, which accompanied dangerous activities like climbing a cliff without ropes, surged through me. The feeling coursed through my body, and I shivered in pleasure, welcoming it back like an old friend. Lucy suspected I might be just the slightest bit addicted to the feeling, but it was a hazard of the job, and really, there were worse things to be addicted to, right?

When I was halfway up the wall, my phone vibrated in my pocket. Ignoring it for now, I kept climbing steadily. It buzzed again and then again, intruding on my concentration. Blowing out a breath, I paused, waiting for it to stop. When it stayed silent for a minute, I resumed my climb only to have it buzz again several times in quick succession as soon as I was within a few feet of the top. Gritting my teeth, I hauled myself up over the top then rolled to lay flat on my back. I yanked out my phone to see what was so important that Lucy would be blowing up my phone when she knew I was climbing, but instead, eight new messages from a number I didn't recognize surprised me. The name declared it *Man of my Dreams*. Caleb must have sent himself a message when he borrowed my phone then stored his number in mine. Annoying? A little. It was also amusing.

Hey. Look. It's the man of your dreams texting you!

Why have you been avoiding me? I thought you were supposed to be helping us acclimatize to CFA.

You're not a very good student guide, you know...

Let's hang out! What are you doing tonight?

I hear the common room at the dorms has a pretty great movie room set up. Shall we watch a movie?

Okay cool, I assume your lack of answer means YES CAL I WOULD LOVE TO so I'll meet you there at 6pm.

...clothes optional

Kidding! (but not really)

The last message included a winky face emoji and I laughed. His messages had all arrived within a minute of each other, clearly not giving me a chance to respond at all even if I hadn't been clinging to a cliff face like a barnacle.

He was right, though. I had been avoiding him for the past few days. Or rather, his brother, and as he and Austin seemed to be a package deal, I had, by association, been avoiding Caleb. Other than a few classes that Lucy and I both shared with them, I was doing pretty well with steering clear. Something about the two of them made me a little uneasy, and I wasn't sure if it was just my exceptionally out of character lack of game when it came to them or if it was the way they seemed to be watching everything just a little more closely than others did.

Biting my lip, I composed a sarcastic response then hit send. *Can't sorry. I'm washing my hair tonight.*

My phone immediately pinged with his reply, *Great! I'll join you!* and another winky face. I groaned—should have seen that one coming. Somehow, I got the feeling he was not giving up easily.

Fine. Meet you in the media room at 6pm. Bring pizza. Also make sure you reserve it or someone else will get in first. I sent the reply then pushed to my feet. The earlier adrenaline still coursed through me—possibly why I gave in to Caleb so easily—but it needed to be burnt off, so I began the steep uphill hike back to my car.

I had worked out the hard way that if I tried to get by just ignoring the increased adrenaline, the effect didn't subside naturally. I always ended up overloading and passing out.

When I say pass out, I don't mean faint. I mean I'd be out cold for a good three days and wake up with a monster migraine. Luckily, I'd only needed to experience that delightful effect twice before working out how to manage it. The overload was the primary reason why Ryan and I had worked for so long.

Despite being a bit of an asshole, an entitled rich kid, he had been genuinely interested in me. His feelings worked well in helping me with my frequent need to burn energy. Sadly, with his absence I would have to make do with substitutes like the grueling trek back up to my car instead. At least I would be staying pretty fit. Thunder rumbled in the distance, and I picked up my pace.

I despised storms.

I made it to my room with enough time to shower off the sweat in my private en suite, *thank you Jonathon*, before the sharp knock at my door. Still wrapped in my towel, I answered and found all six-and-a-bit feet of the delicious-looking Caleb leaning in the doorframe.

"I'm roughly ninety-nine percent sure I said to meet me in the common room." I maintained a stern expression and held back my amusement at his boldness. "How did you know which room was mine anyway?"

Caleb ignored my question and dragged his gaze from my toes to the top of the towel gathered at my breasts. When he finally reached my gaze, his eyes were hot. Breath catching in my throat, I clenched my thighs together and tried to keep my expression bland. At least he had the decency to look a bit guilty.

"I came to let you know the media room is all ours and see what sort of pizza you wanted. But now I see I really should have joined you for that hair washing idea. I thought we were joking, Kitty Kat!" Despite his broad smirk, the words were delivered with a purring, suggestive undertone that made my stomach flip.

Fighting the grin twitching at the corner of my lips, I shoved him out of my doorway. Once he was clear, I shut it and called, "Pepperoni! Extra cheese!"

Taking my time getting dressed and blow drying my hair, I ignored the little voice in my head questioning why I was putting so much effort into my appearance to simply watch a movie in the media room. But just in case, I texted Lucy and invited her along. Something about Caleb screamed trouble. *Better to keep him at arm's length... for now.*

Aiming for the relaxed look, I chose soft gray sweatpants and a black long sleeve top with a V-neck. The cut of the top offered a generous view of my perfectly adequate cleavage, but it was purely a coincidence, I swear. I added a light layer of mascara before heading out to find Caleb in front of the movie screen where the pizzas must have just arrived.

The smell of cheesy pizza made my mouth water and my stomach growl, so I hurried over and dropped onto the floor beside him. He'd laid out cushions so we could access the food easier.

Caleb chuckled. "I guess I'm choosing the movie then?"

I waved my already claimed slice of pizza toward the bookshelf holding hundreds of DVDs beside the projector screen.

He took a minute browsing the options while I started chomping my way through some pizza. Finally, he held up three cases. *The Notebook*, *Schindler's List*, and *Blade*. I made a face at him—what asylum did he escape from? My options were chick flick, sob story, and an action movie? Action movie, duh. Shaking my head, I pointed at *Blade*. He grinned and slid it into the player before rejoining me on the floor.

"Good choice." He smirked.

"Like there was a choice," I snorted. *"The Notebook* and *Schindler's List*? Really?"

He gave me a wide-eyed innocent look. "I don't know where your movie tastes run; that is the whole point of hanging out... to get to know you."

"Mmm hmm," I hummed, still questioning his sanity because he had looked more than a little reluctant to put *The Notebook* away. "You're lucky you brought pizza." I took another huge bite of said pizza and thanked the stars Caleb's snarky brother wasn't crashing our party. I doubted I would have been anywhere near as comfortable feeding my cheese addiction in front of him.

With a snort, he reached over to wipe the corner of my

mouth. "You've got a little sauce..." Then, as though we were trapped in some corny chick flick, leaned in closer. His face mere inches from mine, our breath mingled. It was the most clichéd move in the world, but holy crap. My whole body seemed to quiver in anticipation.

Hell, even his body heat seemed to radiate against my lips. He moved a fraction closer, and I waited impatiently, begging him to just close the gap and kiss me for God's sake! Perfect movie-like moments didn't just present themselves every day.

"Hey guys! What are we watching? Ooooh, *Blade*! Good choice. Yay, pizza too!!" Lucy plonked down on Caleb's other side and started talking a million miles an hour, shocking me into jerking backwards like I'd been burned. *What the Hell, Kit? What happened to keeping him at arm's length? Idiot.*

Caleb sighed, still watching me like a predator, before slowly sitting back and turning his attention to Lucy. "Hey Luce, I didn't know you were joining us tonight."

Lucy shrugged and helped herself to my pizza, the bitch. "I know. Kit called me in as a chaperone 'cause she doesn't think she can resist that sexy body of yours." Yep, my best friend was a major bitch. I was going to kill her.

The sexy boy in question got a sly look on his face, like the cat who caught the canary, and drawled, "Really... how interesting..." Almost gloating, he glanced at me, and heat scalded my face. Damn them both, now I was blushing. "Isn't that interesting, Kit?"

"Oh, shut it, you know you're hot. As for *you*,"—I glared daggers at the blue haired imp beside Caleb—"*you* and I will be discussing this later!"

Lucy just giggled and hit play on the movie, then shushed us as it began.

The three of us watched Wesley Snipes kill vampires for a while in companionable silence and polished off the rest of the pizza. About a third of the way in, Caleb stretched like a giant cat. His shirt rose, revealing the edges of a tattoo curling down the side of his chiseled lower abdominal muscles. Curious about what it depicted, I tilted my head to try and snag a better look. At his amused hum, I snapped my gaze up to see he had caught me gawking. Done with being embarrassed, I met his gaze and asked, "What? I was appreciating the tattoo artist's skill. What is it anyway?"

He smirked then lifted his long sleeve top to give me a better look, and I realized how drastically wrong my plan had gone. So very wrong. But so right.

Shit, did I just drool a little? I wiped my mouth while pretending to scratch my face. *Nope, all clear. Just mental drool.* Because fuck, the boy was ripped. The tattoo in question turned out to be an intricate sprawl of mandalas and lotus flowers that hugged his side and disappeared both higher and lower than I could see. After an inappropriate amount of time ogling at Caleb's naked skin, I forced my gaze away and caught his smug look.

Clearing my throat, I said the only thing I could think of that wouldn't make me sound like I wanted to lick him from head to toe. "Your tattoo artist is very talented. That's a beautiful piece."

His smirk broadened into a full grin. Laughing softly, he dropped his shirt back into place. No mistaking it. Caleb knew exactly what he was doing.

"Guys," Lucy snapped, "Shut up and watch the movie." She took her vampire flicks very seriously and frequently kicked me out if I fidgeted or talked too much.

Even though we went back to watching the movie, I wasn't seeing it. Then his hot breath tickled my neck as he whispered, "I can show you the rest of my ink later." The invitation in his voice left no doubt that to see the rest, clothes would need removing.

I blushed and kept my face forward. Though I refused to answer, it didn't stop the warm shiver racing through my blood.

For the rest of the movie I remained hyperaware of his warm shoulder pressed into mine and every shift of his body. It was maddening. The steadily increasing sound of rain pattering against the windows only amped my distraction. A flash of lightning flooded the room with bright light, followed swiftly by a deafening crack of thunder. Despite having expected it since the storm began, the sound still jarred loose an unpleasant memory. No matter how much I didn't want to remember, I couldn't stop the tension coiling in my muscles or the rapid race of my heart as the past pulled me back into that hellish room. I squeezed my eyes shut tightly and clenched my fists, willing myself back to the present.

"You okay, Kit?" Lucy asked cautiously. She knew how much I hated storms and, even more so, the sound of thunder. I paused a moment before nodding tightly, trying to breathe normally. *It's just thunder.* I repeated the mantra to myself over and over. *It's just thunder.*

Caleb peered at me with a worried expression on his face. "What's going on...?" Another loud crack sounded outside, and I jerked. Locking my jaw, I sucked my lips against my teeth. It was the only way to keep the scream inside. He pressed a gentle hand on my shoulder but glanced at Lucy, not me.

"Kit... doesn't like storms..." she hedged. I needed to get it together. I checked her expression, and her eyes asked me if she could explain further, but I shook my head frantically.

"I'm fine," I squeaked out eventually, forcing my jaw to relax long enough to let out the words. "It's just the thunder."

"You're not fine," Caleb admonished. "You're trembling." He wrapped one of his thick arms around me and tugged me closer into him. I'd have to have been dead to not experience some comfort while secure in his warm embrace. Then the thunder cracked overhead, and I tensed again. His arms tightened as the lights flickered, and then we were plunged into darkness. A pathetic squeak escaped, and I clenched my eyes closed.

"Kit, are you okay here with Caleb for a bit?" Worry discolored Lucy's tone. "I need to go and disconnect my computers so they don't get fried if there's a power surge." Her concern made sense; it had happened before. She'd lost a huge amount of data, and it had taken months to recover.

"Go," I whispered and hated the strained note in my voice, but I didn't move from where I curled into Caleb's hard body. He rubbed soothing circles on my back. Slowly, my shaking subsided, but relaxing took a while. Every time the thunder cracked, I flinched despite my best efforts to keep it in check.

Eventually the thunder and lightning eased, leaving torrential rain and howling wind to continue raging alone.

"Are you okay?" Caleb asked quietly, his mouth near my ear. "Do you want me to go and find some candles or flashlights or something?"

I shook my head against his chest. "I'm good. I don't mind the dark; it's just the thunder."

He slid an arm under me and pulled me the rest of the way onto his lap, hugging me tightly. "Do you want to tell me about it? That was a pretty strong reaction for an ordinary fear of storms."

I said nothing for a while, chewing my lip and debating how much to say. On the one hand, I felt absurdly comfortable with Caleb. Much more so than I should have after only knowing him less than a week. While I didn't get along with his brother, something about Caleb screamed that he was trustworthy. Almost as loudly as it shouted that he was trouble. On the other hand, some memories were just better off dead. I settled on a middle ground and said, "It sounds exactly like the crack of a whip."

Caleb was silent, maybe waiting to see if I would elaborate, but I could feel the tension in his muscles. I said nothing more, and he didn't push. Neither of us moved from our embrace, and he continued to rub circles up and down my spine until Lucy returned with an armload of candles and a box of matches. Of course our school would have candles but not flashlights; God forbid they enter the twenty-first century.

She glanced at me as she placed the candles then lit them. Aware of her concern, I nodded. Once the room was bathed in candlelight, Lucy retrieved a Monopoly box. "We need a distraction until the power is back on."

I groaned because I was *useless* at Monopoly, but reluctantly climbed out of Caleb's lap and selected the little dog as my playing piece. I used a different one every time in the hopes that one would give me good luck, but it had yet to happen and I was on an uninterrupted losing streak against Lucy.

"Also, Kit, on my way back I saw that fox lurking around again outside your room. I warned you not to feed it." She was trying to scold me, but I knew she was just as amused as I was that a wild fox, of all animals, had seemingly adopted me.

"The same one we saw the other day?" Caleb asked, and I nodded.

"I went back later and left him some food. I figured he must have been pretty hungry to be out in the day, and now he keeps coming back for more." I quickly sorted out the game cards and put them in place on the board, then passed Caleb the dice. "Your roll."

For the next two hours, I managed to hemorrhage money to the Monopoly bank and Caleb gave Lucy a solid run for top spot, but she eventually won. She always won at Monopoly.

Bitch.

I was definitely not a gracious loser when it came to board games. The lights popped back on halfway into our second game. The clocks blinked, but it was after midnight and probably a good time to call it a night.

Lucy and I walked with Caleb to the dorm lobby where he high fived Lucy then grabbed me in a tight hug, lingering just a fraction longer than a platonic friend hug. Letting go, I read the twinkle of mischief in his eyes, but all he said was, "I'll see you on Monday." Then he was out the door and sprinting through the rain to his car.

We watched him drive away before Lucy turned to me and snickered. "You're in so much trouble."

Not disagreeing, I groaned, and we headed upstairs for our own beds.

Chapter Five

The weekend ended far too quickly, as always, and when classes started again on Monday morning, I found myself trying to smother a flutter of excitement that my first class of the day was with Caleb. Deep down, my resolve to steer clear of him was really not all that strong. Especially if he made good on his offer to show me the rest of his ink.

Fuck, Kit, it's too early to be drooling over your imagination. I snickered quietly at my own scolding and, with my hip, pushed open the door to the class, as my arms were full of books and a thermal coffee cup. I was way too early, which was entirely unlike me, but the prospect of seeing my green-eyed friend had driven me out of bed much quicker than usual.

"Good morning, Christina." The husky voice seemed to come from nowhere, and I almost dropped my coffee.

"Jesus, fuck! Austin!" My heart was beating so fast it was halfway into my throat, and my temper flared. I hated being surprised; it made me feel vulnerable, and that was the last thing I ever wanted to be again. Despite their identical appearances, there was *no way* Caleb would have called me Christina. "Maybe warn a person when you're about to scare the shit out of them? Fucking hell, I almost lost my coffee!"

"Aw, poor little Princess would have had to go without coffee! The travesty of it all!" His mocking smirk didn't help my temper, *and did he just call me Princess? Pretty sure that was meant as an insult. Rude.*

I huffed and chose a desk as far from Austin's as possible. God only knew why we had gotten off on such a bad foot, but he was making no attempt to rectify it, so why should I?

"Why are you here so early, Austin? Class doesn't start for another twenty minutes."

"Why are *you?*" He countered, and I rolled my eyes at his childish response.

I made an attempt at taking the higher ground by not replying, instead pulling out my textbook and stationary. His fingers drummed noisily on the desk, and I ground my teeth together to stay quiet.

"So, what did you and my brother get up to Saturday night?" Apparently, Austin was in the mood to chat. "We were supposed to go out with our cousin, but he said something urgent had come up. Wouldn't tell us what."

That struck me as a bit odd; it wasn't like pizza and a movie was anything to keep secret. *Maybe it was just an excuse not to go out with the cousin?* To Austin I just shrugged, "What makes you think he was with me then?"

"Please. You must think I'm stupid. He came home after midnight with a huge dopey grin all over his face, and given how he can barely shut up about you, it didn't take a rocket scientist to figure out who he'd been with." His words were spat with a level of disgust that made me frown. *What the hell was his deal?*

"What's your problem, Austin? I thought maybe you were just pissed about being at a new school, but I saw you with your hordes of admirers at lunch on Friday. You're nice to them. So what the fuck did I do to piss you off?"

"My *problem*," he started, but cut off when another student entered the classroom. Candace Watson was pushing hard to beat Lucy for valedictorian, so it was no surprise she was arriving early to class. She sat in her usual seat, directly in front of the teacher's desk, and started meticulously lining up her pencils with an OCD level of precision.

As Austin glared shards of ice across the room at me, making my skin tingle, I turned my attention to Candace who was carefully lining her notebook up perpendicular to her pencils and totally unaware of the conversation she'd interrupted. She was so lost in her own world she probably didn't even realize we were in the room, and she definitely didn't notice how close her can of energy drink was to the edge of her desk.

"Candace, watch out—" My warning came too late as her wrist bumped into the can, sending it flying and soaking her bag with sticky yellow liquid. The poor thing let out a horrified scream, diving to grab the can, but the damage was already done. I could already see the drink pooling on top of her perfectly color-coded notebook.

"No! No no no no no…" She sobbed, frantically trying to shake the book dry, and I rushed over to help her dry it off with my cardigan. It was warm enough inside the class not to need it, and I could get it laundered later.

"Hey, it's okay," I soothed when her panicked breathing sped up enough that she might hyperventilate. "Look, it's not too bad. Just take it down to the restroom and pop it under the hand dryer?" My suggestion was apparently not enough to calm her down as her eyes began welling up and her chin trembling like she might burst out crying any second.

Out of nowhere, the glass fishbowl sitting on the teacher's

desk behind where I was crouched exploded. The back of my head was showered with glass as the water gushed out, carrying Sushi and Roll, the class goldfish, out onto the floor where they flopped around desperately. I sat stunned for a moment, trying to work out what the hell had just happened, while Candace screamed and took off out of the room in tears.

"What the fuck was that?" Austin asked from above me, having smoothly scooped up Sushi and Roll and dropped them into a vase of flowers on the windowsill.

"I have no idea." *But weird, unexplained crap like this was becoming far too frequent. This was definitely not just in my head.*

"You must have bumped the desk or something, you klutz," he sneered. "You should really be more careful; that glass could have hurt someone."

With almost comical timing, the rest of the class began showing up at that moment, cutting off my angry retort. Caleb stepped into the room with Lucy and gave me a confused look. I didn't blame him either; it probably was a bit strange to find me on my knees in a puddle of water and scattered glass with Austin glaring at me from above with folded arms.

"Fuck it. I need to get this glass out of my hair," I grumbled, taking Caleb's hand when he offered it to pull me up, "Let Mrs. Williams know I will be ten minutes late?"

"Sure thing…" he murmured. "I take it Austin can fill us in?"

Austin snorted. "Nothing to fill in. The Princess is a major klutz and knocked over the fishbowl."

I rolled my eyes and flipped him off before leaving the room to get cleaned up. I knew I hadn't knocked that bowl over, though. No one had.

With the fish bowl incident happening so soon after I thought I saw Mr. Gregoric's eyes change, I found myself spending the rest of the week on edge. I was constantly looking too closely at everyone and everything and jumping skittishly at every loud noise, which didn't go unnoticed.

Austin seemed to always be around with a snide remark if I flinched when a door banged too loudly or chalk squeaked sharply on the blackboard. I was still questioning whether it had been my imagination. Had I actually bumped the fishbowl? It was beginning to make me feel paranoid. Not knowing what had caused my *abilities* made me worry what side effects there might be on my brain, and if I actually was imagining all this weird shit, it didn't look good for my mental health.

By the end of the week, my patience had worn dangerously thin, and I didn't think I could handle another hour of playing nice with Austin for his brother's sake. For whatever reason, he had decided I was public enemy number one, and I was done with voluntarily taking his shit. In the interest of avoiding conflict with Caleb, I decided to simply avoid them both and take lunch off campus.

The first half of the day went smoothly; I didn't share any classes with either of the twins before lunch and managed to duck out of the main building as most students filtered towards the cafeteria. I took the long way around to the student car park in order to avoid the lawn where we often ate, in case Lucy spotted me. I was leaving her behind as a sacrificial lamb because she owed me for the stunt she'd pulled last weekend on movie night with Caleb, telling him I had asked her to chaperone. Talk about killing my game, or what little game I had left these days. Caleb, and even Austin to a lesser extent, seemed to have brought out the awkward in me.

Just as I came around the back of the science building, Caleb's familiar voice trapped me, and I pulled up short.

"—really, Austin?" He snorted. "You're hardly one to talk about taking liberties; you've had your tongue so far down Anna Greengate's throat this week you're practically breathing for her."

"Hey. I will have you know that she's extremely useful, which is more than I can say for your little *girlfriend*." Austin sneered this last part, and I could almost picture the look of disgust he so often wore. "What's going on there anyway, bro? I seriously hope you're hitting that because from where I'm standing, she doesn't look useful for much more."

"Shut the fuck up, you ass. You've just got your panties in

a bunch because she reminds you of Peyton." Anger tightened his voice, and I wanted to give him a high five for sticking up for me. Who the hell was Peyton?

Austin growled, then spat, "*Peyton* has nothing to do with this. I just think you need to stop thinking with your dick and focus on why we're here. Now, why don't we cut out of afternoon classes and spend some time in Anna's dorm room? She's been begging for a bit of King Twin Treatment." Ugh, gross. He wasn't serious, surely?

"Ugh, no." Caleb echoed my disgust in his grunt, making me proud.

"Come on, bro. It's been ages... just this once? She's been hinting that she knows something interesting but won't give it up until she gets some." Austin, the dickhead, switched tack and tried cajoling. "Think of the greater good, man."

Caleb sighed heavily. "Fine, I just need to stop by and see Kit first, and then I'll meet you there." *What?*

"Atta boy." The satisfaction in Austin's voice made me want to hit him. What a pig! And Caleb agreeing to whatever the 'King Twin Treatment' was, although it was not hard to imagine... Gross. The idea of both luscious twins in bed didn't turn me on... Not with their ripped bodies and gorgeous ink. I'd bet Austin had tattoos, too...

Woah, where the hell did that come from?

Shaking my head, I snapped myself out of that weird

mental safari. The last thing I planned to do was lust after Austin. Then my heart sunk. Caleb planned to get freaky with Anna. It was stupid; it wasn't like we were dating or anything. Guess all the flirting and banter meant nothing. I'd been friend-zoned and the idea somehow made me sick to my stomach. *Okay stop it, Kit. This is a blessing. You knew you needed to keep your distance from him anyway.*

Fighting the crushing disappointment, I checked to verify the coast was clear then strode to my car. Time to get the hell out of here.

Chapter Six

CALEB

Rolling my aching shoulders, I cracked my neck and rubbed a hand over my eyes. Fuck me, it had been a long day. I can't believe Austin talked me into that crap with Anna. All I wanted was to go and hang out with Kit. I had spent an insane amount of time with her since arriving at CFA, but it never seemed enough, despite Lucy jokingly calling me their third musketeer, which was pretty flattering, considering.

"Oh quit it, Cal. It wasn't even that difficult, and you know it." I loved my twin, I swear I did, but sometimes I honestly wanted to deck him. The "King Twin Treatment," as Austin liked to call it, was nothing quite as bad as it sounded. We had discovered a year or so ago that loads of girls fantasized about having a threesome with identical twins, but when push came to shove they rarely went through with it. The anticipation and lead up, the flirting and dirty talk, always seemed to be enough to have girls spilling their guts on any questions we managed to subtly slide in.

"It was exhausting. It always is, putting on a show like that. You know I'm not as good of an actor as you. And her information wasn't even worth it! What did we learn? That the gym teacher turns a blind eye to students cutting class if they pay him and that Mr. Gregoric is using a false identity? That could be for a million reasons. She gave us shit, and you know it." I was constantly snapping at Aus these days, even without meaning to. Ever since we'd arrived at CFA, he had been acting like a total dick. The way I'd heard him speak about Kit made me want to throttle him. The reaction concerned me, considering it was a pretty extreme feeling of protectiveness for a girl I barely knew.

"Whatever, bro," Aus muttered, but I could tell by the tightening of his mouth that he was disappointed.

"You know she's probably going to tell the whole school that she slept with both of us." I shuddered at the thought. Not that I didn't like occasionally sharing with my brother—we shared DNA for God's sake—but I would just never go there with Anna Greengate. Something about the high-pitched, screeching sound of her voice made my skin crawl. The fact that Aus didn't seem bothered by her spoke volumes to how messed up he still was from Peyton's bullshit. Austin was already walking a thin line by making out with Anna in public, but at least I knew my brother had enough standards not to have actually followed through on half the shit she was bragging about.

"So?" My dickhead other half put on a mulish look. "Why are you suddenly so concerned with what these people think of you? We will hopefully be gone from here soon, so what difference does it make if they think you're a man-whore? Or is it a certain clumsy, airheaded redhead that you're worried about?"

I punched him in the arm, a bit harder than playful but not hard enough to make him hit back. Asshole had a point; I *was* worried about Kit hearing Anna's bullshit. I had looked for her at lunch, but Lucy had said she was studying. Clearly a lie, but I couldn't call her out on it without being a dick.

"Whatever, bro," I repeated his line back at him, not wanting to have yet another argument about my friendship with Kit. We had done that enough since meeting her, and it was getting old. I knew we wouldn't be in Cascade Falls for long, but I also didn't see the harm in enjoying myself while we were here.

Being around Kit made me insanely happy—more so than I'd been in a really long time—so I wasn't letting Austin's stupid, girl hang-ups fuck with that. As it was, I had been making the most of every opportunity that presented itself to spend time with her, even though she didn't seem interested romantically. It had seemed we might have had something—at least the night of the storm. Yet after? Well, she'd gone out of her way to keep our interactions platonic since then, so I was fairly sure I'd been friend-zoned.

I decided to give it a day—*can't look too desperate*—and text her tomorrow if I didn't hear from her before then. Failing that, I'd stop by her room on Sunday. We had spent a bit of time in there this week studying, so I didn't feel like it would be *too* invasive for me to drop by over the weekend.

Chapter Seven

KIT

I hauled myself over the lip of the building and collapsed on the rooftop for a minute to catch my breath. Definitely too much pizza this week. After hearing the twins talking about Anna the day before, I had really gone all out for lunch and practically rolled myself into my afternoon classes I was so full. I was paying for it now, though. Mental note: eat more salad, damn it!

"All right," I huffed into my Bluetooth headset. "I'm up. That was harder than anticipated."

Lucy chuckled on the other end. "I told you not to eat so much this week, fat ass!"

"Yeah, yeah." I blew out a breath, then rolled to my feet, "Okay, where is this entry point?"

The taps of Lucy's keyboard accompanied her directions guiding me to the center of the roof near the air conditioning motors. The ventilation shaft would give me access after Lucy deactivated the alarm system. While waiting, I checked my phone and saw a message from Caleb. I'd managed to avoid him completely the day before, then left early to get to the job site, where I had spent all day on surveillance until the building emptied of workers.

Not that I particularly wanted to hear about his afternoon with his brother and Anna, the lucky bitch. What? I was only human and not a blind one either.

Hey, where were you yesterday? I couldn't find you at lunch. It only took him a whole day and a half to reach out. Too busy perhaps?

I tapped out my reply and hit send. **I'm sure you had enough company.**

There was a pause before his response pinged through. **You sound jealous.**

Shit. I do. **Not jealous, just not sure we have the same taste in friends.** The last thing I needed was to focus on drama, so I added another text before he could respond. **I'm in the middle of something, catch up tomorrow maybe.**

Maybe? He added a frown-face emoji.

I didn't bother to reply. Silencing the phone, I slid it back into my pocket.

"You're clear," Lucy announced. Good timing.

With a small screwdriver, I opened the ventilation grate. After securing a rope to one of the pipes, I used it to shimmy down the shaft.

It was a tight squeeze, but not impossible. In the interest of time-saving, I tucked my body tight into a pin and dropped rapidly, using my gloved hands on the rope to slow my descent.

"Ten more feet," Lucy advised, tracking my location. I continued my slide until she said, "Now."

Her timing was perfect; I was right in front of the vent I needed. I waited a beat. If there was a problem, Lucy would have me hold. With a kick, I opened the vent and descended into the server room. Waiting for Lucy's app to do its job, I held in place. Once it showed the room as being clear, I located server seven and plugged in a handheld laptop. The only reason I was here, instead of Lucy simply hacking them, was because these servers had no external network access. The laptop possessed its own Wi-Fi uplink. Lucy logged into it remotely and began hacking the passwords I'd need to select targeted files on the server.

Waiting for the file transfers was boring, so I clicked through the files. Maybe what we were taking wasn't any of my business, but I was curious. What was stored here that someone would actually pay such an exorbitant fee to retrieve?

The first three seemed pretty much what one would expect: electronic paper trails for huge sums of money moved into offshore accounts and property bought under false names. The fourth file, however, sent a cold chill along my spine.

I scanned through the document and then slowed to read it again. Stomach churning, I swallowed the bile burning along my throat. The filename seemed innocuous enough, just a sequence of numbers and letters—similar to the other files.

"Lucy?" I exhaled her name. "Can you just read me the client's requests again?"

"Sure. Is there a problem?"

I answered with a grunt because I didn't know if we had a problem yet.

Lucy rattled off a series of filenames in sequence. The file bothering me definitely fell on that list. Crap.

"Kit, what's going on? You've got me worried, girl."

It wasn't a question of whether or not I should tell her but if I could manage the unsettling terror filling my veins. "I've just clicked into a file which has nothing to do with money. It's a series of memos discussing a black market genetics experiment focusing on enhancing human abilities with specific mentions to enhanced strength and speed... Luce, it doesn't look like they're using willing participants or that there is a very high rate of success." My heart rate kicked up as I relayed the information. "There is specific mention in one of these notes about how reckless the scientists are being and how many 'subjects' they have needed to terminate or that have died during the experiments. It all seems to be referencing a successful experiment from the eighties that they're attempting to replicate..."

"Hon, that sounds like..." She trailed off, but I knew what she was saying. It sounded like me. *Maybe this was what caused my abilities. Was I the product of some sort of lab experiment?* "What are you going to do?"

I chewed my lip and weighed my options for a minute. I could finish the job, pass along the files to some shady person who would do who-knew-what with the information, or I could delete the file in question and pretend it never existed.

No contest.

Decided, I pulled an extra pen drive from one of my pockets. Like the Boy Scouts, I was always prepared. Sliding it into an open USB on the laptop, I copied the file for myself. After that, I made the unilateral decision to delete the file off the server and from our client's package. The folder stayed, but the actual file was gone. I needed to shield Lucy, and the folder's presence meant we'd technically fulfilled the contract. Without a doubt, it was the right thing to do. Nothing good would come from either party having the information.

"I'm done," I told my partner, and none of the trembling in

my hands reflected in my voice. "I've taken a copy for us and deleted the original. I'm heading back out now."

"All right," she said gently. "Let me know when you're safely clear, and I will reactivate the alarm. See you back at school in the morning." She probably wanted to say more, but thankfully she left it alone. My best friend never pushed me until I was ready to talk.

Mind in chaos, I cleaned up the physical signs of my presence before returning up the ventilation shaft. While it was deeply concerning that someone was conducting these experiments, this could be the answer to what had given me such unusual abilities. Part of me couldn't wait to investigate further, but the sensible part reminded me that from what I had seen, there weren't many clues to go on.

Chapter Eight

The whole drive back to Cascade Falls was spent turning this new information over and over in a search for meaning. It was too much of a coincidence to not have something to do with my own talents. There surely couldn't be too many other orphans running around with superhuman abilities. Not that I had ever considered my strength or speed to be superhuman, just... extra. The one part of that memo that my mind kept tripping on was the total absence of anything healing related. The way I healed? That definitely leaned more towards the super side of human. So it didn't make sense.

If that was how I'd come to be enhanced, wouldn't they have also been trying to replicate my healing?

My head was beginning to pound, and my hands shook as I arrived in town. The sun was rising, so rather than head straight to the school, I went to the gym. Need to burn off the extra adrenaline overrode everything else. An old boxer named Rusty owned the gym, and he was always up, with the gym open before dawn.

At the gym, I parked and grabbed my bag. Once inside, I called out to Rusty so he'd know I was there. He grunted a response from his little office in the corner of the large, open space. It only took me a couple of minutes to change in the ladies' locker room. Hands still trembling, I settled in to work with my favorite punching bag, Old Betsy.

I loved coming in early when I had the entire gym to myself. I didn't feel the same level of pressure to hold back my punches, so it allowed me to burn through my excess energy much quicker. Rusty never mentioned anything, but I'd noticed not long after I began coming here that Old Betsy had been reinforced with an extra skin and the chains were heavier than on all the other bags.

An hour later, my mind had quieted and sweat coated me. Taking a step back from my bag, I noticed the gym had begun to fill with people doing their workouts.

Being a small town, I recognized most of the gym regulars.

Yet the tall, muscular man chatting with Rusty just outside his office was a complete stranger. I would have noticed him before. He was taller than Rusty, so probably around six foot four, and broad across the shoulders with heavily muscled arms wrapped in brightly colored tattoos. The stranger's dark hair was shaved short. Dressed in a black singlet, which hugged his sculpted body, he seemed to ooze violence and danger as he prowled towards me.

Wait, what? Why was he coming towards me? Rusty was bringing that lethal Adonis with a smug smile over to my corner of the gym. Too late to pretend I wasn't ogling him; he'd already noticed. Crap. I used to be so smooth; what had happened to me? Face flaming, I looked away while stripping off my gloves. A long drink of water could give me a moment to fake composure until I could make it.

"Mornin' Kit," Rusty rumbled. "This here is Cole Bennett; he's new in town."

New guy had deep, slate gray eyes—*seemingly bottomless but intense* was nowhere near adequate to describe them. They were cold and hard, adding to the air of danger around him even more than his powerful frame.

"Hi. Kit Davenport." I smiled introducing myself, but my voice cracked, making me cringe. I held out my hand for him to shake, and when he grasped it in his massive mitt, I had to suppress an icy shiver of fear.

"Cole here used to be semi pro in the MMA scene. I was just saying to him that you might be looking for some lessons in that area. Perhaps you can also show him around town a bit, seeing as he's new? Maybe take him for a drink at Pete's Place?" Rusty waggled his eyebrows at me. Was the old goat trying to play matchmaker?

Amusement vied with embarrassment, so I said, "I'm sure Cole has better things to do than get the tour of our postage-stamp town with a *high school student*, Rusty. And as a *high school student*, it would be highly illegal for me to drink at Pete's Place."

Cole raised his brows, and Rusty let out a loud snort. "Girl, you're nearly nineteen; you ain't no normal high school student. Everyone knows that old drunkard will turn a blind eye to anyone over eighteen so long as no one causes trouble!"

At the mention of my actual age, Cole regained his predatory look. Biting my lip, I looked him over slowly. Fuck me, where do these guys keep turning up from? First the twins, now the hulk.

Nope, this one scares the crap out of me. I had more than enough on my plate dealing with Caleb and his dickhead brother. "Thanks, but no thanks," I said with a firm shake of my head.

Cole shrugged, then tilted his head as he spoke for the first time. "Let me know if you change your mind. I could do with a local guide."

Was it too much to have hoped he had an unattractive, girly voice? Instead, his voice was like rough, smoky scotch with a menacing undertone that frightened the pants off of me. And not in a good way.

"Sure thing," I said with a tight nod. "Excuse me, I was just leaving."

Then I headed to the locker room. I wasn't running, at least not on the outside. Pace steady, I took a quick shower before dressing. On my way out, I refused to look in Cole's direction, and almost instantly my mind was back on the stolen memo.

Did it have anything more useful in it? I had read it three times while in the server room, so I practically had the whole thing memorized, but maybe I had missed something. I would need to get Lucy to take a look at it soon.

Chapter Nine

Back in my dorm room I made sure to hide my USB in the false bottom of my sock drawer, just in case. I was exhausted from both the night's activities and my early morning workout, so I stripped and fell face-first onto my bed.

The sound of knocking at my door intruded after a painfully short amount of sleep. Rolling over, I glared at it. Hopefully whoever was there would go the hell away. To my crushing disappointment, the knocking continued. After throwing my blanket back, I staggered over to the door without fully opening my eyes. The damn knocking needed to stop.

"What?" I snapped, slamming the door open and wishing a painful death from a thousand paper cuts on the sleep invader.

"Well, if I knew this was how you answered your door, I would have woken you up sooner," Caleb drawled, running his gaze up and down my underwear clad figure. Scowling, I slammed the door in his face. He was not worth losing sleep over. Crawling back under my fluffy duvet, I sighed.

Seconds later, my door clicked open then closed and a man's heavy footfalls crossed my floor before Caleb's solid frame pinned me beneath him and squashed the wind out of me. He dragged the blanket off my face and grinned down at me.

"Good morning, sunshine!" he sang, looking far too pleased with himself.

"Fuck you, Caleb; it's too early for your bullshit," I growled, giving him my best dagger glare. With my arms pinned under the covers, I couldn't push him off. At least not yet. "Why are you so goddamn chirpy anyway?"

"Aside from having just seen you in your underwear? Because that alone would be reason enough." His grin turned flirtatious. "You never replied to my message, so I thought I would come over and take you out for lunch."

The night before rushed in, filling in the exhausted

crevices. After the shock of the memos, I'd given Lucy the all clear then ignored my phone. So I'd never answered him, and he should have taken the hint.

"I'm busy today; why don't you go see if Anna and your brother need some company?"

Caleb's grin spread even wider. "Holy shit, you are jealous! You made it pretty clear we were only friends; why should it matter who I get naked and sweaty with?"

"I'm not jealous." *I definitely am.* "I just thought you had better taste than bitchy little Anna Greengate."

Skepticism filled his eyes, but instead of pursuing the conversation, he rolled onto his side. Settling in next to me, he spooned me through my blankets and started poking me in the side.

"Come on, get up! It's almost the afternoon, and I'm hungry!"

Shrugging off his prodding, I burrowed deeper into the duvet. My sides were insanely ticklish, and I had zero desire to share that weakness with him. When I tugged the pillow over my head, the asshole jerked it away.

"If it makes you feel better, I would have much preferred a feisty little redhead instead..." He murmured as though trying to seduce me, his breath hot on my neck. My toes curled and thighs clenched at that smooth, chocolaty tone. Shoving backwards, I dislodged him even as I got off the bed in an attempt to gain a little distance.

Stop it, Kit. You're not attracted to him. He's trouble for you, remember? Think about unicorns or roller-skates or cheese... Fuck, I'm hungry.

"All right, lunch. Let's roll. I'm ready." I propped my hand on my hip in my best casual, we're-just-friends pose.

He smirked in satisfaction, making no attempt to hide his enjoyment of my figure. Oh, right, I was still only in my bra and panties.

"After I get dressed." I scooted into my bathroom, gathering up as much of my dignity as I could on the way.

After a quick *cool* shower, I found myself stuck with whatever clothes were left lying around my bathroom. It would serve him right if I went out in a towel, but I wasn't sending that message. *Not attracted to him.* Maybe if I told myself that enough times, I might start believing it. Luckily, I had most of the components of a full outfit, with skinny jeans and a forest green V-neck sweater that hugged my body in a flattering way.

Back in my bedroom I found the dangerously sexy fiend sprawled on my bed, seemingly asleep. When I padded closer, he cracked his eyes open. Ignoring him, I grabbed some socks and some low-heeled, over-the-knee, black suede boots. If I happened to bend over to zip them up in what I hoped was a somewhat alluring way, it was purely coincidence. I swear.

"Come on, Kitty Kat; let's go before I decide I'm hungry for something else," Caleb insinuated as he abandoned my bed and led the way to the door.

We signed out with campus security then took my car down into town. I'd had enough exercise at the gym not to feel guilty about driving such a short distance, and I wanted to be quick so I could get back and look at that memo again.

Grabbing a table in the little local diner, I chomped my way through two of their massive burgers as well as a large side of fries and around five cups of coffee with cream and sugar. He watched with amusement as I polished off the last few fries from my plate and licked my fingers. I didn't apologize, not when I had been starving.

"So what were you doing last night that you couldn't text me back?" he asked, slowly working through his own remaining fries.

Breaking and entering probably wasn't the appropriate answer in this situation, so I just raised my eyebrows in what I hoped was a mysterious expression and said, "This and that."

Luckily, I was saved from further questioning by the arrival of an extremely pissed off Lucy.

"What the hell, Kit? I have been calling you all fucking morning! Are your fingers all broken or something?" she screeched, red-faced and uncaring about where we were.

I tried not to smile; she really was cute when she was mad.

"Ahhh nope, fingers are all fine, thanks Luce!" I held them up and wiggled them at her to demonstrate.

"Then I can't think of any other reason why you wouldn't be answering your phone!" She practically seethed.

Right, still haven't checked my phone. In fact, it was probably still sitting on the passenger seat of my car. Luce had every right to be upset. We had protocols in place for a reason, and I'd gone off the grid without letting her know I'd made it back safe and sound. For all she knew, I had been caught on my way home and might currently be rotting in a cell or getting the snot beaten out of me.

"I'm sorry, Luce; I really didn't mean to worry you." I gave her my very best puppy-dog eyes. I really did feel awful for breaking protocol, and I knew she was probably dying to look at the stolen memo. "Come and join us? Caleb's buying. Aren't you?" I gave him a pointed look, and he sighed before passing Lucy a menu.

"Sure, just sit down, Luce. I may be already used to your unique way of yelling obscenities with love, but the rest of the diner is looking at you like you might start throwing plates." He snickered at her as she looked around in shock, as though she was only just noticing all the other customers, and quickly slid into the booth beside me. Snagging a passing waitress, she placed her usual order of a burger and fries with a coke.

"What were you doing this morning that would have

Lucy so worried about you?" my far too observant new friend questioned, and Lucy froze beside me. She always was pretty awful at lying when asked a direct question. Luckily, he had asked me instead because I had no issues with my poker face.

"Sleeping," I replied with confident eye contact. "You know that; you rudely woke me up, remember?"

"Woah, what?" Lucy coughed on the glass of water a waitress had just delivered for her. "Why was Caleb waking you up, Kit?" Her scolding glare spoke volumes to why she clearly *thought* Caleb had woken me up, and I threw a fry at her.

"Not like *that*." I laughed. "I was asleep, and this asshole decided to knock like crazy on my door, then let himself in and kept annoying me until I got up." Caleb grinned broadly, and Lucy snorted.

"Good work, Cal. She would probably still be passed out if you hadn't."

"I live to serve," he teased.

The waitress returned with Lucy's soda, and as she placed it down, a small spark seemed to fly off her fingers, hitting a condensation ring on the table and hissing into a little puff of steam. I gasped and looked around to see if anyone else had seen it, but neither Caleb nor Lucy were paying any attention to the waitress. She herself had clearly seen something though, as her face had drained of color and her eyes were like saucers.

"M-must just be static electricity," she stammered, meeting my shocked gaze with her own and hiding her hands behind her back. "Let me know if I can get you anything else." It was an obligatory statement but not one she intended to wait for a response on as she scurried back to the kitchen.

"What was that about?" Caleb asked, looking confused. "You can't get a static shock from a wet glass." I had absolutely no idea how to explain what had just happened without sounding insane, so I just shrugged.

Lucy's phone vibrated loudly on the table, and she picked it up to read the message. Her mouth twisted with disgust as she scanned the words, then looked up at Caleb through narrowed eyes.

"Did you seriously sleep with Anna Greengate on Friday?" she exclaimed. "God damn, Cal. I know she's hot but that girl is just plain nasty! Even I wouldn't go there!"

Caleb rolled his eyes and sighed. "Where did you hear that?"

"It's all over school; she's apparently telling anyone who will listen. What gives? I thought she was with your brother."

"She is," a whiny voice interrupted us. "But that doesn't mean I can't double down right?" As though she was Beetlejuice, there stood Anna herself at the end of our booth with her perfectly styled blonde hair, fake tan, and permanently stuck-up facial expression. Worse yet, she seemed to be sporting her new favorite accessory.

"Hey, bro." Caleb greeted his twin. "We were just talking about you. It seems Anna here has been telling people about our *study session* on Friday." There was a thread in his tone that clearly told Austin to sort it out. Austin just shrugged and sat in the booth beside Caleb, dragging Anna into his lap and giving me yet another unreadable look.

"Like I care what anyone in this shit show of a town thinks of me." he sneered, dismissing me and turning to his brother. "I don't understand what the hell we are still doing here anyway."

"You know why we are here: because our *cousin* says we should learn more about the people of Cascade Falls and what makes this town so *special*." Caleb's words were delivered through gritted teeth, and I watched them with a frown. There was definitely subtext to that statement; I just didn't know what.

"*Special?*" Austin snorted. "There's nothing *special* here except a couple of kids who are good at sports and some pretty little rich girls who are easy lays."

I half-expected Anna to be offended by such a callous statement from her boyfriend, but she just giggled and batted her heavily mascara-clad eyelashes at him.

"And then of course there's Kit," she said, shooting me a nasty smile.

Here it comes... She was probably about to out me as a poor, damaged orphan. Anna and her like loved to rub it in my face that I didn't belong at CFA, but before she could continue, Austin cut her off with a cruel laugh.

"There is nothing *special* about Christina, unless you count either her ability to look good in that hideous school uniform or her skills in spending her daddy's money on ridiculously expensive shoes as some sort of talent? God knows she and Lucy can't have two thoughts to rub together in those vapid little brains of theirs or they wouldn't be a year older than the rest of the senior year." Austin's eyes were cold as he spat these words out.

"Except," she managed to squeak out between giggles, "Kit doesn't have a daddy, do you Kit? You don't have any family. No one loves you because you're a giant freak." Austin went still and frowned, even as Anna continued her cackling.

"Austin," Caleb barked, "shut your girlfriend up. No one wants to hear this verbal trash, from her *or* from you. I think you owe Kit and Lucy an apology."

Austin just glared back at his brother, making no move to deliver the apology, but he did clap a hand over Anna's glossy lips when she opened them to speak.

I clenched my jaw. It was none of their business, yet Lucy seemed to think it needed explaining. "Jonathan adopted Kit when we were thirteen."

Dammit. Tears threatened at the pained quiver underscoring Lucy's words. Every time I think I'm used to it, something rips open the wound which won't heal.

"And for your information, *Austin*," Lucy snarled at the darker twin, the shake in her voice warming to anger. "We are behind because we had a shitty fucking upbringing. And I have an IQ of one hundred and forty three, you asshole. Come on, Kit." After shoving away her plate, she grabbed my hand. With a tug, she pulled me from the booth, and we left.

I didn't look back, not even when I heard Caleb swear in a low, almost inaudible voice.

Chapter Ten

Following our run in with Austin and his bitchy girlfriend over lunch, both Lucy and I managed to successfully duck Caleb for a couple of days. We needed the space. Although it was his brother who was at fault, it just seemed easier to avoid both of them. We went to lunch in town and switched up our after school study location. By Wednesday, I was actually getting a bit sick of it and kind of missed my sexy new friend, but I wasn't willing to forgive and forget with Austin so easily.

Between Lucy and me, we had spent hours poring over the memo which was my first ever lead on finding out what made me unique. To my crushing disappointment though, it seemed like one giant dead end, and Lucy, for all her computer genius, could find nothing further for us to pursue.

"I think I have one more avenue to try," she announced while we walked down the hill into town. We hadn't even been talking about the disappointing lack of clues, but she was unnaturally attuned to my thoughts, as always.

"Oh? Do tell," I prompted, eager for *any* suggestions.

She nodded, chewing her lip, "I'm sending it off to some dark net friends." My step faltered at her statement. She had made some waves in the "dark net," the illegal underworld of the internet, with her hacking skills, and several organizations had been trying to recruit her lately. The fact that she was asking for their help was *huge,* but I knew better than to try and talk her out of it. She reacted really badly to me *wrapping her in cotton wool*—her words not mine.

"Okay... let me know how it goes?" I frowned, trying to convey my concern, and she just smiled and shrugged. I guessed that was that.

Just then, a sleek, silver car pulled up alongside us, and the passenger window rolled down.

"Hi, Kit!" The driver called out, and I bent to see who it was, as I didn't recognize the car.

"Uh, hi... Mr. Gregoric?" I frowned in confusion and glanced at Lucy to see she was equally confused, with raised brows.

"Did you girls need a lift somewhere?" He smiled in what was probably intended as a friendly way, but I could swear his teeth were looking awfully sharp again. The effect it had made me feel a bit too much like Little Red Riding Hood for comfort.

"Uh... no. No, we're fine. It's a nice day for a walk," I politely declined, biting back my instinct to educate him on how wildly inappropriate it was for a male teacher to be offering lifts to female students.

"Are you sure? I'm heading to town anyway, and you wouldn't want to be late back to class after lunch!" He delivered the words with a laugh, but it just served to send an uneasy spike through my gut.

"We're sure, Mr. Gregoric!" Lucy chimed in, "Have a nice day!" Grasping my elbow, she started walking again, and his car idled for a minute before taking off once more.

"So weird," I muttered to Luce.

"Totally agree," she responded.

Lucy and I had eaten at the diner three days in a row, so we decided to head to the other end of town for pizza at the little Italian restaurant owned by the least Italian people I'd ever met.

"Hey, Kit!" Hearing a masculine voice call my name as we wandered down Main Street surprised me. Pivoting, I found tall, dark, and dangerous from the gym jogging toward me. As it had when I first met him, my heart rate spiked sharply, and my palms broke out in nervous sweat.

"Hey, Conor. What's up?" Hopefully my joking insinuation that he was Conor McGregor, current UFC champion of the world, would ease some of my own discomfort at his presence.

"Cute. But Conor McGregor is a lightweight." He grinned, but the smile did nothing to soften his features. His gaze held mine for a beat, then he nodded to Lucy and extended a hand. "Hi. I'm Cole."

Lucy took the offered hand, giving me a sly smile, then turned back to Cole. "Lovely to meet you... Cole, was it?" He nodded. "I can't believe Kit hasn't mentioned you to me. Where did you two meet?"

"At the gym, Sunday morning." He absentmindedly cracked his knuckles, and I saw a web of old scars across the backs of them. Made sense—Rusty had said he was semi-pro in the fighting scene—but I thought they used gloves to protect their hands. A shiver ran down my spine as I watched his hands flex.

"Well, nice seeing you," I told him with a polite smile. "We were just on our way to lunch so..." I tapped Lucy on the elbow to encourage her to say good bye, but she was still staring up at Hercules.

"Yes, we're getting pizza. Would you like to join us?" She

beamed up at Cole, and I stifled a groan. *Fucking hell, Lucy. What are you playing at?*

"Lucy, I'm sure Conor has better things to do than eat with us kids." I answered before he could, giving her a glare to try and shut her up.

Rather than take a hint, Cole focused on Lucy. "I could eat."

A small, surprised squeak escaped my throat at his response. The man was dressed for a workout but wasn't actually sweating, which suggested he had to have been on his way in to, not out of, the gym. *Holy shit, he makes gym gear look good though.*

His tattoos were nothing short of beautiful, not to mention the body beneath them. Dragging my attention back to his face, my breath caught. Under his intense inspection, I began to understand how small animals felt when confronted by a hungry wolf.

Clearing my throat uncomfortably, something I seemed to be doing a lot of recently, I spun on my heel and led the way to the restaurant.

Throughout lunch, Lucy maintained an unrelenting level of chatter. Cole stoically fielded her inquiries with one-word answers, which left me plenty of time to watch him from the corner of my eye. The raised lines of several thick scars were hidden beneath the bright colors of his tattoos. *What had happened there?*

Toward the end of our pizzas, someone loomed into my line of sight at the corner of our table. I glanced up, expecting to see a waiter clearing plates, then let out a loud gasp, drawing Lucy's attention.

"Holy shit," she exclaimed. "Si?"

The young man standing at my elbow was lanky in a malnourished way, with sallow skin and limp, dark red hair, but he was still unmistakably our former friend Simon. Shock held me rigid. Neither Lucy nor I had seen or heard anything of him in five years. Our whole world had changed in a matter of hours in one single night. Yet his presence... it filled me with unrelenting guilt. Clearly, he hadn't fared as well as we had in the aftermath.

"Did you need something?" Cole demanded with an edge to his voice, which thankfully gave me a minute to gather my wits again.

Simon ignored his question but flicked a small smile to Lucy and murmured, "Hey Luce, nice hair." Then stared at me with his mud-brown eyes. "Kit. Hey. Can I speak with you? Outside?"

Still speechless, I nodded and followed him out to the sidewalk.

"Si, what... how... where...?" Okay, so my voice was back, but it didn't mean I was coherent.

He smiled at my babbling then hugged me tightly.

Really tightly.

"Jesus, Kit. You have no idea how good it is to see you!" He was still hugging me, and it was becoming a little awkward. I was pretty sure he'd just smelled my hair, too. *Who does that?*

"What are you doing here?" I asked, pulling out of his embrace as politely as I could manage. "How did you find us? Lucy looked for you a few years ago but couldn't find anything on where you'd ended up after everything..."

He ignored my question and gave me a weird, lopsided smile. "You look real good. Guess you pulled up pretty well after we all split up, huh? And you managed to stick with Little Lucy. Good for you guys. You always were like sisters..."

"What are you doing here, Si?" I asked again gently. I didn't want him to think I wasn't happy to see him; I was. But it was very out of the blue, and he seemed super cagey about something. He continued to stare at me, then eventually looked at what I wore. I sincerely hoped I just imagined that lecherous glint as he took in my school uniform.

"I wanted to warn you about something," he started, making eye contact again and beginning to freak me out with how rarely he blinked. "But you look like you might need to be back at school soon? So maybe we can meet up later when you have more time?"

I nodded cautiously. "Maybe Pete's Place around eight? It's up the street. I just have to be back to school by curfew at ten."

For a moment, his smile lit his sallow expression and reminded me of the caring little boy I used to know. He hugged me again, a little longer than comfortable, before disappearing down the street.

Confused as hell, I headed back inside to rejoin Cole and Lucy.

"Kit..." Lucy started, then trailed off as though at a loss for words, her mouth hanging open and a frown pulling at her pixie-like face.

"I don't even know." I shook my head then rubbed my eyes, suddenly feeling exhausted with the weight of everything on my mind. "It was weird. He wants to tell me something important, apparently."

"So, why didn't he?" Cole frowned as he cracked his knuckles, which seemed like an unconscious habit of his.

"No idea. He made some lame excuse about not having time. He wants to meet up later instead, so I guess I will find out then?" I bit into one of my remaining slices of pizza but found it stone cold. *So disappointing; cold pizza sucks.*

"Kit, this seems like really weird timing. Given... you know..." Lucy was wide-eyed and a little pale. She was referring to the timing of Simon suddenly turning up so soon after we stole the memo that might explain my existence; it couldn't be a coincidence. My heart sank a little at the panic on her face. I needed to stop putting her in these situations.

This whole game, *being The Fox,* it was my messed up way of dealing with my traumatic childhood, and I should never have dragged her into it. When it had all started though, after chewing my way through seven therapists in six months, I just didn't want to be alone with my issues. So we had created The Fox.

"Where are you going to meet him?" Cole asked me with narrowed eyes, and I hesitated a moment before replying. His knuckles were still clenched, and from the set of his jaw, I wouldn't put it past him to show up to try and keep me safe. *Overprotective alpha male.*

"Doesn't matter." I dismissed his question, then responded to Lucy. "I agree; the timing is way too coincidental. I'll meet him and find out what's going on tonight."

My best friend knew me well enough not to try and tell me not to go, so instead she just said, "Be careful, will you? You're too bloody reckless."

I grinned at her with affection. "Always." Cole just scowled at me from across the table. He clearly wanted to push the issue further, but I avoided eye contact.

"Lucy, we should get going, we have biology next, and I heard a rumor this morning that there might be a pop quiz."

Chapter Eleven

Later that evening, after a grueling afternoon of pop quizzes and three hours of studying with Lucy in the school library, my brain was fried. Arriving back at my room after leaving a fresh plate of food out for the stray fox, I glanced at the time and groaned. I was going to be running late to my meeting with Simon.

I showered quickly, then raced around my room hunting for something to wear and smacked my big toe hard into the leg of my desk. "Jesus fucking Christ!" I screamed. When had that moved?

I took a deep breath, trying desperately to get a grip.

All afternoon my mind had been in turmoil, running through all the weird things that had happened recently. All the new hot guys arriving in town, my possible mental break with seeing Mr. Gregoric's eyes change, and the waitress shooting sparks. Simon…

Simon's sudden appearance was *almost* more worrying than my possible insanity. He seemed so different from the boy I had known in the foster home. His eyes were cold and hard, and the lecherous way he had looked at me made my gut churn in disgust. I had no idea what might have brought him here after all this time, but it definitely sounded more specific than just "tell me what you've been up to for the last five years."

As kids, Simon had been like an older brother to Lucy and I. The three of us had stuck together through a lot and leaned on each other for support almost daily for over a decade. When Suzette's fucked up operation was shut down and all of the kids re-homed, Luce and I had been heartbroken to lose touch with him.

Which brought me to another thing bugging me. *Why had he barely even looked at Lucy? She'd been just as much a sister as I was…* Back then, he and I had shared the job of protecting her. She was small now, but when we were younger, she had been tiny, helpless, and an easy target at the foster home. His lack of interest in her today just didn't sit right.

Still remembering the less than brotherly hug Simon had given me, I decided to dress down in an oversized hoody and old, faded jeans with a tear across the knee. They were the sloppiest clothes I owned, so would have to suffice. Once dressed, I sat on the floor to lace up my black and white converse boots. Right as I got to the top of my first boot, my bedroom door flew open, whacking into me, and I snarled.

"Crap! Sorry Kitty Kat, I didn't expect you to be sitting on the floor behind the door." Crouching down, Caleb apologized and looked me over as though checking for injuries.

"What the hell, Cal? You don't just go barging into girls' rooms unannounced!" I scowled. *I can't believe I have to educate him on the concept of privacy. Typical male.*

"Sorry, I've only ever lived with guys, so I'm kind of used to just barging into each other's space whenever we want." He shrugged but at least had the grace to look a bit sheepish.

"What if I had been naked?" I rolled my eyes, rubbing my knee where the door had hit. *I doubt he will suddenly start knocking; he's already too friendly with me to backtrack into politeness.*

With a sly look, he winked at me. "Who says that wasn't what I was hoping for?"

"What are you doing here, Caleb? I'm just on my way out." Determined not to be charmed by his relentless flirting, I finished tying the lace on my first boot.

"You've been avoiding me." He pouted adorably. "I miss you... We haven't spoken since my dickhead brother and his bitchy little girlfriend treated you like crap, and it's been killing me. You know that's not what I think of you, right?"

I sighed, retreating to the bed to deal with the second boot. "Yes, of course I know. I just couldn't deal with seeing the two of them again and knowing how he *always* seems to be around you at school, I figured it was easiest to avoid you both."

He rose from his crouch and took a seat at the end of my bed. Lifting my unlaced booted foot onto his lap, he slowly and precisely laced it up, alternating with a massage of my calf muscle with his strong fingers.

"I get it," he said eventually. "But I don't like it. Can we just avoid him together?" Finished with my boot, he stretched his long body out alongside mine and tucked a piece of hair behind my ear.

Guilt panged through me. I'd lumped Caleb in with his brother. "I'm sorry. I shouldn't have been avoiding you, too. I've just had a lot on my mind recently, even before that scene with Austin and Anna. Honestly, what they said wasn't anything I'm not used to, but it upsets Lucy to hear that shit, and I'm just a bit protective of her."

Caleb propped his head on his palm and gestured with his free hand. "Well, go ahead. Why don't you tell me about what's got you down, and maybe I can help?"

I stared into his emerald green eyes for a minute, considering what to say. I was already late for my meeting with Simon, but Caleb made me feel warm and fuzzy inside and I wasn't ready for this moment to end.

"I found out some information recently," I said, choosing my words carefully. "Something which might help me find out who my biological parents are."

"Hmm." He looked thoughtful. "What do you know about them so far?"

"Nothing. I was left abandoned on the side of the road when I was five and with no memories except my first name and date of birth."

"And what is this information that makes you think it could help?"

Lips compressed, I shook my head slightly. I wasn't willing to share the specifics about my unusual talents or the possibility that I was the result of some sort of genetic experiment.

"How did you and Lucy end up here?" he asked, seeming willing to follow my lead. "You guys never talk about yourselves much. I didn't even know you were adopted until that showdown with Austin."

I grimaced as unpleasantness teased at the edge of my memory, but I forcefully pushed it back in its mental box before the pain could get the better of me. "The woman in charge of our foster home was involved in some pretty bad shit. One day the whole place was raided by a private intelligence agency then shut down. After, all the kids were split up and re-homed. A few of us, like me and Lucy, struck it lucky and found really great caregivers. Jonathan, my 'dad' is a pretty important guy and didn't really have the time or skills to raise a damaged teenager, so he sent me here, then offered to pay for Lucy to come here too so I wouldn't be alone. A really lovely older couple in California adopted her, but they aren't very wealthy, and they were overjoyed to have Lucy attend school here. It's an education they wouldn't have normally been able to provide. She spends every holiday with them, and I think they genuinely love her, which is awesome."

Caleb frowned. "Jonathan sounds like a real gem." His tone didn't match the statement; he actually sounded angry.

"He is." I laughed. Jonathan was an amazing guardian, but the role of 'father' just hadn't come naturally to him when applied to a damaged thirteen year old. We'd had a bit of a rocky start but since then have grown into a comfortable rhythm. I wasn't stupid enough to think he didn't keep track of my comings and goings, like any parent, but he trusted me enough to give me an illusion of freedom. "He took me in simply because I remind him of his sister, but he has absolutely zero parenting skills, so believe me when I say this solution worked best for everyone involved."

Caleb hummed under his breath and started twisting bits of my hair between his fingers. We fell silent for a bit, and I almost purred under the light tug of his gentle fingers in my hair.

"So where are you headed to tonight in such serious boots?" he asked, breaking the quiet.

"Oh, crap!" I jolted upright. "Shit, I must be so late now! I'm supposed to be meeting up with an old friend for a drink in town."

"An old friend?" Caleb arched an eyebrow at me, a note of jealousy in his tone.

"Yes, actually someone from my time in foster care. Showed up completely out of the blue today and says he needs to warn me about something important."

"That sounds kind of sketchy, Kitty Kat. Maybe I should come with you?" He echoed my own thoughts about Simon's unexplained arrival.

"Thanks, but I'll be fine." I smiled at his concern. "I'll text you when I'm home safe. Lucy has already told me about seventeen thousand times to text her, so I can just copy-paste it to you." I stuck my tongue out, and he gave me a mock scowl.

I was almost an hour and a half late when I finally reached Pete's Place. Simon had chosen a table near the back of the bar and had taken full advantage of Pete's relaxed policy towards checking IDs. Sliding into the booth opposite him, I eyed the empty glasses on the table. *Just how many had he had?*

"You're late." he slurred, narrowing his beady eyes at me.

"Sorry." I smiled, not in the mood to start an argument. "I got caught talking to someone at school. It looks like you found something to do while you waited, though?" I raised an eyebrow at his inebriated state. *As if this whole encounter isn't strange enough, he has to add alcohol to the equation. Okay, Kit. Just... work out what he's doing here and leave. Fast.*

"School." He sneered. "That's a fucking fancy-looking school you and Luce go to, huh? Bet that costs a pretty penny."

He didn't seem to actually ask a question, so I said nothing and waited for him to get to the point.

"You know, you always were a good-looking kid. But you sure grew up well." He flicked out his tongue to wet his lips, and I suppressed a grossed out shudder that someone I thought of as family was looking at me like he was imagining me naked.

"Si, what are we doing here? You said you had something important to warn me about?" The whole situation skeeved me out, and I hated the idea that my "brother" only made me more uncomfortable the longer I spent with him.

He didn't immediately respond, but continued to stare.

"You know, I had the biggest crush on you when we were kids."

My stomach sank. *Did he intend to get those feelings off his chest before telling me why he was here? Ugh.*

"I even started looking forward to the beatings and abuse because I knew that afterwards you'd be there to look after me."

"Si, that's just..." My skin crawled, and I was at a loss for the right words.

"Beautiful. I know." He cut me off with a creepy smile then sipped his drink.

"Sick. It's *sick*, Simon. The shit they did... how could you think that anything made that worthwhile?"

He slammed his glass down hard on the table, making a loud bang, and I jumped.

"How dare you?" he hissed. "How dare you call how I felt for you *sick*? I was a little boy in *love!* I would have put up with far more than that for those moments when you held me afterwards." His voice climbed in volume and anger as he spoke. Pete, the old guy who owned the bar, gave me a meaningful scowl. *Time to get Simon out of here.*

"Of course," I back-pedaled in a soothing voice. "I'm sorry. I didn't mean to upset you. Why don't we get some fresh air and continue talking outside? Then maybe you can tell me what you came here for?" I coaxed him up out of the booth and took the quickest exit, out the back door leading to the alleyway running behind the row of stores where the bar sat. The alcohol must have dulled his reaction time. It wasn't until we were outside that he even seemed to register we'd left the bar.

"What? Now you're too ashamed to be seen in public with me, Kit? What's the problem? What's so wrong with a man confessing his childhood love to his long-lost friend?" He was yelling now, invading my personal space. Little flecks of his spit were hitting me in the face, and I backed up a step to get away from it.

"That's just it, Si. I was your *friend*. Nothing more. Some seriously bad shit happened to us back then, and it's understandable that you might be experiencing some sort of, I don't know, misplaced emotion? But I've never considered you anything more than my friend and brother." I tried to keep my voice gentle but could hear the outrage leaking through. This shit was getting out of hand. "Is that what you came here to tell me? That you used to have a crush on me? I don't believe that is what you came to say."

He laughed; a more scornful sound I'd never heard. "No. No, what I have to say is much more... life threatening, shall we say? But suddenly I'm not feeling in the most sharing mood."

It was futile to argue with a drunk, so I pushed off the wall to leave. "This was a waste of time."

Simon stepped into my path, blocking my exit. "What do you think you're doing?" he snarled, his saliva hitting me in the face once again.

"I'm leaving, Si. You obviously aren't going to tell me this big secret you've got, and you're making me super uncomfortable, so I'm not sticking around for it to get any weirder." I tried to ease past him, unwilling to use any of my extra strength on someone I considered family. No matter how bat shit crazy he was acting. He shoved me back against the wall, the rough contact making me instantly regret my decision to not hurt him, then plastered his mouth to mine like some sort of overgrown octopus under threat.

He tasted like beer and garlic as he forced his wet fish of a tongue into my mouth. Enough. I shoved him off me, uncaring of how much force I had to use.

"What the *fuck*, Simon?" I screamed, horrified at the unwanted intrusion and his blatant disregard for consent. "Are you fucking deaf? Have you not heard a word I have said? I am *not attracted to you*!"

The last thing I expected from him in that moment was a violent backhand. The blow against my face startled me more than anything else. My head smacked backwards against the brick wall, and my knees went to jelly. Shock overrode everything, and my mouth burned where my lip was split.

Who reacted like that? Mentally deranged people, Kit, you fucking idiot. I wasn't dealing with my brother anymore—this man was a stranger.

A dangerous one.

"...could have saved you!" he raged on in some insane tone wavering between madness and fury. "But *you*... you just have to be such a little bitch, don't you? You used to be such a nice girl, *Kit.*" He cackled as he sneered my name. "Kit, the Foxy Girl, Patron's favorite. No one could ever gain as much favor as adorable, skinny little Foxy with her perfect fox-red hair and porcelain white skin that showed up the marks so beautifully. I guess they were right about that part." He touched my face where he had just struck me. No doubt I already had a rapidly expanding bruise. I slapped his hand away.

"You know, it wasn't hard to track you down. You've been leaving your little foxes all over the country for years, just *begging* someone to connect it back to you. But no one ever did, did they? Until me. I knew it was you as soon as I heard about them." His eyes narrowed, a cruelty in them I'd never imagined. "A notorious thief dubbed 'The Fox' because of the little plastic foxes left at the scene of every crime. Let's not forget who first taught you how to steal, sweetheart."

"I have no idea what you're talking about." Denial was my best defense, and I used a calm voice to support it. "I am just a normal high school student. I barely even remember those parlor tricks you taught me."

"That's *bullshit!*" he screamed. "*Stop lying to me!*" He reached out with curled fingers as though to grab me, and I readied myself to avoid the contact.

Out of nowhere, Simon's hand was snatched away from where he had it stretched toward me and wrenched up behind his back in an arm lock. He let out a high-pitched scream and tried to turn his head to see who was holding him.

The way the shadows were falling, I couldn't see much except a nice pair of men's shoes and suit pants. Whoever he was, the person growled something in a menacing tone against Simon's ear. Whatever he heard, Simon nodded frantically. The Good Samaritan released him, and Simon staggered away, pausing a few steps down the alley and glaring poison at me.

"I'll be seeing you *real* soon, Foxy Girl." Then he took off out of the alleyway at an unsteady jog.

Chapter Twelve

"Are you okay?" The stranger asked in a soft British accent, holding out his hand to help me up. After I accepted it, he pulled me to my feet with ease.

"I had that under control," I muttered indignantly, brushing the dirt off my ass and fighting back embarrassment at being saved like a damsel in distress.

"Uh huh, it sure looked that way." He chuckled and touched a gentle finger to my chin where my split lip dripped blood.

At the bold and unexpected contact, I studied my

unnecessary savior. From what I could tell in the dimly lit alleyway, his dirty blond hair was cropped short in what can only be a slightly grown-out military cut, and his strong jaw was shaded with stubble. My earlier guess at his dress slacks had been correct as he wore an expensive looking charcoal suit with a white shirt, sans tie underneath, open a few buttons at the collar. Most arresting though, were his eyes. His eyes possessed the most unusual shade of gold with flecks of emerald green in one and fiery orange in the other. Even as I stared at him, he took a fabric square from his breast pocket and gently dabbed at my lip. The contact stung, breaking my trance. I hissed in pain.

"Sorry, love." he murmured, a sexy smile lifting one side of his full lips. He tucked the handkerchief back in his pocket, then ran his finger lightly over the spreading bruise under my eye and across my cheekbone. At the light caress I shivered, and a faint whimper escaped my throat. My body flushed with the same heat I had experienced when meeting both the twins and Cole. *What the hell is happening to me?* As though surprised, his brow raised, and then a wolfish, calculating glint shimmered in his mesmerizing eyes.

"Tell me," he said in a voice like honey. "What was that all about with your intoxicated friend there?" As he spoke, he slid his other hand confidently around my waist and took a step forward, forcing me back a step and planting my back against the wall once again. Only this time, I wasn't complaining. *Why wasn't I complaining? He was a total stranger, no matter how sexy!* It was like I was possessed by a succubus or something. He was tall, and in my flat-shoed boots I needed to crane my neck to look up at him.

"Huh?" I asked, having totally forgotten the question. *Smooth, Kit. Real smooth.* His throaty chuckle vibrated through my body as he leaned in closer and brushed his satiny lips against my ear, then more firmly over my pulse point. The muscles along my spine quivered as a surge of adrenaline rushed through me, leaving me a pathetic, panting mess.

"Why did your friend just refer to you as 'Foxy Girl'?" the delectable stranger questioned against my skin in his panty-dropping voice, and I melted a little more. Not enough to lose my brain entirely, though it was getting close.

"Because of my hair color, obviously." Only a half-lie, since it was how I first got the name.

He pulled back from my neck and gave me an assessing look. His eyes flicked from my hair to my face, and then he seemed to take his time memorizing my features. He ran his rough thumb across my lower lip, and I tried not to moan, still riding high on the hormone rush.

"How curious." he muttered, then abruptly pulled back, leaving an ice cold void where his body had been.

"Be seeing you around, Fox." He winked one stunning

golden eye, then strode his fine ass out of the alley without so much as a backward glance, leaving me gaping after him.

What the hell just happened? My mind felt like scrambled eggs, all awash with shock and betrayal and frustration. Not to mention the confusion at how uncharacteristically docile I had just gone under the sexy British stranger's hands. I lifted my fingers to touch where his thumb had caressed my lip, and I froze, a cold spike of fear jolting through me. The split in my lip had completely healed, and I would be willing to bet the bruising under my eye was totally gone now too.

Fuck.

Chapter Thirteen

Absolutely shattered, I hid in my room back at school. The weird events of the day, from lunch with Cole, Simon's reappearance, Caleb's drop by and his tenderness—then the insanity of Simon in the alleyway—*what the hell had happened to him?* Then the Good Samaritan in the alley, he took my breath away.

Exhausted, I fell face-first into my pillow. I wanted to just go to sleep and escape it all. If I did, however, I wouldn't be very comfortable. Flopping onto my back, I unlaced the boots one by one before kicking them off the end of the bed. The jeans took some actual effort to wiggle out of, and then I let them hit the floor.

Everything else could stay. I quickly tapped out a message to Lucy, letting her know I was back and would explain when I saw her in class the next day, then sent a briefer one to Caleb as promised. Within seconds I was fast asleep.

Jolting upright—a minute later or an hour? I had no idea—I looked around my dark room. What had woken me? Fatigue warred with grogginess, so I hadn't been asleep for too long, but I was a light sleeper, so something must have made an out-of-place noise.

A subtle scratch and click in the near silence—someone was working at picking the lock on my door. Adrenaline flooded my system, chasing away the sleepiness.

Come on, Kit, think. What are the options?

I could head out the window. Regardless of my enhanced speed, this moment spent being indecisive had eliminated that as an option. A tumbler had already clicked; one more and the door would be open. It was my room, and I was awake, that gave me the element of surprise.

Positioning myself to the side of the door, I waited. Seconds later, the last tumblers surrendered. The door opened slowly, admitting a large man in a ski mask.

I launched a swift upper cut to the intruder's jaw, intending to knock him out. He went down, but the three behind him surged forward. *Dammit!* I danced backward, delivering several more hard punches, but even as a second man went down, two more landed on me. I had to spend more time blocking their blows than hitting them.

A crash into the back of my head sent me to the floor. Smart-asses tried to pin me, but before I could respond, one of my arms was wrenched behind my back. Zip-tied.

Dammit.

Slamming my head back, I struck one of them in the face. I didn't get to enjoy the satisfying crunch of bone and his snarled swear words before something sharp pierced my thigh and my body went ridged. The last thing I heard before succumbing to the blackout was one of them saying, "The package is secure."

Chapter Fourteen

WESLEY

The large screen showed twelve boxes of static flickering a few times, and then one by one the static boxes were replaced with live camera feeds showing various views of Cascade Falls Academy.

"All right, boys," I muttered into my Bluetooth headset, leaning back in my office chair and running my hand through my shaggy blond hair, "We are up and running on cameras one through ten. How are we going with eleven and twelve?"

"On it now," Cole responded. "Should be done in a couple of minutes if Austin quits his crying." The snickering laughs of my team, everyone except Austin, could be heard on the open line.

"Shut the fuck up, Cole," Austin grumbled. "I still think River's wrong. There's no way—*no way*—that simpering idiot is the thief we're looking for."

"Aus, don't be such an asshole," Caleb snarled down the line, "You clearly don't know her at all, so don't go making assumptions."

"Obviously, neither do you," he sneered in reply to his twin, and Caleb said nothing. Austin had a point; Caleb had been spending all his free time with the girl for the past two and a half weeks and hadn't once suspected she was our mark.

"Children. Cut it out," River, our team leader, snapped at them. "I don't think any of us were expecting The Fox to be a teenage girl. Let's get these cameras set up, and hopefully we can get the evidence we need."

I coughed to cover a laugh at hearing the twins chastised. They should have known it was her. Her name was Kit, for fuck's sake. Surely I wasn't the only one who knew a kit was a baby fox? Then again, maybe I was. I sometimes forgot that my mind stores all kinds of random knowledge. Aside from that clue, though, we were way off base with the profile we'd been working off for the identity of "The Fox."

"I bet you a hundred that you're wrong on this, River," Austin grunted, not willing to give it up so easily. "She doesn't have it in her to pull the jobs we've seen."

"Done," the Brit accepted. We all knew he would; River was never one to back down from a wager, especially when he knew he was right—and I suspected he would be walking away a hundred dollars richer tonight.

The last two cameras flickered online, and I started clicking through them all, one by one, to ensure they worked correctly. Camera five showed movement, and I enlarged it to watch more closely. It was three in the morning; there should be no one moving around other than my team, and the people on this feed were definitely not my team.

"Aus, you are soon to be a hundred dollars poorer because we have suspicious movement on camera five. Four masked men currently picking the lock on Kit's bedroom door," I warned them.

"Locations?" River barked, and everyone reported their positions. "Austin, Cole. You're closest. Head toward the window in case they take that exit, and Caleb and I will take the main entrance."

Confirmations flowed over the line. I watched the security cameras as the team ducked into and out of feeds, while keeping one eye on the cameras showing Kit's door and window.

"Window," I updated them. "It just opened, and I can see a gloved hand on the sill."

Austin and Cole darted across the lawn visible on camera three. They were moving fast, but they were still a decent distance out.

"Yep, coming out the window. Four guys, and one of them carrying the girl over his shoulder. She looks unconscious."

Caleb cursed at the update.

Austin and Cole raced into view on camera nine and immediately pounced on the masked men. A combination of surprise and their superior training helped the pair to swiftly disable and subdue Kit's four assailants. The boys quickly zip-tied their hands and feet, and then Cole bent to check on Kit where she had been dropped during the violent exchange.

"She okay?" I asked hesitantly when he didn't immediately report her status. Cole still didn't answer, taking a few more seconds to check her over.

"Think so." I should have known better than to expect him to elaborate. Cole was never one to waste words. River and Caleb arrived on camera view and checked the bound intruders.

"Cole, take the girl back to our house and get Wesley to look her over. We will take care of these four," River assigned, and we all confirmed again.

Holy fuck, that was unexpected! When River had told us he'd found our mark, it had sounded too easy, so I really should have seen something like this coming. It was a shame we hadn't thought to put cameras around the student dorms earlier, but by all witness accounts, as well as the profiler report, The Fox should have been much older and male.

I hope she's okay... they probably sedated her. I trusted River and the boys to get information out of the goons as to what they might have used, just in case she needed an antidote.

Chapter Fifteen

KIT

Rolling over, I moaned and buried my head in my pillow, which oddly smelled exactly like Caleb. All vanilla and cinnamon like some sort of giant cookie. Why was my head pounding so hard? What the hell had I done last night? The last time I'd woken up this bad, I'd had a hard night on tequila, but that didn't seem right.

Awareness rushed in, and I froze. Masked men. Attacked. Where was I? Who were they? Slowly, I cracked open my eyelids to assess the situation—definitely not in my room anymore. I didn't seem to be restrained in any way, but to be certain, I moved my wrists. Opening my eyes more, I glanced around the room. For all appearances, it was an unexceptional bedroom. Designed tastefully with stained wood furniture and complimentary colors, but totally devoid of any personal effects that I could see. More importantly, though, I was alone.

What the hell is going on? Who forcefully kidnapped someone only to put them into a super comfortable, cloudlike queen size bed that smelled really weirdly similar to Caleb, then didn't stick around or tie their prisoner up?

I sat up, then hissed as a wave of dizziness washed over me and a sharp headache started throbbing. I hated headaches.

I was still dressed in what I'd gone to bed in, so I thanked fate that I had fallen asleep in my sloppy hoody. On my bottom half, I was in nothing but tiny bikini briefs. I made the effort to get out of the bed. I needed to know where I was and what was going on.

Padding over to the dresser against the wall, I pulled open the top drawer and found a pair of men's track pants, which I pulled on and immediately felt less vulnerable. The door to the side of the dresser opened smoothly, revealing a compact bathroom. Thank God! My bladder wanted to cry with relief. At least my kidnappers weren't making me pee in a bucket or something barbaric like that. *Always nice to get the civilized kidnappers.* Not that I had ever been kidnapped before, but things could always be worse.

Always.

Finished, I washed my hands then returned to the bedroom. There were two more doors to try. One of them led to a closet full of men's clothes, so the other must be the way out. I slowly rotated the handle, expecting to find it locked, but it turned easily and glided open silently.

Okay, these were either the worst kidnappers in history, or something else was going on here. I looked around the bedroom once more, noticing a CFA tie draped over the mirror and a graphic print T-shirt crumpled on the floor that I'd seen Caleb wearing recently. All clues pointed to the room belonging to Caleb. *How the hell did that happen?*

Was he one of the masked intruders? Why would he do that to me? They hadn't been at all afraid of inflicting damage while taking me from my room last night. *What a dick!* I could have been really badly injured, and they had no way to know I healed easily. *Was this his idea of potentially the worst practical joke in history?*

Boiling with indignation, I stormed out of the bedroom and down the hallway, intent on finding my *so-called* friend and demanding answers.

Angry, I strode out into a large, open-plan living-dining area with a kitchen set on the far side. A huge marble island separated it from the rest of the space. The décor was that of a mountain lodge, all exposed wood and soft furnishings in earth tones. It looked like it had been fully designed as a show home rather than by people who actually lived in the space.

"Caleb!" I shouted, after spotting his back poking out from behind the open fridge door. "What the fuck is going on?"

The fridge door slammed shut with a jerk, and the man spun around to face me.

This guy was young, maybe my age, and much slimmer than the twins, although his frame was hard to make out since he wore an oversized, crumpled flannel shirt over a white T-shirt with what looked like a coffee stain down the front. His hair was blonde and shaggy but in more of a "forgot to cut it" way rather than a style, and he sported square, black framed glasses

"You're... not Caleb," I said, pointing out the obvious. I'm not entirely sure how I had mistaken him for my solidly built friend. He pushed his glasses nervously up his nose as his green eyes darted to something behind me.

"Kitty Kat!" Caleb exhaled against my ear before sweeping me up in broad arms and twirling me around. The force sent a painful spike into my brain. I smacked him in the arm until he let me down, then clutched my head and groaned.

"Shit, sorry babe, I wasn't thinking," he apologized as he led me over to the couch and eased me down to sit. "Are you okay?"

Before I could answer, a glass of water was pressed into

my hand, and then a palm holding two white pills appeared. I looked up at the jittery blond guy, and he gave me a tight smile.

"Aspirin," he explained. "For your head. You were jabbed with a pretty run-of-the-mill tranquilizer, but it leaves a bit of dizziness and a headache the day afterwards."

"Thanks." I said on reflex and warily accepted the pills. I really needed the aspirin. "Now, one of you needs to explain what the fuck is going on here. Why did you kidnap me in the middle of the night while wearing ski masks? Is this some sort of joke? Because if it is, I'm not laughing. And what the fuck were you thinking *tranquilizing* me? Even if it was 'run-of-the-mill,' it's so incredibly not safe to do shit like that!" I yelled, beyond pissed off at the whole damn thing. *Of course* I knew it wasn't a joke, they were clearly with *one* of the groups hunting *The Fox*. I wasn't going to volunteer up any more information than I needed to, though. It seemed like denial was my best tactic until I knew where we stood. They may not yet know it's me.

Caleb grinned. "Stop giving us that look, Kitty Kat. You're not scary."

I narrowed my eyes at him, growing more incensed by the second, and the other boy made a strangled noise in his throat.

"Agree to disagree, Cal," he muttered under his breath, then retreated to the kitchen.

I returned my attention my so-called friend. "Start talking."

"Okay," he said, puffing out a sigh and running his hands over his face. He looked exhausted. "So, I think *obviously* it wasn't us who kidnapped you. My jokes are way funnier than that. Luckily for you, Wesley," he said, gesturing towards glasses-guy before continuing, "happened to notice those guys breaking into your room, and alerted us in time to ride in on our white stallions to save you."

I stared at him, waiting for him to elaborate, but he seemed to think that summed it all up.

"Can't believe I have to ask the obvious questions here. How did *Wesley* happen to see this going on in the girls dorms at God knows what time of morning when I am ninety percent sure he's not a student? No offense, Wesley, you don't look like the type who would be paying a late night visit to anyone's bedroom." My assumption of his character proved correct when his face flamed red.

"Ahhhhhhh...." Caleb stalled, clearly trying to think of a plausible lie. "Wesley works in IT and surveillance and was doing a routine update of the CFA security system?" Was that a statement or a question?

Fine. I decided to play along. "Oh really? How fortunate for me. Tell me, where were these cameras that showed my room? Because I've checked the locations of all the security points, and none are near enough to even see that hallway, let alone my specific door."

"Well...." He looked over my head at Wesley for help.

"And when you say 'us' who are you talking about?" I continued before he offered another weak excuse. "You can't seriously expect me to believe *Austin* came to my rescue?"

"Actually," Wesley piped up helpfully from the kitchen, "he did!"

I raised an eyebrow at Caleb, and he ran a hand over the longer middle section of his hair, causing it to stand on end.

"Okay, so Austin and I aren't technically students at CFA..." he began, and I got the feeling he was finally telling the truth. Sitting back, I motioned for him to continue. Caleb narrowed his eyes at me as if to remind me I *wasn't* in charge here.

"We work for a company called Omega and we're here on a job. Of sorts. To... find someone... Austin and I were enrolled as students to gather information..." He spoke slowly, as though choosing words carefully, but I had a feeling about where this was headed. *That goddamn bloody tracker*. I might be able to play ignorant for a bit longer, but chances were, my cover was already blown wide open based on the way Caleb currently avoided eye contact.

Fuck, he probably hates me now if he has worked out I'm a criminal. My heart sank a little but I reinforced my emotional walls, putting on my cool, calm confident act. Hearing they worked for Omega Group helped with the calm part. They were the only "good guys" currently hunting *The Fox* so this was definitely the best of a bad situation.

"Interesting," I commented mildly. "And who were you gathering information on... exactly?" His gaze snapped up to meet mine, offering the confirmation I needed.

Crap, dammit.

"Mr. Gregoric, to be honest. Although it seems our intel was just a little off base..."

I snorted a laugh, relaxing a bit while Caleb frowned at me, clearly not seeing the funny side. I can see why they would have suspected him, though. Coincidently, he had shown up at the same time as I had returned to Cascade Falls with that damn ring. Not to mention his sharp-toothed smile and weird behavior in town. Man definitely gave me the creeps.

"All right, what gave me away?" I asked, dropping the pretense. Maybe, hopefully, I still stood a chance of him letting me go if I kept things friendly.

Actually, that isn't a totally unreasonable idea, and would be a real kick in the face to Omega Group.

"Oh, I see we're done playing innocent now?" Caleb smirked.

I shrugged. *What's the point?* "If you had evidence, I wouldn't still be sitting here. So you've obviously worked it out but based on rumor or hearsay, so I ask again, what gave me away?

I know for a fact my tracks were covered impeccably well."

"They were," Wesley muttered, sounding confused. "I'd really like to ask you about how you managed a couple of your jobs..."

I mimed zipping my lips. "Trade secret."

After giving Wesley an inscrutable look, Caleb rose and said, "The rest of the team will be back soon; I'm sure they will want to explain it themselves, if you can handle waiting a bit?"

"Sure," Not like I didn't already know more than they did, "In the meantime, do you have anything to eat? I'm *starving* and is that coffee I smell?" I grinned at Caleb and prayed he didn't see the worry in my eyes. *Come on Cal, it's just me. Your friend. You want to help your friend, don't you?*

He watched me with suspicion for a moment before he sighed and stood up. "Fine, I'll make you food but only because I know how crabby you get when you're hungry. Wes just brewed fresh coffee, too."

Hope flared in me as I saw him giving in to our flirty friendship rather than the whole criminal/superspy dynamic. The sooner I could convince him to let me go, the better.

"Thank fuck, I thought you would never offer. It was all I could smell when I came out here!" I groaned and followed him over to the kitchen as though pulled by a beautiful caffeinated magnet. Wesley watched me suspiciously but Caleb didn't seem to notice. He pulled out a bowl and began mixing batter for pancakes. Have I mentioned lately how much I love him? Pancakes and coffee were breakfast heaven.

"So, where is your douchebag of a twin anyway?" I asked after downing my first cup. Wesley refilled it for me politely while Caleb poured pancake batter onto the griddle. The first sizzle had my stomach growling.

"He and the others are dealing with your would-be kidnappers."

I paused, cup halfway to my mouth, and frowned at him.

"Sorry, what? You have them? I want to see them!" I exclaimed, slamming my cup back onto the counter and sloshing precious liquid out.

"Why?" Caleb glanced over to meet my gaze. "Do you know who sent them?"

"Of course not! That's why I want to speak to them, to find out who the fuck tried to have me kidnapped! Isn't that obvious?" I tried to hold my temper in check. Of course, they weren't going to let me, their mark, interrogate prisoners but it wasn't an easy concept to swallow.

He looked at me for a minute, as though weighing my words, then nodded. "Well in that case, we are working toward the same goal. We are considerably more qualified for interrogation than you, so just trust that we know what we're doing."

Just as I was about to irrationally lose my temper at a situation that couldn't be changed, the front door banged open. Austin stalked in wearing a moody expression, followed by Cole from the gym, and... what the hell, the good Samaritan from the alleyway? If I were honest with myself, I wasn't even surprised, really. It would have been way too much of a coincidence that all these beautiful, mysterious men would suddenly show up in my small town at the same time. Not to mention be so interested in me.

"I guess I should have seen this one a mile away," I remarked. "River, I presume?" I addressed the mystery man, recalling the name of the twins' "cousin" that they were living with. He answered with a sharp nod, all business. Had I completely imagined our heated encounter after Simon's nutty behavior the night before? God, had it only been the night before? Felt like a million years ago.

"So, I take it you heard considerably more of Simon's ranting than you let on? Nice of you to wait so long to intervene." I rolled my eyes. *I guess that explains what gave me away.*

"I thought you said you had it under control?" he reminded me, his all-business façade dipping for a moment as a teasing look entered his mismatched, liquid gold eyes.

Biting my tongue, I avoided revealing my lack of retort by freshening up my coffee.

Shit, not good. This guy looks like he'll be way harder to talk around than Caleb.

"You've already met the twins of course, and I assume Caleb had the decency to introduce Wesley?" River continued smoothly. "And this is Cole Bennett, the last member of our team."

"We've met," I stated, meeting Cole's steel gaze then quickly looking away, still unbelievably unnerved by the wild danger living in his eyes.

All four guys turned to look at Cole with surprise on their faces, and he gave them an unapologetic look.

"We had pizza," he deadpanned. Then, when they continued to stare at him, he shrugged. "What? I didn't think it relevant."

River shook his head in disbelief and pointed sharply at Cole then both twins as he said, "The three of you are on punishment detail for a week for having our mark literally under your noses and not working it out. Now, Christina—"

"Kit," I interrupted. Austin snorted. *Asshole.*

"Kit then, can you tell me who those men were that tried to kidnap you last night?" River certainly didn't beat around the bush.

I frowned at him. "I thought you would tell me. Haven't you interrogated them?"

"We did." He grimaced. "Unfortunately they were

equipped with cyanide capsules, and as soon as they realized we were experienced in interrogation, they took their own lives. Which begs the question, what have you gotten mixed up in that hired goons would rather die than squeal on their employer?"

Stunned, I didn't answer. What the hell *had* I gotten myself mixed up in? Kidnapping; that wasn't too unexpected from the people we stole from. But hired mercenaries willing to die rather than be questioned? That was insane. I shook my head.

"I swear I have no idea who they were. How do I know they're not something to do with you lot? Seems like an awfully big coincidence that they show up within weeks of all of you!" Yes, I was grasping at straws here but I'd always maintained that the best defense was a good offense. I stood a much better chance of wiggling my way out of this if I feigned ignorance as to who their employer was.

River stared me down, his face impassive, "And what about your friend from the bar? Seemed like he had a vendetta. He even hinted that something bad was heading your way. You don't find that coincidental?"

My shoulders sagged, and I propped my elbows on the kitchen counter. He was absolutely right. Simon turning up here out of the blue and railing on about some big secret that he needed to "warn" me about only hours before someone attempted to kidnap me? Jesus, I thought it was bad enough he'd tried to force himself on me, but now this? Nauseated, I clapped a hand over my mouth.

"Kitty Kat, are you okay?" Caleb appeared at my side and rubbed circles against my back. Sucking in a few deep breaths and leaning into his comforting warmth, I got my shit together. As much as I knew that things were different between us now, we had grown really close lately. I wasn't ready to give up that closeness just yet and it seemed, neither was he.

"He's right. This must be connected to Simon." *Dammit, Simon.* "I have a feeling I know what this is about."

I pulled away from Caleb and refilled my coffee cup. The caffeine helped with the headache. Retreating from the kitchen, I curled up in the corner of the big couch. I waited until the guys all followed me and found seats before I started talking again. River's jaw clenched, as though he would prefer to give the orders rather than let me usurp his authority. Tempting as it was, I didn't stall a bit longer just to piss him off. Definitely a control freak, that one.

"Last weekend I had a job which required *procuring* some files from a secure server in an office building," I began, but I didn't make it far before Austin interrupted with a derisive snort.

"Steal. You stole files from a secure server. Let's call a spade a spade here." He sneered, and it took a lot to resist the urge to punch him in his arrogant face.

"*As I was saying*, one of the files wasn't the financial records I'd been contracted to retrieve." I kept Luce out of it, for now "It was a series of memos referring to some illegal human genetics trials with unwilling test subjects." Several brows rose, but the other guys said nothing even though they looked thoughtful.

"So why kidnap you?" River pushed.

I imagined it had something to do with my own possible ties to those Frankenstein projects, but I wasn't ready to let these boys in on that little tidbit just yet, so I pasted on my best wide-eyed innocent look and shrugged.

"I don't know. Maybe because I took the file for myself and deleted the originals?" *Yes, good thinking on your feet, Kit. Sounds plausible.*

"And what do you intend to do with this stolen file?" River continued to run the conversation, giving me a fair idea of why he was their team leader. The guys seemed natural in how they deferred to him in this situation, listening silently and trusting him to take charge.

"I..." *plan on using it to find out who I am.* Being careful with how much I was sharing, I said, "I was planning on investigating further. They're killing people in these experiments, and it can't be allowed to continue. It's what any decent person would do." *Except we had already hit a dead end... they didn't need to know that, either.*

He watched me for a minute, as if pondering my half-truth, making me sweat.

"How do you plan to do that?" River asked finally.

It was a good question; aside from Lucy's connection in the dark net, we really had no further plan of attack in mind. Not that I was going to admit that to this group of specially trained field operatives. They were definitely going to make this difficult. Maybe I could deflect with questions of my own?

"Perhaps *you* should be telling me a little more about why I should trust the five of you? How the hell do I know you're not the bad guys here?" *Yes, Kit. Good deflection.*

River dipped his head to me. "Fair enough. I can understand your concern. My team and I are agents with the Omega Group, a private intelligence firm which is often contracted by various government factions as well as civilians requiring assistance. Have you ever heard of us?"

I maintained my poker face. They certainly weren't *expecting* me to have heard of them—I could tell by their relaxed expressions—so I tactfully didn't contradict their assumptions.

"River," Austin snapped, "Why are you explaining anything to her? She's a criminal. It's our job to take her in to OG headquarters and be done with it."

River cast a warning look at Austin, who shut up and glowered at me with his arms folded over his chest.

"My reasons are not up for discussion at this point in time, we can speak later if you disagree." River turned back to me to continue his explanation. "No, I didn't think you would have heard of us. Well, it's safe to say we *are* the good guys. I would offer to give you references, but then everyone would know we had found the infamous *Fox,* and you'd be staring down a very, *very* long prison sentence. Is that what you want?"

Well this sounds hopeful... Could he seriously be considering letting me escape? Why? I was never one to look a gift horse in the mouth, so I took a leap of faith, praying it would work out. If it did, it would be well worth the gamble, given both mine and Lucy's futures were at stake.

"Very well. In answer to your earlier question, I don't have a specific plan as of yet. I was kind of counting on the memos I found to contain some clues as to a starting point or some sort of lead." I shrugged. It was mostly true; that was exactly what I had been counting on. I just omitted the part where Lucy was sending off for outside help.

None of the guys commented, though River continued to study me with his unnatural eyes. Unnerved, I glanced away, and my gaze landed on Cole. He looked so furious I suddenly wanted to be in another room.

"All right, here's what's going to happen," River announced, breaking the tension. "You're going to give Wesley this file so he can examine it for further leads. From there, my team will investigate. You will stay out of it; however, I think in the interest of your own safety you need to remain here under our watch for a while. You can still attend classes during the day. We already have Caleb and Austin enrolled, so they can keep you safe. But you'll return here at night. Your dorm has proved how easy it is to infiltrate."

I opened my mouth to protest, but he cut me off with a slice of his hand.

"Let me make this perfectly clear to you, Kit. We were sent here to find and detain an internationally wanted thief-for-hire, and it seems to me that we have found our mark. As it currently stands, we don't have the evidence necessary to detain you, *however*, I have absolutely no qualms about making my team stick to you like glue for as long as it takes to find that evidence. Now, either that means we find it and take you in, or you keep your pretty little nose clean and hang up your fox fur coat, so to speak. We still win because you will no longer be *procuring* items that don't belong to you. Or you can play nice, let us protect you until we are sure the threat against you is cleared, then I will give you a fair head start to change locations before we begin hunting you again."

Shock held me captive for a moment. "Sorry, this makes no sense. Why are you so willing to help me? I thought your job was to haul me in, not help me escape? Is this part of the game?"

"What game?" He tilted his head and gave me an intense look.

"Nothing," I backtracked, in case I had this all wrong, "Never mind." He seriously *was* offering me a chance to make my escape if I cooperated in the interim. Seemed like a no-brainer. They may not have any evidence on me yet, but they knew who I was and it wouldn't be all that hard to connect Lucy, which made the decision easy. While I was willing to gamble on my own future, I wasn't willing to gamble on hers. I had to take any and all opportunities presented in order to wiggle out of this mess, regardless of their motivations.

I nodded slowly. "Very well. I want to be involved in the investigation, though. I think you and I both know I have skills that will be useful."

Lips compressed, he studied me for another beat then gave a sharp nod. "Done. Caleb, take Kit to gather some clothes and retrieve this file for Wesley." He stood, then adjusted his rolled up shirtsleeves "Cole and Austin, we have some bodies to dispose of. Let's move."

With that, the three of them swept out of the house, and I was left with Caleb and Wesley once more.

ChapteR SixteeN

The run back to school was uneventful. I packed a bag of clothes and then fished the pen drive out of my hiding place while Caleb was distracted looking at my meager decorations. I wanted to see Lucy and tell her what was going on, but she was in class, so I decided to text her instead. When we arrived back to the house, River had returned from "disposing of bodies," however the fuck one went about doing something like that. He told us to take it easy for the rest of the day but not to leave the house again, so I curled up in one of the cozy armchairs in the living room and pulled out my phone. It was a ballsy move, discussing our crimes in front of their faces and it made me snicker to myself.

We've been caught, my first message to Lucy said, with an emoji of a monkey covering his face. I didn't have to wait long before my phone buzzed with her response, and I bit back a smile when I read it.

Balls. Let me guess, the fucking tracker in the ring? Hers was accompanied by an angry face.

Yep. I was never going to hear the end of this from her. *Of course* the one time I slipped up, it had to lead the *good guys* straight to our doorstep.

Was it Omega Group? she replied immediately, and I glanced up to make sure none of the boys could see my screen.

Yep, I replied again and rolled my eyes when my phone buzzed again quickly.

LOL, guess you lost that bet! At least it was the good guys who caught us. Lucy and I had known for a while that several different agencies were chasing us, and Omega Group was the only one with honorable intentions. The others were hired by our so-called victims. Seeing as all of the items we targeted were already stolen, they couldn't exactly call the police like any normal robbery. Instead, a few of them had hired mercenaries to try and stop us, so given the alternatives, I too, was glad it had been Omega that had found us first. We had our own inside knowledge which gave us total confidence they legitimately were "the good guys." Another message followed closely. ***Who was the agent? Someone we know?***

I snickered to myself as I sent my reply. ***Yep. Caleb...***

Just a single gasping face emoji came back at me so I continued. ***...and Austin***

Well, duh. They are twins; it stands to reason, her matter of fact response read, so I kept going, dragging it out for dramatic effect.

...and Cole

Another gasping emoji

...and two others that I haven't had a chance to tell you about yet. So... a whole team, not just a single agent. There was a bit of a pause this time before Lucy's reply buzzed in my hand.

A whole team? I'm kind of flattered. Omega must think we are pretty badass to send a team this time.

You're taking this really well, Luce. I pointed out the obvious, a bit surprised by her lack of concern.

I figured it'd happen sooner or later. You know how good their agents are! Don't worry, girl. I have a plan. She sent me a winking emoji, and I rolled my eyes again.

"What do you keep rolling your eyes at?" Caleb asked, jolting me from my text conversation. I looked around the living room and noticed River, Cole, and Austin had disappeared again, and Wesley was working on a laptop at the dining table.

"Huh? Um... just Lucy. Being Lucy." I smiled an innocent smile, and he narrowed his eyes at me suspiciously.

"Speaking of Lucy, does she have anything to do with your life of crime?" He cocked his head, skewering me with his intense green gaze.

"Ummmmm..." I stalled, quickly tapping out a message to her.

Do you want me to keep your part secret?

Her response, thankfully, came immediately, saving me further stalling on Caleb's question.

Don't you dare, you bitch! I want credit where credit's due! Besides, all for one and one for all, right? If they've caught you they may as well catch me too. And don't forget I have a plan! Send Caleb to come pick me up after school, 'kay? Got to go, class is starting. She signed off with kisses so she must be pretty confident in her plan.

She's never steered me wrong yet, so better trust her on this.

"Yup, Lucy's involved." I answered Caleb's question succinctly. "She wants you to go pick her up after class so she can be involved. Girl has just the worst case of FOMO."

"What's that?" Wesley frowned, coming over to join us.

"Fear Of Missing Out," Caleb replied for me. "For a smart dude, you still need to get out more." Wesley blushed adorably under Caleb's teasing but nodded in agreement.

"So Lucy's involved?" Caleb turned his attention back to me, and I held my palms up in surrender.

"She can tell you herself." I shrugged and didn't elaborate.

"Holy crap," Caleb whispered after a brief pause, staring at the ceiling. "It makes so much more sense now. How you've been getting through security systems and remotely disarming door codes at the same time as physically accessing the areas. Lucy's a fricking genius." Wesley gave a fake cough, and Caleb added, "Not that you're not too, bro. Just... a different skill set."

Wesley huffed then asked me, "Hey, what happened to the tracker in that hideous yellow ring? That piece of nano-tech took me months to construct."

Oops. I cringed as I admitted, "Uh, I might have dropped it in a glass of Coke."

His face fell like I'd just told him I ran over his dog, and my stomach sank. *Fuck, I feel awful now.*

"I'm really sorry. I panicked when Lucy found it, and it seemed like the best thing to do at the time... In my defense, it did kill the signal, right?"

He nodded slightly with a sad puppy look on his face. "It's okay. I expected something bad when the signal cut out so abruptly. I'm going to go work on these memos." He waved my USB then slunk out of the room with a dejected slump to his shoulders. I kicked myself a little for ruining his hard work, even though it had been for my own safety.

"So you were investigating Mr. Gregoric, huh?" I turned to Caleb, changing the subject. He laughed, hanging his head.

"Yes, we were, and it was so damn boring. He fit the profile to a T, and the fact that he arrived in Cascade Falls at the same time as the tracker…" He sighed. "I'll have to give the company profilers shit for this one."

"Aw, don't be so hard on them. Lucy and I have actually left a couple of false witness statements over the years since we started. It was sort of just a coincidence that Mr. Gregoric matched our made-up Fox." I yawned heavily and stretched out my stiff neck. I still wasn't feeling one hundred percent, but it was mostly just exhaustion. "Shouldn't you be leaving soon to go get Luce?"

"Trying to get rid of me? Not to worry, I just texted Austin and asked him to pick her up."

I raised my brows at him. "Are you sure that's the best idea?" Lucy held just as much affection for Austin as I did, so I was a bit concerned only one of them would make it back here alive.

"They'll be fine. Don't worry so much, Kitty Kat." He laughed and ruffled my hair. I pulled away sharply.

"Don't you *Kitty Kat* me, Caleb King. You've been lying to me since the day we met, and I'm supposed to just pretend that is okay? Uh-uh. I don't think so." I scowled at him to mask my own self-doubt. *Had our whole friendship been an act for him? Fuck, I feel stupid right now.*

"Oh really, Kit Davenport? I might point out I wasn't the only one who was lying," he countered, correctly.

Damn, he had a point.

"So where does that leave us?" I chewed my lip, nervous to hear his response. I had grown really close with him in the past weeks and had genuinely felt like we had known each other for years.

"Look." He released a heavy sigh, running his hand across his face. "I know I didn't tell you our real reason for being at CFA, but everything else, everything with us, it was all one hundred percent real. Wasn't it for you?"

I nodded slowly, and a rush of relief washed over me, making my stomach flip happily.

"So now what?" I asked, and he yawned.

"Can we just chill for a bit? I was up half the night rescuing you from kidnappers, and I'm beat." He pouted adorably and I laughed.

"Sure thing. I'm pretty tired myself."

He flicked on the TV, but within minutes his gentle snores filled the room, and I took an indulgent moment, studying his handsome features while he dozed. *It should be illegal to be that good looking. Ugh, these boys are going to fry my brain with all their sexiness. If my brain wasn't already fried... I still needed to work out if I was imagining all the weird shit lately.* I stifled a yawn of my own and rubbed my eyes. *Just a short nap surely won't hurt...*

I was woken some time later when a loud car pulled into the driveway. A bouncing ball of blue hair came flying into the room and launched at me.

"What the fuck, Kit! You almost got kidnapped? And Simon hit you? I'm going to murder that motherfucker! Fuck! How could you not have called me? That was a dick move! You didn't mention *any* of that in your messages earlier!"

I smiled at her colorful language and hugged her back.

"Aw, it's okay Luce; I'm fine now."

"No fucking shit. And now I hear Caleb and Dickface over there are part of some secret intelligence organization? I mean, that's kinda cool, but what is with all the secrets these days?" she railed, sending Caleb a stern glare and flipping Austin off when he muttered something under his breath. I stifled a laugh at her act that she had no idea who Omega Group was. *Not such a bad actress after all, Luce!*

"That, I only just found out about. So don't go blaming me for keeping secrets," I defended myself and simultaneously threw Caleb under the Lucy-bus. Lucy grunted and then snapped her fingers in the air. She reached into her backpack and whipped out a slightly bent manila folder.

"I went by your room this morning looking for you, and

this was stuffed under your door. I was going to give it to you in class, but obviously you weren't there." She handed the folder over to me, and curious, I opened it.

Inside was a small stack of papers and a handwritten note paper-clipped to the top of the pile, which read: *This might help with what you're searching for - N.*

I flipped through the papers, including various blueprints and maps of somewhere called "Blood Moon Genetics Laboratory." On one of the floor plans, there was a large red circle drawn around the room labeled "Records Storeroom." While I looked through papers, Wesley had resurfaced and was trying to peer at them from over my shoulder. When I was done, he reached for the papers at the same time as Lucy did, and it was like a scene from *The Quick and The Dead* as they stared each other down.

Before they decided on pistols at dawn, I split the pile in two and gave them each half. Both set up on the kitchen island with their laptops. Their quiet chatter faded to a hum in my mind as they communicated in tech jargon.

"Who is 'N'?" Caleb frowned, looking at the note that accompanied the documents.

"I have no idea," I murmured and took the note back to study the handwriting. "Lucy, could this have been one of your, er, contacts?"

"Could be." She frowned. "It is sort of their style." I

seriously hoped it was one of her dark net friends just delivering information because otherwise this was another person of undetermined intentions who knows more about me than I do.

"River will want to know about this," Austin announced and left the room while dialing on his cellphone.

"Do we trust that this info is legitimate? What if it's a trap to lure you in since their kidnapping attempt failed?" Caleb frowned, and I had to admit he had a point. Then again, what other choices did I have? I desperately wanted to know what gave me these abilities, and this was the only lead I had to go on.

"Leave that to us!" Lucy called out. "We will verify all these documents before we act on anything."

"She means," Wesley corrected, "Leave that to me. There's no way in hell I'm letting Lucy anywhere near our company databases."

Lucy rolled her eyes and muttered something under her breath that I didn't catch but Wesley blushed red again.

Caleb and I joined them and attempted to help with looking through the documents but kept getting glared at by the pair of super-geniuses, so eventually we gave up. It seemed like Lucy and Wesley were having an unspoken race to see who could piece together the clues fastest.

Caleb and I watched two movies before Lucy let out a

loud yawn, stretching and cracking her neck dramatically. Wesley's bespeckled face popped up from his own screen, and he announced he was going to make coffee. We had already ordered in Chinese for dinner earlier in the evening and it was getting late, but my love for coffee knew no time limits, and I eagerly hopped up to join Wesley and Lucy in the kitchen.

Waiting for the coffee to brew, Wesley turned to my pixie-like friend with a thoughtful look on his face.

"Why do you do it?" He asked her with interest. "You clearly have a lot of talent for this work, so why are you using your skills to commit crimes?" I froze, not liking where this conversation was heading.

"None of your fucking business," Lucy snapped, her earlier contented expression slamming closed. I mentally begged Wesley to let it go, but he seemed to lack the social experience needed to understand when best to back down. Rather, her refusal to explain seemed to fire him up. It appeared as though Lucy was being an unreasonable hothead, and she was, but Wesley didn't realize that he had just hit on a really sore subject.

"No, I want to know why you and Kit choose to be the bad guys in this world," he pushed, a stubborn set to his jaw. "You both have the potential to do a lot of good, and yet you squander your gifts committing crime, and for what? Money? Surely that can't be it. I mean, even just based on the school you're attending, it's pretty obvious you aren't exactly poor. So help me understand why you would want to steal priceless items from innocent people?"

His hands shook a little, and his cheeks were stained with mottled color as he asked these questions, which made me wonder if there was more going on here than we knew. Regardless, he didn't realize the hornet's nest he'd just kicked with those words. I knew my best friend well enough to know she wasn't going to back down, so was praying Wesley would.

"Innocent people?" Lucy hissed, slamming her hand down on the countertop, and Wesley jumped. Still, the foolish boy didn't know when to stop.

"Yes." He stuck to his guns. "Innocent people. What have they ever done to deserve you stealing from them, other than being rich? As far as I'm aware, being wealthy isn't a crime."

Lucy flicked her outraged gaze to me, and I gave her a tiny headshake. Her lips tightened, and she slammed her laptop closed before shoving it roughly into her bag along with her half of the documents.

"Kit, I'm going back to the dorms. I'll keep working on this from there, but I will not sit here and listen to this bullshit." She slung her bag over her shoulder and then spun back to Wesley, poking her angry finger in his face. "And as for you, fuckface, I advise you keep your fucked up opinions to yourself until you know the whole story. How do you know for sure that this

Omega Group you work for is actually doing good? For all you know, you're all criminals yourselves."

His face turned red at her accusation, but he didn't get a chance to retaliate before she stormed out of the house. Austin has just come back in and caught the end of the argument, so he groaned and picked up his keys again, telling us he would take Lucy home.

Wesley and Caleb both stared at me with confused and shocked expressions on their faces in the aftermath of hurricane Lucy, but I was too tired to get into this with them, so I just shook my head and muttered, "Story for another day." I lifted my coffee for another sip but yawned loudly. Caffeine never seemed to keep me awake.

"Where am I sleeping?" I asked the boys, and a sly, sexy grin spread across Caleb's face. I had no doubt he was about to offer his bed, with him in it, which was more tempting that I cared to admit.

"Take my bed," Cole rumbled from behind me. I tried not to jump and casually turned to look at him. He was in the process of pulling on a T-shirt, and I caught a glimpse of chiseled abs and more ink before his steely gaze locked on me. "I'm heading out on a job now so won't be home until late tomorrow."

Wesley nodded in agreement. "Actually, that's likely to be the case for at least one of us most nights, so there should always be a bed free if you don't mind playing musical pillows?"

"Fine by me," I said. "I can sleep pretty much anywhere, so I'm good!"

"Second door on the left," Cole rumbled, jerking his head towards the hallway. "You're welcome to sleep naked." He winked one of his danger-filled eyes at me then headed out to the garage, leaving me gaping in shock.

"Did he just make a joke?" I stage whispered to Caleb, who was standing closest to me.

He snickered then said, "I don't think he was joking."

"I'm not sure what scares me more..." I mumbled as I dragged my ass down the hall to Cole's room.

Chapter Seventeen

The next morning before school, I was in the kitchen having coffee with Caleb when River joined us, leaning against the counter with his arms folded.

"Kit, we need to organize some training for you," he announced. "If you intend to participate in this investigation, then I need to know you can hold your own if necessary. Cole mentioned seeing you at the gym; do you already have any fight training?"

I shook my head, chewing my lip. "None. I only took up boxing as a... er... stress reliever."

River sighed, and a heavy frown creased his brow. "Maybe you should just leave it to us."

Outraged, I opened my mouth to protest, but Caleb paused the imminent argument by placing a hand on my shoulder.

"River, I'm sure we can train her. She must have some skills from all those Fox jobs," he reasoned, and River raised an eyebrow at me.

"I do." I nodded. "And I am a really fast learner."

"Fine. But I reserve the right to pull the plug if I don't think you're up to scratch," he told me in a no-compromise tone.

"Deal," I agreed quickly, before he could change his mind. "So when do we start?"

"Tomorrow. You three have school today, so we can start on the weekend then continue in the evenings during the week." River nodded a greeting to Austin, who had just joined us in the kitchen.

"You're not seriously still making us attend that school, are you River?" he grumbled, yawning and pouring himself a coffee.

"I am," River confirmed. "Kit needs around-the-clock protective detail until we can deal with whoever tried to kidnap her. I have already called the Headmaster this morning and moved the two of you into all of her and Lucy's classes. I expect you to keep an eye on Lucy too, just in case they go for her." Austin surprisingly didn't argue, so River turned back to me. "The best way for you to learn will be to train with the best. Cole will teach you combat, Caleb will educate you on blades, and Austin will teach you to shoot."

"Couldn't Caleb just teach me both blades and guns at the same time?" I asked, screwing my face up. Honestly, I would rather shoot myself in the foot than *learn* from *Austin*. Caleb coughed over a laugh, and Austin murmured something under his breath that sounded like he agreed, but River gave us all a sharp look. The twins noticeably snapped to attention, shoulders pulling back and their faces serious. I was shocked to find I was also sitting a bit straighter in my seat.

"Austin *will* be teaching you to shoot because he is our team's best marksman and because he will not disobey a direct order. Will he?" River barked at us, and Austin looked suitably chastised for his childish behavior.

"No, sir," he responded, and River turned his attention to me.

"Understood," I whispered, feeling a bit chastised myself. River cocked an eyebrow at me, as though expecting something more, and then I added, "...sir?"

He nodded briefly then turned away but not before I caught the small smile on his lips and heated look in his golden eyes. "Good. I'm glad that is settled. Now get to school or you'll be late."

I woke up Saturday morning with a flutter of excitement in my belly. I was going to learn some real skills today! The day before at school had dragged, first because I now had to deal with Austin in *all* of my classes, and second because I ended up with detention for skipping school the day prior. I couldn't even argue seeing as *sorry, I was recovering from a kidnapping* probably wouldn't have been a believable excuse.

I tried to rein in my excitement as I skipped out to the kitchen and sang, "Good *morning!*"

"Shhh," Caleb shushed me, eyes wide. "You'll wake Wesley." He pointed to the blond boy who was slumped over in an armchair, breathing deeply, and I smiled at how peaceful he looked.

"Late night?" I asked with a whisper, and Caleb just shrugged.

"I wouldn't know; I just woke up myself. Has Cole come back in yet?" I shook my head. I had slept in Cole's room again as he was still off on a job but hadn't seen any sign of him in the brief time I had been awake.

"Guess that means you've got me for lessons today!" He grinned at me and handed me a huge cup of coffee, the sweetheart.

"Sweet." I hummed into my coffee happily. "Knives, right?

So cool."

He snorted. "Not that cool, I'm sorry. You can't learn how to fight with them until Cole teaches you how to fight without them first. So, until he gets back, I will be giving you more of a theory lesson. History, safety, cleaning... these are all the important things you need to know before you're allowed to actually handle them."

I gave him an exaggerated pout. "But Caleb, that sounds *so boring!* How will I learn unless I can get a feel for it physically?"

"Don't you worry, Kitty Kat. I've got you covered." He winked at me and disappeared for a minute, returning with a heavy looking case, which he placed on the table in front of me. As it turned out, he had a perfectly dull, wooden knife for me to handle until I was ready for the real ones. *Not at all what I had meant, Caleb, and you know it.*

For what felt like the next twenty hours, but was probably closer to four, I was drilled and grilled on all aspects of the delicate blades he placed on the table in front of me, without ever being allowed to actually touch them. Eventually he told me we could take a break for lunch and that when we came back he would teach me how to correctly hold them.

I gasped dramatically. "You mean, *touch them*? Surely not!" He rolled his eyes at my teasing and headed into the kitchen to make us sandwiches.

While we were eating, Cole arrived home and we filled

him in on River's training schedule. He agreed with Caleb that learning to actually fight with blades needed to come after I learned some basic combat, so he offered to take the next three days solid, seeing as he shouldn't need to do another job so soon.

I frowned as a thought occurred to me. "I thought you were doing me?" They both looked at me with raised eyebrows at how suggestive the words sounded.

"I mean, I thought your 'job' was tracking down 'The Fox,'" I clarified in order to sound less sexual or potentially conceited.

"We are," Cole confirmed, answering my original question with a fierceness that made me quake a little in my seat. "But our company couldn't justify simply sending us all out here on what could have been a wild goose chase, so we also have another mission in the area involving a possible human trafficking operation."

I stared, wide-eyed. That was the most words I had heard him say in one sentence so far, and I could get used to the sound of his gravelly voice. We had human trafficking in this area? I couldn't imagine it happening in Cascade Falls—there just weren't enough people—so he was likely talking about Seattle, which was our nearest city.

"Right. So, that's what you guys are working on now that you don't have any foxes to hunt?" I teased them, and they smiled. Or rather, Caleb smiled and Cole twitched the corner of his lip up, which I was fairly sure was his version of a smile.

"Exactly," he confirmed. "So we should thank you for cooperating; it means the twins can quit playing teenager and actually help on this case."

I looked sharply at Caleb. "Wait, how old are you then?"

"Twenty-one." He grinned. "My youthful glow allows me to pass for younger."

I snorted a laugh. I'd known they looked way too hot—er *old* to be in high school.

"What about the rest of you?" I asked Cole, and he caught my gaze.

"Twenty-four for me, twenty-five for River, and twenty for Wesley," he confessed, drumming his fingers on the counter.

"Wesley's the baby," Caleb joked. "Although I guess that's technically you now."

"That's all right with you, isn't it, Kit?" Cole was still watching me and practically purred my name. "Lucy did mention you liked older men."

"What?" I spluttered, almost choking on my sandwich, as I had just taken a big bite. "When the hell did she say that?"

He grinned wolfishly. "At lunch when you went outside with your slimy friend. She had *lots* to say while you were gone."

I rolled my eyes. Either he was lying to wind me up, or he wasn't and Lucy had blabbed way too much info about my sex life or current lack thereof. Either way, not much I could do about it now, and I wasn't about to walk into a trap here trying to guess what she might have said, so I just narrowed my eyes at him and made a humming noise like I couldn't care less. He held my gaze, and there was a wickedly amused glint in his. Crap, she really had blabbed. I was going to have to kill her. On the upside though, these small moments of emotion cracking through his terrifying façade were helping me become less afraid of him with every interaction.

I was saved from this awkward turn of conversation when Austin walked into the kitchen. Never thought Austin'd save me, but nonetheless I'd take the wins where I could get them.

"I'm heading out to do some groundwork on this case," he announced to the boys. "Christina's shooting lessons will have to wait, or one of you can do it."

"Ummm, sitting right here," I pointed out, waving a hand in his face. He simply scowled at me like I was something gross on his shoe before he stalked out of the house.

"What the fuck is his problem with me?" I asked, offended. I swore he was getting worse every day.

Cole and Caleb exchanged a long look, then Caleb offered, "He has issues."

"No shit," I retorted, but let it go as they obviously didn't intend to elaborate. "Come on; let's go play with sharp things!"

I led the way back to the living room where we had been having our lesson, and Caleb yelled behind me, "They're not toys!"

Chapter Eighteen

Over the next week we fell into a comfortable rhythm of school during the day, then studying with Lucy for an hour or two, then back to the house and alternating training between Cole and Caleb. My time with Caleb was slow-going. I definitely had no natural skill with knives, but my lessons in combat with Cole went exceptionally well, despite me still getting occasional chills when his cold, emotionless mask slipped into place while demonstrating a move.

Some big development happened in their other case that kept Wesley, Austin, and River fairly busy. We scarcely saw any of them, so I continued sleeping in River's room most nights while he was out. That in itself was a bit odd, as I hadn't seen him for days. Yet I knew he must have been in and slept during the day because each time I returned to his room, the bed was tightly made with precise corners and the pillow smelled of fresh soap and pine trees. Against my better judgment, my trust for these men was slowly growing, despite the cloud of secrets surrounding each and every one of them.

In the early evening a week since my failed kidnapping, I was sitting on the porch swing, wrapped in a blanket against the cold and awaiting my weekly catch-up call with Jonathan. The last time I had spoken to him was before heading out to meet Simon, and I felt like I had aged a year in that time. The screen of my phone lit up with his familiar face, and I smiled, answering the call.

"Hi *Dad*," I teased and was rewarded with a chuckle down the line.

"Kit, don't. It's weird, like me calling you *daughter*." He snorted, humor underneath his words. I wrinkled my nose, despite knowing he couldn't see me.

"Yeah, that is weird. So how're things?" I decided to keep the topics light; he didn't need to hear about all the strange shit going on with me lately. Jonathan had an insanely high-pressured job, so I always hesitated before dumping my crap at his doorstep as well, despite his continued encouragement that it was okay to do so. Telling him now that I was seeing things like teachers eyes changing species or waitresses shooting sparks wasn't going to help his stress level. The kidnapping attempt and my current living situation, I was *definitely* not going to mention.

"Things are good here. I have a feeling we might be picking up some valuable new employees soon, so I'm excited. How is school? Are you still on track for your early graduation?"

I chuckled. *Not exactly early, more like late.* Lucy and I were technically a year behind because we'd had such a rough start to our schooling. But we'd caught up really fast and were on track to graduate half way through our current academic year. Not that Lucy couldn't have already graduated two years ago. It was painfully obvious she was staying just to keep me company, which gave me the guilts every time I thought about it. She was nothing if not stubborn though, and despite numerous arguments on the subject, she was determined to stick with me.

"Yeah, should be. I had a day off last week with the flu"—*attempted kidnapping is similar to the flu, right?*—"but didn't miss much, and Lucy's being a gem to study with me every night after school."

"That's good to hear. Hey, sorry to cut this call short, kiddo; I have someone calling on the other line. You'll be home for Thanksgiving, though, right? I'm planning a party at the townhouse." Our "home" was Jonathan's absurdly over-the-top four-story townhouse in New York's Upper East Side. Neither of us spent enough time there for it to actually feel like home, but it was where we spent the holidays together.

"You bet! I love your parties. Speak next week," I confirmed.

"You know it. Try and stay out of trouble, yes? Love you, kid." His voice held a warmth that I doubted many people would ever hear from him.

"Love you too, Jonathan!" I grinned and ended the call. I sat for a minute before heading back inside, turning the events of the past week over in my mind. Ever since that damn ring with the tracker, everything had been going bat shit crazy, first with the memo alluding to my own talents, then with Simon's craziness, the failed kidnapping, moving in with the guys...

Although in fairness, things had been slowly sliding into crazy town ever since my eighteenth birthday when I'd started seeing things that couldn't possibly be real, like Mr. Gregoric's eye shift or the waitress shooting sparks. I was still pretty sure the fish bowl at school had spontaneously exploded too, but there was just zero explanation for *any* of these things. Unless I wasn't actually going insane and the supernatural did exist? It really wouldn't be such a stretch to imagine, considering my own abilities... *Ugh, this is giving me a migraine.*

I had been making sure on the nights I wasn't training

with Cole to spend some time on the treadmill, just in case my adrenaline decided to spike, but so far so good. My growing unease, now that I was thinking over all the weird shit of late, suggested I would be wise to spend the time before dinner in the gym.

Just in case.

By the weekend, I was getting really anxious about our lack of progress with the blueprints left by the mysterious "N" so was having a bit of a mental pity party when I came out for breakfast.

"We found the location of the testing facility," Wesley said casually while munching through a bowl of cereal. I dropped the piece of toast I was buttering and stared at him, waiting for him to continue.

He blushed and avoided eye contact with me while he pushed his glasses up his nose. "It's about three hours north of here, in the middle of pretty much nowhere. There's only one road in and out, so it will look pretty suspicious if we just drive straight up to the gates. Lucy and I think the best way in will be to park at a rest stop on the main highway and hike the rest of the way up through the forest."

I was pleased to hear Lucy had been playing nice and even more pleased to hear we finally had an idea for where this mysterious records room was located.

"That's awesome news; thank you Wesley." I smiled at him, and he blushed pink.

"Looks like we should go hiking today!" Caleb sang, probably as excited for the change of scenery as I was.

"There's a waterfall maybe about five miles from here if you want to go check that out?" I suggested, and he nodded eagerly.

"I'm in," Cole grunted. "Wes?"

Wesley shook his head vehemently. "Count me out, guys. I have work to do." He finished the last of his cereal before he headed to his room.

"Looks like it's just us three musketeers again." Caleb set his dishes in the sink and headed toward his room to get dressed, slapping my ass playfully on the way past. "Hurry up and get dressed, Kitty Kat. We want to get there and back during daylight!"

"Yeah, you're going to want to make it a quick one," Wesley told me, looking at his laptop. "Forecast is for rain and high winds later this afternoon, but not until four, so you should have plenty of time if those two don't fuck around too much."

"Got it. There and back." I finished off my coffee and went to change.

The three of us set a brisk pace, which didn't allow for much conversation, but as we came within a few hundred yards of the falls, I sped up a bit until I was right behind Caleb.

"Race you to the end!" I called out to him as I bypassed him and jogged up the trail, aware of his pursuit hot on my heels. I dialed back my speed to a more believable level but still beat him there by an easy margin.

When he arrived, panting and gasping, I stood on a rock overlooking the deep pool at the base of a majestically cascading waterfall. He joined me, staring down at the clear water.

"Beautiful, isn't it?" I remarked, watching him stare down at the water as he murmured in agreement. "It's deep too. Often in summer we would come out here to go swimming so don't worry; there aren't any submerged rocks or anything."

He frowned at me, confused. "Why would I worry about—?" His silly question was cut short as I shoved him into the water. He surfaced spluttering and gasping, swearing revenge at me, so I guessed it must be pretty cold. I had only ever been swimming here in summer, but even then it hadn't been particularly warm. I laughed, but my enjoyment was cut short when two strong bands of steel wrapped around my waist and sent me flying through the air. I plummeted into the icy pool alongside Caleb.

"Holy mother-fucking shit fuck ass and balls, that's cold!" I shivered, coughing out water and shoving my wet hair out of my eyes while treading water. Seconds later, there was a loud whoop from above as Cole cannonballed into the water.

"You two are weak!" he yelled. "It's not that cold!" He began a lazy stroke over to the waterfall then dove underneath it.

I was shivering hard when Caleb swam over to me, and his warm arms snaked around my waist.

"You deserved to get thrown in. Call it karma in the form of that giant weapon of a man." He chuckled in my ear.

I spun in his arms and scooped my hand across the surface of the water. I swiped up a sheet of water to splash him in the face, but he ducked, swimming backwards away from me. The immediate rush of freezing water that filled the void where his body had been caused my shivering to kick up a notch, and I whimpered, reaching out and clinging on like a little spider monkey.

"S-s-so c-c-cold," I stuttered out, smooshing my face into the side of his neck. "Keep me warm, hot stuff." His chest vibrated with a soft laugh, but he obliged, running his hands up my back and beginning to rub firm circles along my spine with his strong fingers. I puffed out a soft breath as my muscles softened under his touch and my body melted into his. He lowered his face to the curve of my neck and feathered a kiss across my cool skin. My skin pebbled as he pressed his lips more firmly. I let out an involuntary moan when his hot tongue flickered over the pulse point, and I arched my back, pushing my hips more firmly into his. He hardened against me. Breath catching in my throat, I lifted my head from his shoulder and tilted my face toward his.

"Kitty Kat..." he whispered, a hair's breadth from my lips. "You're turning blue." It took a second for his words to sink through the foggy haze of my arousal. Then, he was swimming us to the edge of the pool and calling out for Cole.

The big man swam over and hopped out beside us without a word. His sharp gaze darted all over me, pausing on my face where my teeth were chattering hard and I could imagine my lips were a little blue. I had that type of skin. It seemed our brief flash of playfulness was already gone, and he was back to being a serious, scary bastard.

He nodded sharply at Caleb and rumbled, "Let's move."

"We need to get you home and warmed up before you get hypothermia," Caleb told me, and I growled in indignation at being treated like a damsel in distress.

"I'm fine. You're both just as cold as me."

They both gave me an odd look, and Caleb explained, "Kitty Kat... we've both spent a fair bit of time training to withstand extreme temperatures."

Oh, I hadn't thought of that. Damn logical men. I was still grumbling about the interruption to what could have turned into a very heated moment. Out of the water, my shivering seemed to climb in intensity and my teeth chattered loudly.

"Yeah, fair enough. Let's move." I acquiesced and followed Cole back up to the trail, where he set an accelerated pace to get us back. With impeccable timing, dark rain clouds started rolling in, and within minutes we were getting pelted with rain.

"At least we couldn't really get any wetter!" Caleb joked from his place behind me on the trail.

"Didn't Wesley mention high winds too?" Cole asked back, and Caleb groaned.

"S-so long as there's no th-thunder," I muttered from behind my chattering teeth. Caleb increased his speed to walk beside me on the narrow trail and squeezed my hand reassuringly.

Chapter Nineteen

After that, the wind picked up and my hands started to go numb. By the time we reached the house, even the boys were shivering. Whose stupid idea was it to go swimming fully clothed in October? Oh yeah, mine. Bad idea, Kit. My hands were shaking so badly I fumbled the handle three times before Cole reached past me and opened it. We spilled into the kitchen in a cold, wet puddle, and Wesley looked up in surprise from the stove where he had started dinner.

"What the hell have you three been doing?" he exclaimed in a very un-Wesley-like tone. "Whose idiotic idea was it to go swimming fully clothed in October?"

"Hah!" I snorted. "That's what I was wondering too!"

Cole and Caleb both gaped at me in disbelief before loudly protesting that I had started the whole thing, which was technically true.

Wesley cut them off, telling them to go and dry off. "As for you"—he gave me a stern look—"you're bordering on hypothermia. Come with me; I have a bathtub in my bathroom."

He led the way down the hall to his room, which I'd actually yet to step foot in seeing as he was usually holed up in there working on his computers. It was a big room but pretty much like I expected it to look, with a huge desk covered in monitors and various tech gadgets. He politely ushered me through to his bathroom and the biggest bathtub ever, sitting under a picture window showing a stunning view of the mountains. I perched on the edge of the tub while he ran it for me, dumping a healthy dose of bubble bath in, which filled the room with the scent of jasmine. It was such a sweet, unexpected gesture that it left me lost for words.

"Are you, um, okay to get..." His earlier bluster seemed to have subsided, and he was back to being awkward and shy. I blinked up at him owlishly, his words taking way longer than they should to sink through my brain. "You know, undressed," he continued, blushing furiously. "I can call

Caleb if you need help?"

I smiled with numb lips, suddenly realizing why he seemed so nervous. "I'm fine. Thank you though." I stood and stripped off my shirt, which made his face flame even brighter red before he spun away.

"It's important you don't fall asleep in the, ah, bath so I'll just, um, sit outside the door and talk to you. If that's okay?"

"Fine by me," I told him, and he retreated out of the room, leaving me to finish stripping down and get into the water. My stiff fingers made slow work of my clothes, but eventually I got them off. Stepping into the deep tub, I hissed as the hot water met my freezing skin. Slowly I lowered myself in, inch by inch, letting my skin adjust to the heat at each interval, and by the time I was fully seated, I was already feeling almost normal. Wesley said something from the other side of the bathroom door, but it was so muffled I couldn't make it out.

"I can't hear you!" I yelled out to him, "Just come in here if we're going to talk!"

There was a pause, then the door cracked open an inch. "I can't come in there!" he replied through the crack. "You're, um, you know... naked!"

I laughed. How different he was from the rest of his team. I doubted they shared his hang-up about seeing a naked woman in the tub.

"I'm completely submerged in bubbles; I promise you

won't see a thing, except for my arms."

There was another pause, and then the door opened farther, admitting a very pink Wesley, who shuffled in with his eyes on the ceiling until he sat with his back against the tub near my feet. Once situated, he flicked a quick glance at my face and nodded.

"You're still a little blue, but your cheeks have more color now." He sounded relieved.

"I'm feeling loads better. Thank you for letting me use your tub." I was genuinely grateful; it had been forever since I enjoyed a good soak, and I'd really been insanely cold. He bobbed his head in acknowledgement.

"No worries. I know it's not super manly, but I love bubble baths," he admitted.

"So what were you trying to say before?" I prompted, reminding him he had been trying to ask something through the door.

"Oh, yes, I was just asking what you wanted to talk about. It's so easy to fall asleep in a warm bath after a prolonged cold exposure that I thought it best to keep you talking." Made sense, and I could very easily drift off in this heavenly tub.

"Why don't you tell me about how you came to work for Omega Group?" I suggested. It was something that I had wondered about with all of the boys, but no one had volunteered their stories yet. A sad smile crossed his face, so I wasn't surprised when he shook his head slightly.

"Maybe later," he said softly. "For now let's just keep the topics a bit less heavy. Also, I need you to be talking or else it defeats the purpose."

"Okay, sounds fair. What do you want to know about me?" I sank a little lower into the water, getting my cold shoulders submerged beneath the bubbles.

"Ummmm," he said as he dropped his head back onto the ledge of the bath and stared at the ceiling. "What's your favorite color?"

I let out a giggle which was very unlike me. I blamed the cold. It was affecting my brain. "Really, Wesley? You know next to nothing about me, and you ask what my favorite color is?"

He tilted his head slightly to look at me and shrugged. "Have to start somewhere."

"I suppose you do. Okay, uhh, blue I suppose? Like, dark blue. Sapphire. You?"

"Green," he replied decisively. "Favorite food?"

"Cheese." I grinned. "Melted cheese. Doesn't even need to be on anything, I'd just eat it off a plate if necessary."

"Weirdo. Mine is curry."

"As if that's not weird!" I laughed. "Okay, how about your favorite animal?"

"Crows. They're one of the smartest animals on Earth,

you know. What about yours?"

Was that really a question? "Fox, duh."

He blushed again. We continued back and forth with our meaningless questions until one struck a chord with me.

"Favorite childhood memory," Wesley asked, and my body tensed. All pretense at relaxing fled.

"Getting adopted," I whispered, and he turned sharply toward me.

"Shit. Sorry. I didn't mean to..." He looked horrified at his blunder, so I forced a small smile to show I wasn't mad.

"It's okay. I assume the twins didn't tell you. Lucy and I grew up in foster care until we were adopted when we were thirteen. It wasn't... the kind of place for good memories."

He looked thoughtful for a minute then blurted out, "My brother got shot."

I cocked my head to the side, searching for the right response, but thankfully he continued.

"I was fifteen, and he was eight. We went down to our local grocery store to get some food for dinner, and while we were there, some asshole tried to rob the place at gunpoint. He was pointing a pistol at the cashier, demanding he open the tills, when a customer tried to be a hero and disarm him. As the guy got knocked to the ground, he started shooting. Just randomly pulling the trigger and firing. Everyone was screaming and yelling, so it took me a minute to realize my little brother wasn't. One of the bullets had caught him in the back, and he was lying beside me on the floor, slowly bleeding out. It seemed like it took forever for the police to arrive and arrest the guy, and even longer for an ambulance to get there."

He fell silent, and my curiosity burned. "What happened to your brother?"

"He lived, but the bullet was lodged in his spine, and they couldn't get it out. He's now paralyzed from the waist down."

I sucked in a sharp breath. *That poor kid.*

"We were already living in a trailer park as it was, with Mom working two jobs to just keep on top of things, so when we found out how much the hospital bill was, not to mention the cost of ongoing care for Grant..." He smiled sadly. "I started doing some dodgy shit online, hacking bank databases and moving money around. I had no idea how to cover my tracks; I just wanted to take care of my mom and Grant. Eventually it all caught up with me though, and I was offered a choice of juvie or community service within Omega Group. No prizes for guessing which option I chose. After I worked off my required hours, they offered me a spot in their training program with the opportunity to join a team. It turns out they had been keeping an eye on me since I had started hacking and arranged it that theirs was the only 'community service' option offered instead of the normal way it's done. Anyway, the money I earn all goes back to supporting my brother.

This year I managed to get all of his medical bills cleared and moved him and my mom into a new house with ramp access and everything." The pride on his face when he spoke about all he had done for his family transformed him.

"So that explains your argument with Lucy?" I guessed, and he grinned.

"Uh huh. So." He cleared his throat, shaking off the intense moment. "What about tattoos? Do you have any?"

I leaned back in the tub once more, accepting the change in subject.

"Nope, none. But I've always wanted one. Maybe I'll have to ask Caleb and Cole where they get theirs done because they're stunning. Like, unbelievably beautiful."

Wesley snickered like he knew something I didn't. "You should ask them some time. Their artist is very passionate about his work."

"I'll do that," I murmured. "How about you? Any ink under that circus tent of a T-shirt?"

He looked mildly offended at my description of his clothes. "Actually I do. All of us use the same tattoo artist, so I assure you it is equally as 'beautiful' as theirs."

"Can I see it?" I grinned, knowing he would probably say no, and he didn't disappoint.

"Maybe another day."

The bath had begun to cool, and I was more than warm

enough to be done, so Wesley excused himself to rescue our dinner.

Chapter Twenty

I finally saw the remaining members of the team again one Saturday morning at breakfast in the midst of an argument with Caleb over which one of us deserved the last pancake. River came in the front door with Austin not far behind. They both pulled up stools at the counter where the four of us were already sitting. Everyone's body language sharpened just the tiniest bit, and I used the distraction to swipe the pancake in question and swiftly licked it all over while Caleb stared in shock.

"I licked it, so it's mine," I gloated and set it on my plate to be drowned in syrup.

Caleb's outraged expression turned heated, and he smirked at me. "Well, by that logic..."

I choked on my mouthful of pancake at the opening I'd created with my innocent statement. Crap. Luckily, River saved me further embarrassment.

"That's enough, you two," he interrupted sternly. "First off, I need to get a couple of hours sleep, but then I'm heading back to the city to pick up some things. Kit, you and Austin will be coming with me to start your target practice at the shooting range. Despite the fact that we have been a bit under the gun with our current caseload, it is unacceptable for you not to know how to shoot if you're to be included. Caleb and Cole, you will be picking up where we left off, Austin and I will take a few days to recuperate, and Wesley, you keep working on your current task. Everyone clear?"

There was a chorus of "yes, sir" around the kitchen island. When River looked at me with a raised brow, I fought back a smile as I bobbed my head submissively and murmured, "Yes, sir." I didn't imagine the flame in his gaze this time.

He made a pleased *hum* and pushed up from his stool. "Austin, get some rest. We leave in five hours."

The shooting range was quiet when we arrived in the late afternoon. When River left me with my biggest fan, he ordered us to be civil to one another. I wasn't sure *civil* was possible for either one of us, but perhaps we could get by with minimal interaction.

Austin signed us in and set us up at the far end of the booths before pulling two different sized handguns from the case he carried.

"I assume you've never handled a firearm before?" He sneered at me. Great, the training session would go well with his attitude.

"You assume correctly." I gritted my teeth and added, "*Asshole*," under my breath. After all, I really did need to learn how to shoot, regardless of the teacher.

He rolled his eyes. "This is going to be slow going. Okay, here's what you need to know before we begin....." He proceeded to rattle off a crash course in gun safety without once stopping to check that I understood or followed what he was saying.

Finishing his lecture, he picked up one of the guns and pointed to each part, naming them. "Barrel, slide, safety, magazine, sight, trigger. Got it?"

I nodded, memorizing every piece.

"Here's how you load it," he said as he added a series of efficient hand movements and a full magazine clicked into place. "Flick the safety off, aim, shoot." Demonstrating as he spoke, he fired the gun without any more warning, and

I jerked. The sound echoed in my ears and left them ringing. Austin gave me a look as though I was a simpering idiot, and my face flamed in embarrassment.

"Your turn. Think you can handle this, Princess?" His condescending tone contradicted his concerned expression, although why he would be concerned was a mystery to me. *I must be reading him wrong.* Clenching my jaw, I kept my anger in check and my mouth shut as I took the gun. Replicating his movements, I checked the gun then aimed it at the paper target and squeezed the trigger lightly. Nothing happened. I frowned in confusion, glancing first at the obviously faulty weapon and then at my surly teacher standing behind me. Eyes narrowed and his lip curled in contempt, he reached over my shoulder and clicked off the safety.

Whoops.

I tried again, and the kickback on the gun sent the bullet wide. It didn't even graze the edge of the paper target. As expected, Austin snickered behind me. Judgmental bastard. Boiling, I tried again. The shot went wide again.

"Great shot, Christina." The smug comment was anything but a compliment. "I'm sure the people in the next lane would appreciate you not hitting their target though."

"As amusing as I'm sure you find this, I might point out that River gave you a direct order to *teach me* how to shoot. Not stand there with your finger up your ass laughing at my inexperience," I reminded him.

His glower gave me a small sense of satisfaction. At least I could hit that target.

Grudgingly, he began to show me the correct way to hold the firearm, how to stand, how to aim, and how to absorb the recoil so as not to jerk the gun when firing. His hands were confident and firm on my body as he adjusted my position, but he didn't linger a second longer than what was strictly necessary. Once I was able to grasp these concepts, my aim improved remarkably. The closer I came to hitting the center of the target, the surlier Austin became.

After firing the gun several hundred times, or so it seemed, my cantankerous mentor declared it was time for a break. I gratefully pulled off my earmuffs and raced back out to the entry lobby where I'd seen a sign for toilets. My bladder had been on the verge of bursting for close to an hour, but I'd refused to ask *him* for a break.

Coming back out of the ladies feeling much fresher, I spotted River standing with his back to me, so I snuck up behind him.

"Back so soon, *Sir*?" I teased, hoping to get another one of *those* looks out of him, but instead as he spun to face me, a flash of panic tensed his expression for a millisecond before lust heated his eyes, reminding me of how he'd looked at me the night we first met.

"Sweetheart," he purred in his sexy British accent, sliding his strong arm around my waist and pulling me in close to his body. "Didn't I tell you only to call me that in the bedroom?" His husky laugh wrapped around me before he glanced over my shoulder. "Women, huh?"

"You didn't mention you had a girlfriend." A rough voice with a heavily Eastern European accent answered him. Curiosity road me, and I casually turned in River's embrace to see who was speaking. He was a heavyset man, shorter than River by almost a head, which explained why I hadn't seen him when I approached. The other man's face was engulfed in a dirty brown beard, and he had a thick scar running through one eyebrow.

I smiled sweetly, playing along. "It's a new relationship."

River hummed in agreement and introduced me as Emily. I offered the man my hand to shake, but he snatched it up and pressed a lingering, wet kiss to my knuckles. Fighting a shudder of revulsion, I leaned back into River's chest, and he tightened his grip on my waist.

"It's a pleasure to meet you, Emily. I am Sergei." He ran his rat-like gaze all over me, and it made me feel dirty just standing there. Something told me Sergei was not a nice man. I smiled politely back at him but linked my fingers through River's at my waist and clung tightly.

"Tell me, what is a pretty little thing like you doing in a

gun store?" He asked the question mildly, but something told me he was smarter than he was letting on. Maybe River and I hadn't sold the idea that we were together.

I took a gamble by playing the stereotype and giggled like an airhead, scooping my long hair over my shoulder then running my hand down the length, which drew Sergei's attention to my chest. "Oh, we aren't here for me, silly! I could never shoot a gun; they're way too scary. I just love seeing my man here handling these big, dangerous weapons. It makes me so.... hot...." I bit my lip like a fucking twit and wiggled my backside against our stern-faced leader. River's breath caught, and triumph surged through me. Huh, River wasn't as unaffected by me as he seemed.

"Well, with that in mind, Sergei, I hope you'll understand if we excuse ourselves?" River drawled, tugging me away without waiting for a response.

He didn't let go of me until we were back on the shooting range and at the end booth where Austin was waiting. When we got to him, River released my hand and puffed out a breath. Rubbing his hand across his permanent three-day stubble, he surprised me with a laugh. Humor wasn't the response I'd been expecting.

"Shit, love. You're not a half-bad actress."

I glowed at his praise, not mentioning that it didn't really require a huge amount of acting skill to act turned on by the idea of him firing guns. He was in another sharp suit again today, and my imagination drooled a little at the rugged James Bond look he pulled off oh so well.

Austin looked confused, but River filled him in on the details of my meeting with Sergei. Though he appeared concerned, River said nothing more on the subject.

Chapter Twenty One

Once again, I was sparring with Cole in the basement gym and growing increasingly frustrated at my inability to best him. I had been dialing back my strength to a more believable level, but even so, he commented a couple of times that I seemed unusually strong for my size. Even when I did allow a little extra oomph behind my fists, he still won due to his superior training from his days in the UFC. Not to mention the fact that he weighed probably three times what I did, so it would be a little obvious if I were able to pin him easily. It was the weekend, so I had insisted on a much longer session than we had been managing after school during the week, and my body was feeling it already.

"Stop," he commanded suddenly, even as I gritted my teeth and clenched both my jaw and my fists in frustration. "Just stop. You're getting all fired up for no reason. I have *years* more experience than you and significantly more body mass. You're not going to beat me any time soon, so stop stressing out over it. Besides, I doubt you'll often come up against someone with my training."

He considered me with his fierce eyes, and I shifted awkwardly. For the most part during our training I'd been able to avoid his gaze, but every now and then I found myself pinned to the spot by his intense focus. My palms grew clammy, but thankfully he broke his musing quickly.

"I have an idea," he said before roaring up the stairs. "Caleb! Get down here!"

The thundering of footsteps down the narrow staircase announced Caleb's arrival, and he bounded into the room with a lazy grin on his face.

"What's up, big guy?" he asked, flicking a glance at me in my workout clothes.

"I need you to fight Kit. She needs to test herself against someone different," he rumbled, perching himself on one of the weight machines.

"Sure, sounds fun!" he accepted without an ounce of

hesitation, then immediately launched himself at me. The sudden flurry caught me off guard, but he wasn't taking me seriously. Reacting, I had him in an arm bar within seconds. When Caleb tapped out, Cole huffed a disappointed sigh.

"Should have known you would go easy on her," he grunted, then turned his face toward the stairs again.

"Austin! Get your ass down here!" he bellowed, and I swore the walls quivered.

The three of us waited while Austin made his lazy way down the stairs then completely ignored me as he looked at Cole. "What do you want?"

"Fight Kit," Cole ordered succinctly.

Austin raised an eyebrow. "You're telling me... to hit the princess?" A cruel smile crept over his face, and suddenly this didn't sound like such a good idea.

"I'm telling you to try," Cole rumbled, getting comfortable on his perch again.

"Uhh, are you sure about this?" Caleb sounded even more concerned by this turn of events than me, but Cole silenced him with a stony glare.

I stepped back out onto the thin mat covering the concrete floor and tightened the Velcro on my thin cushioned gloves while Austin strapped on the pair Caleb tossed him. Bouncing lightly on my toes, I twisted to keep him in my sights as he prowled around the edge of the mat like a caged tiger. Very different from his twin, Austin didn't seem to have any qualms about inflicting maximum damage on me.

He seemed to size me up for a moment then, entirely without telegraphing the motion, he darted in and clipped me in the side before swiftly dodging my return strike. I swallowed a groan of pain; he hit *hard!* Hearing a disappointed grunt from the sidelines, I picked up my game and refocused on the fight with Austin. Channeling my dislike of him into my moves, I managed to land a few punishing hits. Unfortunately, he was quick and very calculating and landed far more punches than I did. His satisfied smirk after each blow left me furious.

Letting my anger fuel my moves, I was able to catch him off guard and sweep his feet out from under him. Down didn't mean out. Cole had taught me that the hard way. I followed through with a punch to the jaw intended to knock him out, but the slippery bastard rolled out of the way right at the last second. Too late to stop my momentum, my closed fist plowed into the thin mat, and the sickening crunch of bones snapping filled the air.

Letting out a strangled noise of pain, I curled around my damaged hand, breathing hard and waiting for my familiar rush of adrenaline to heal me, but all I felt was anger and frustration. God damn it.

"Oh come on, Princess," Austin sneered. "Don't tell me you're giving up because the floor gave you a *boo boo.*"

I ignored him, closing my eyes tight and clenching my jaw. Sweat beaded on my forehead, and I took some deliberately slow breaths, trying to manage the pain.

"Shit, Kitty Kat, are you okay?" Caleb rushed over to me and gently peeled my injured arm away from my chest so he could inspect it. "Fuck," he cursed, seeing the odd angle of my wrist and rapidly swelling fingers.

Tears tracked down my cheeks as he yelled at Cole to check where Wesley was and smoothly swept me up in his arms to carry me upstairs. I was generally pretty good at handling extreme pain with a stiff upper lip, but it had been a really long time since I'd been hurt this bad, and my control threatened to slip entirely.

As Caleb cradled me, careful not to bump my hand, Austin's indignant anger followed us. "How hard were you planning on hitting me?"

Chapter Twenty Two

In the living room, Wesley and River were sitting around the table poring over the papers and blueprints that my mysterious helper had left me. They rose as we burst up the basement stairs, and Wesley sent Cole to fetch the first aid kit from his bathroom.

Caleb set me down gently on the couch but continued to hover, his hands on my shoulders, until Wesley glared at him.

"Caleb, back the hell up man. You're stressing me out," he snapped. "Go get me one of those floppy icepack things from the freezer."

Sitting on the coffee table, Wesley took my arm, holding from the elbow, and laid it across his lap. With precision, he peeled away my gloves as Caleb came running back in holding the ice pack.

"Can you move your fingers?" he asked me quietly, and I shook my head, still unable to speak. Cole returned with the first aid box, and Wesley fished out a roll of bandages and started gently wrapping the flexible icepack around my hand. I whimpered quietly in pain while he worked.

"We need to get you to a hospital for x-rays," Wesley told me, but River frowned at me from behind him. He looked pointedly at my hand, then back at my face with confusion in his expression. He was probably recalling how I'd healed myself in the alley.

Before he could comment or ask about it, I said, "River! Can I speak with you?" Surprisingly, I could handle the pain now that the offending limb had been wrapped up. He twitched his eyebrow up, as if to say there was nothing stopping me, so I grit out, "In private?"

Confusion reigned, but I dodged eye contact with anyone. At River's sharp nod, I forced myself upright and ignored the throb in my hand as I followed him to his bedroom. Once inside, he shut the door firmly.

A door wasn't much of a barrier, and I didn't want the others to overhear us.

"All the rooms in this house are sound-proofed. You can only hear between them if the doors are open. Your secrets are safe in here." The reassurance helped.

Though relieved, I had no idea where or even how to begin explaining this, so I lurked near his dresser, inspecting the impersonal decorations while River stood with his arms folded, watching and waiting for me to speak.

"Kit. What do you want to tell me?" he prompted. *Maybe he hadn't noticed my healing after all?*

"Uh," I stammered. "Um, actually it's nothing. Don't worry. We should get to the hospital like Wesley said."

"Stop," he commanded as I tried to slide past him and leave the room. His forceful tone sent a shiver through me. "I think you were going to tell me why your wrist isn't healing like your face did in that alleyway?"

No such luck. He did remember. Crap. Nothing in his ruggedly handsome face suggested I couldn't trust him. Retreating to his huge bed, I perched on the edge of it. At this point, what choice did I have anymore?

"Okay, so it's not an exact science or anything, but as far as I can tell, I can only heal myself during a surge of adrenaline. Or rather, I call it adrenaline, but it might be something else; I haven't exactly asked a doctor about it, you know?"

River nodded slowly, choosing to sit in an armchair near the bed. Elbows on his knees, he leaned forward and studied me.

"So what causes this 'adrenaline surge' to happen? Why did it happen in the alleyway with a minor injury but not now with this more serious one?"

"Ahhh well..." I dodged meeting his gaze and glanced at the rug. It was a nice rug. Very fluffy. "So, it usually happens when I'm in some form of danger or scared or, um, you know... excited." God damn my body for the hot flush at the idea of River getting me *excited,* but the memory of his lips on my skin still haunted me.

He cleared his throat, his expression thoughtful. "So... that night with Simon..."

"I was definitely scared!" I said firmly, lest he correctly assume it was another emotion fueling my healing that night. "And it would seem that today, despite how much of an utter fucking dickhead Austin has been to me, I never actually felt like I was in any real danger. I mean, I was scared of what I had just done to myself, but anger and frustration were my primary emotions, and from experience I've found my little trick only works off my most dominant emotion at the time."

He frowned at me for a moment before speaking. "Clarify."

I sighed. I hated trying to explain this because it barely made sense to me as it was. "As far as I have been able to work out, it has something to do with the adrenaline rush I get from dangerous or exciting situations, but in this situation with Austin, I was mainly just pissed off at him and myself for letting him get to me like that. So no adrenaline, therefore no healing."

"Hmm." River didn't say more while he processed the information. Standing abruptly, he loomed over me, and my breath caught at his nearness. "Your wrist looks pretty badly broken, and it will definitely exclude you from this mission to the testing facility until it heals."

No one was excluding me. "What do you suggest then? None of you scare me like that; my foolish subconscious seems to trust you all too much."

He leaned forward, placing his palms flat on the bed on either side of me, forcing me to lean backwards a little. My gaze went to his sensual mouth like a moth to a flame.

"But excitement should work, hmm?" His question sent another shiver through me.

My pain-addled brain could hardly comprehend that we were heading in the same direction I was currently fantasizing, but I was definitely not objecting.

Flushing, I managed a nod as I didn't trust my voice. He leaned in closer, pausing when his lips were close enough to mine that a deep breath would push us together, and my eyelashes fluttered shut.

"Well," he whispered, his warm breath fanning across my mouth, "if it will help, it seems rude not to try. Don't you agree... love?" As he purred the endearment, I lost my tenuous hold on dignity and closed the distance between us. River rewarded my choice with a low growl as his mouth closed over mine.

He snaked a hand up to grasp my hair, gripping firmly and controlling my head as he teased my lips apart and delved in, exploring my mouth with a confidence that made my knees shake. His solid body pushed against me until we were flat on his bed, and I hiked my knee up to brace against his waist. Taking advantage of the space created, he moved his hips in line with mine and coaxed a breathy moan from me as his hard length rubbed me through our clothing. Drunk on the smell of pine and the taste of his lips, I touched his face then hissed at the sharp pain in my hand.

He pulled back and studied me and then my hand. "Well, that won't do now, will it?" he murmured as his hot mouth descended to my neck. With a smooth motion, he encircled my good wrist and brought it above my head where he pressed it firmly to the comforter. Then he raised my bad hand to join it.

"These," he said as he tapped my unhurt palm lightly, "are not to move from here. Am I understood?"

"Uh-huh." Willing to agree to anything right now, I groaned. He paused, pulling back from my sensitive throat and looking me sternly in the eye.

"I don't think I heard you correctly. I said, am I

understood?" He quirked an eyebrow, and his gaze was a metallic inferno. I fought a grin, trying to give him my best serious expression. *Such a control freak.*

"Understood, *Sir*." I exhaled the obedience, and he made an animalistic growl, roughly pushing up my tank top and deftly flicking open my front clasped bra. Cupping my full breasts in his palms, he locked his mouth onto one of my tight nipples. His hot mouth sent a fluttering of pleasure through me, and I made a noise of encouragement. He took his time, rolling my sensitive peak in his mouth while his fingers tweaked the other. He gave me a firm nip with his teeth, pinching the other side simultaneously, and I sucked in a sharp breath of pleasure. I bucked my hips impatiently, and he clicked his tongue at me in warning before lazily trailing kisses further down my belly. By the time he reached my waistband, I was a whimpering mess. He peeled down my yoga pants and panties together with excruciating patience then threw them across the room before running his strong hands back up my naked thighs.

"Please..." I begged, desperately trying to keep my hands in place. River placed a teasing kiss against the crease at the top of my thighs, and I mewed.

"Please... what?" He smirked, lightly running his fingertips along my wet folds.

"Please, *Sir*." I gasped, and he rewarded me by sinking a thick finger inside. He rumbled a satisfied noise and licked a slow line to my throbbing bud, then sealed his lips around it and stroked me with his tongue.

The stinging itch of my bones knitting themselves back together again distracted me, but the sexy Brit between my legs ramped up the intensity of his strokes. Alternatively sucking and flicking my clit with his insistent mouth while his powerful fingers pumped into me, he captured my attention. He slid another finger in, and I moaned loudly, nearing the edge. No way I could last much longer. The tension coiled within me, and my heart thundered like a wild horse. When he scraped his teeth across the sensitive bundle of nerves, I shattered. A loud cry ripped from my throat, and I grabbed River's broad shoulders with curled fingers. My nails bit into his flesh as I held on as the orgasm quaked through me. Time ceased as I rode the waves, and then I collapsed, a boneless puddle of pleasure.

The smug smile on River's face greeted me as the spots cleared from my vision. He nuzzled his rough stubble on my thigh then lifted to take a long look at his shoulders where several bright streaks of blood stained through his crisp white shirt.

"It would appear that my kitten has claws. I take it your hand is feeling better then?" he inquired wryly, giving me a heated look. "You disobeyed a direct order. I have half a mind to tie you down next time."

Shuddering from arousal at this suggestion, rather than the fear, I stared at him.

River moved along my body then claimed my mouth once more in a forceful kiss. I reveled in the rough scratch of his facial hair on my soft skin. Sliding my newly mended hand under his shirt, I caressed his velvety skin and enjoyed the steely strength of his muscles beneath. Eagerly, I unbuckled his belt and flicked the button open on his pants, desperate to return the favor. Then a sharp knock on the door interrupted us.

We both froze, but when the sound didn't repeat, I slipped my hand inside his pants. I had expected to encounter more fabric, but instead all I found was bare skin. *Wonderful.* I wrapped my hand confidently around his thick shaft, and the knock came again, more insistent this time. I bit my lip, looking at River for a decision. With a sigh, he dropped his head heavily to my shoulder.

"Bugger." He groaned, then slowly rolled off me and buried his face in a pillow. We both lay still for a minute, and I prayed whoever it was would give up, but the knock came a third time. Giving in to the inevitable, I rearranged my bra and tank top before looking around for my pants. River still had his face in a pillow, so I jabbed him in the ribs, and he popped his head up in question.

"Where are my pants?" I asked, trying not to laugh at

the situation. He reached over the far side of the bed and retrieved them from the floor. When he returned my pants but kept my panties, I raised an eyebrow. He simply winked then tucked the turquoise lace into his pocket before he zipped his pants and buckled his belt. I dragged my pants back on and grinned wickedly at the knowledge that we were both now going commando.

"You're going to need to explain that." River nodded towards my freshly healed appendage, and I agreed. I needed to tell them everything; it was past time for it, and they'd proven themselves to be trustworthy. Or as trustworthy as I was likely to find under the circumstances.

I checked my appearance in the dresser mirror, but my face was still flushed and my lips were swollen red. It wouldn't be hard to guess what we'd been up to. I was still running my fingers through my wild hair when River opened the door.

"Everyone is getting worried out here. Kit's wrist looked really bad, and Wesley is adamant she needs to go to the hospital." It was Caleb, and he glanced from my flushed face to River's un-tucked, bloodstained shirt.

"Tell them not to worry; Kit will explain in a minute," River responded in a tone that brokered no arguments. "We'll be there shortly."

He shut the door again without waiting for Caleb's reply, and my stomach churned with guilt. River must have seen something in my expression because he crossed the room to cup my face in his hands.

"Do *not*," he commanded, "feel guilty. You're not dating anyone, so you've done nothing wrong, Kitten."

The new nickname made me smile. I wouldn't mind showing him my claws again sometime soon, but at the same time, I couldn't fight the sick feeling of hurting Caleb.

"All right," I sighed. "Let's go and get this over with. Believe me, this story is going to take a while." I dreaded having to rehash the past, but at the same time strangely looked forward to eliminating some of the secrets between these men and me.

Chapter Twenty Three

In the living room the whole team was gathered and wore expressions of concern. Or rather, Caleb, Cole, and Wesley look concerned, and Austin just appeared... irritated? Maybe? His expressions were becoming harder to read by the day.

"If you're done having a cry, Christina, the boys would like you to go get checked out so the rest of us can get on with our day," Austin drawled. I smothered a small grin. My flushed face must have looked like I had been crying. Silly boy, I'm not that weak.

I didn't grace him with a response; instead, I went to

the couch and made myself comfortable on the opposite end from Cole. Once seated, I unraveled the bandage on my wrist, despite the sharp protests first from Caleb then Cole. I hadn't realized the scary guy had a soft side, but it made my mouth quirk in a little smile as I finished unwrapping the bandage. Once done, I held up my hand and flexed it a few times, showing them it was good as new again.

Stunned silence blanketed the room. I had their full attention.

"That's not possible," Wesley blurted out, the first to recover. "I examined it. That was a really bad break; you should have needed surgery!"

"Or maybe she was just being a drama queen and you need new glasses," Austin contributed helpfully.

Wesley glared at him and defensively pushed his glasses up his nose.

"No, Wesley's right," I defended him. "It was a pretty bad break, and not just my wrist but a few bones in my fingers too." Four baffled expressions turned in my direction, all except River's. He'd been there as it healed.

"So I guess I should explain a few things about myself..."

"You think?" Austin snorted, and Caleb hurled a cushion at his head then indicated for me to go on.

"I have a couple of unique abilities I've been keeping quiet about that contribute to why I've been able to accomplish such seamless thefts." Wesley's eyes lit up with interest; it had been bugging him that he couldn't work out some of my access points. I considered just how much I should share, but then decided to rip off the Band-Aid. "I have a somewhat exaggerated strength and speed, and as you can see, I can heal myself."

Cole grunted thoughtfully. "You seemed pretty strong for your size."

I coughed out a laugh. "Actually, that's nothing. I've been deliberately holding back to a more normal level. Same with my speed."

"Can you explain how the healing works?" Wesley prompted, curiosity burning in his face. The academic in him had to be just dying to pick me apart.

"Well, obviously I've never volunteered myself for testing or anything, but as near as I can tell, it just requires a trigger, much like an adrenaline surge, so for lack of a better scientific description, that's what I think of it as. When I'm feeling scared or in danger or really excited, I get this, sort of, rush of adrenaline through my body that heals up any injuries I have at the time. It needs to be a really strong feeling to trigger it though, which is why I didn't immediately heal my wrist. I was predominantly pissed off, and that emotion doesn't seem to cut it for the whole healing thing to work."

They were quiet for a moment, probably turning the idea

over, and one by one, it was like awareness rippled over them as they put two and two together to work out what River and I had just been doing to have healed my wrist. His face was like granite, giving nothing away, but I know my lips were still swollen and my face was hot.

I cleared my throat in the awkwardness that followed, then continued, "Anyway, the information I found on my last job did point to illegal human experiments, but what I didn't mention is that the results they're trying to replicate sound suspiciously similar to my own skills. I thought that if I could gather more info, then maybe I can learn more about who, or what, I am or maybe even who my birth parents are."

While I'd been speaking, I'd pulled my legs up on the couch and hugged my knees. Needing to make a conscious effort to look less pathetic, I relaxed my hold and simply tucked my legs to the side, but my hands were trembling, so I clasped them under my knees.

"How did you work out that you had these abilities?" Caleb asked gently. No way I could get away without telling the whole dreadful story.

I closed my eyes for a second and slowed my breathing. I *needed* to tell them this. "As you know, Lucy and I lived in a foster home until we were thirteen." I opened my eyes, avoiding eye contact, but I caught Caleb's nod from the corner of my eyes. "Mother Suzette's, she liked to call it. Sounds lovely huh? Well, not so much. Mother Suzette was a cruel, greedy woman who saw the children under her care as an easy payday. She had a circle of 'patrons' whom she had met through some charity fundraiser. They provided her with substantial donations in exchange for time alone with the kids. She made it a point to take on children who already had a history of abuse before entering the system."

Someone sucked in a horrified breath, but I had barely even begun. Cole gently lifted my feet onto his lap and wrapped his massive paws around them in a rare display of affection and comfort. Having his physical manifestation of support while I recounted this story aloud for the first time since it had happened was oddly cathartic, and I gave him a grateful smile.

"Not that I had been, as far as I know. I actually have no memories before I was found on the streets when I was five. Just my name and age. Anyway, Suzette's patrons all had their favorites among the kids, and the rules were that they were each only allowed one hour per week, so they were careful to choose wisely. They would then be taken to a room with no windows and locked inside for one hour. During that hour, they could do whatever they liked, no questions asked so long as there was no damage that couldn't be covered by clothing. Once the hour was up, the door would be unlocked and they were expected to leave immediately."

The memory of that horror-filled room already threatened to suffocate me. My palms began to sweat and my breathing spiked, so I slammed a steel door on my emotions and disconnected from the words. It was the only way I was going to get through the next part.

"When I was eleven, one of the newer patrons chose me. He was attracted by my red hair and started calling me Foxy because names would have been too personal for child abusers. I was taken down to the little room with him and locked inside. They didn't need to use force to get us in there, we truly believed we had no other choices, that bad things happened to kids who fought back. He was a huge man but not all fat, and I was a tiny, malnourished stick of a thing. Once I heard the lock turn it was like something snapped inside me and I was no longer the docile little girl I had been raised to be. I lashed out at him, fighting like my life depended on it. He laughed at me and tried to bribe me. He offered me all sorts of things that he thought a kid would want, but I was too far gone to play along like was expected. I swung a punch at his face and it broke his nose, knocking him unconscious."

A mutter intruded, but I didn't focus on whoever spoke. In my mind all I could see was the Patron's irate, sweaty face.

"Of course, the door was still locked and there was no other way out of the room, so I sat there, curled up on the corner of the bed, crying hysterically and hoping the man wasn't dead.

I knew Suzette was going to punish me. Kids didn't fight back against patrons, it just wasn't done. Not if you valued your life. He eventually woke up and he was furious. I was still curled up and crying so I didn't see him get up until his hands were around my throat. He kept choking me until I passed out, then when I woke again my hands were bound with his thick leather belt. I started screaming but that made him laugh and he began hitting me. Over and over, pounding blows down on me. Luckily, Mother Suzette kept guards around, under the pretense of 'family' and they busted in, dragging him off me before I was killed. The last thing she needed was to be investigated by social services for a dead foster kid."

I paused for a breath, and the sensation of Cole rubbing calming circles on the balls of my feet invaded my awareness. His face was downturned, so I couldn't see his reaction.

"So that's how you discovered your strength?" Caleb prompted, hurt in his eyes for the little girl I was.

I nodded. I didn't want their pity. "It's grown since then, but that was the first hint I had of it. No underweight eleven-year-old girl should have been able to knock out a man of that size with one hit. When they dragged me out of that room, I was broken in more places than I could count, my face a bloodied mess, and I was barely breathing thanks to a broken rib piercing my lung. Mother Suzette tossed me back in our bunkroom and left Simon and Lucy to care for me. I knew it was a punishment for what I had done, but also she would have needed to come up with a plausible explanation for the emergency room when they inevitably asked questions."

Another breath, each one cost me, but they also kept me in control as I continued, "I was terrified, thinking I was dying, but my body slowly healed. The bones clicked back into place and knitted together, and my cuts all sealed up. By morning, you couldn't tell anything had ever happened, except for the blood stained sheets of my bunk. It was impossible to hide, and Mother Suzette saw an opportunity. She contacted the same patron, who we called Mr. Gray. All the patrons had color names as they never gave us their real ones. He came back the next week, paying that bitch twice the normal rate; Lucy had overheard them discussing it in the hall. The guards came for me this time, and I stood no chance against three of them as small as I was. They took me back to the room and used handcuffs on my wrists and ankles, locking me to the metal frame bed. I was panicking and screaming at them to help me, but it was like pleading with a brick wall. Then Mr. Gray came in. He saw my perfectly unblemished skin and got this... sick, twisted smile on his face. That was one of the longest hours of my life, and by the end of it, I was begging for death. But of course my traitor body healed itself once more overnight and by morning, I was good as new. It was beyond fucking terrifying. He had always made such a show about being *kind*, making the kids *like* him so they wouldn't understand how depraved he really was. But there was no more need to pretend with me and I saw him for the monster he truly was."

While I had been speaking, someone had pressed a cup of coffee into my hand, and I gratefully took a long sip.

"Something tells me it doesn't end there." Caleb said, his voice dark and queasy.

A bitter smile stretched my lips. "It doesn't. His visits became a regular occurrence. Each time he pushed the limits further to see how much I could take, but everything healed eventually. Sometimes it took days, but sure enough, by the time his next visit rolled around I was back to normal, perfect and unblemished. In the beginning I fought back, hard, but Mother Suzette knew how to keep me in line. She promised me that if I went willingly, let them shackle me and play out their perverted desires, then Lucy would be safe."

Protecting my best friend when I couldn't protect myself? It was a deal I could accept. "She would never be chosen and never have to suffer the same treatment as I did. After months of this, he couldn't keep his secret any longer and told one of the other patrons. He too began visiting me, and I only had half the time to heal before the next session. Every now and then they would get bored and try something new. Nothing was off limits." I shuddered, the emotions seeping through the steel door I had slammed them behind, and a slow tear rolled down my cheek. No one spoke for a while, and the tension lay thick in the air. Cole continued rubbing my feet, but his hands shook and energy seemed to coil around him as though he would rather have them wrapped around someone's throat.

"How did it end?" Wesley asked, a sick look on his face.

I smiled, for real this time. That day had been the best one of my life. Hands down.

"Someone must have reported something to the right people, and a private detective agency began investigating. It took them a while to gather the evidence they needed, but eventually they acted. It was late at night and there was a huge storm outside—I remember because the cracks of thunder and the sound of the whip Mr. Gray was using on me seemed to just *melt* together. The agents swept through the building silently, all dressed head to toe in black and heavily armed, taking out Mother Suzette's guards and arresting anyone there that wasn't a kid, then keeping the kids detained until Child Protective Services could arrive. After that, all of us kids were split up, mostly into other foster homes, or the lucky ones like Lucy and I were adopted out. I was thirteen; that's how I ended up with Jonathan."

"Thirteen?" Wesley squeaked. "For two *years*...? What happened to these 'patrons'?"

"They all walked free," River answered for me. "They were

some very influential and wealthy men, and they paid off the right corrupt people in order to get off entirely scot-free."

I raised my brows at him. How did he know?

River looked back at me with pain in his eyes. "Cole and I were in training with Omega Group at the time and heard about it from some of the senior agents. I remember looking it up later and the details haunted me for weeks."

Cole's hands tightened on my feet, but he didn't look up. Now wasn't the time to push him, so I hurried on with my story.

"That's right. Someone tipped Mr. Gray off with just enough time to wash the scene of any material evidence, literally, so the case against him was an easy one to pay his way out of. Anyway, after Lucy and I were reunited at CFA, we created 'The Fox'. It started out pretty small scale, minor break-ins and such, mostly just causing an annoyance, but as we got better, we started getting contacted to steal for other people. We ignored most of them, but then one caught our attention and we saw an opportunity. It was for a painting, a Monet, utterly priceless and guaranteed to hurt the owner if it were taken."

Caleb grunted in surprise, "I remember hearing about that one. Some filthy rich businessman in Toronto right?"

I grinned at the memory. "It sure was. We only steal from a select list of targets, and I leave the foxes behind so they all know it was me. The Monet belonged to Mr. Gray, and since then we have expanded to all of the former 'patrons'. It's not much, but I know it infuriates them, and until I can think of a way to get real revenge, this keeps me satisfied."

"How do you know they understand the message behind those little foxes?" Wesley queried, still a bit pale behind his glasses.

"Lucy taps their communication for a few days after each theft. After the Monet, they knew it was me. Mr. Gray was the one who named me Foxy after all. It's a warning to them that I'm still out here and haven't forgotten, and it keeps them on their toes. Every now and then, I'll break into one of their homes and leave a fox, just to show that I can get to them anywhere and at any time."

"Fuck," Wesley groaned. "That fight with Lucy... and I said you were stealing from innocent people... I need to call and apologize. Are you...?" He hesitated, as if unsure of the social etiquette in this situation, so I waved a hand to tell him to go.

Caleb scooped me up from where I was sitting then took my seat, settling me back into his lap, his strong arms wrapping around me in a tight embrace. Cole claimed my feet once more, and I didn't spill my coffee. Win-win, I supposed.

River stood. "I have errands to run. You're safe here." Then he leaned down and pressed a lingering kiss to my cheek. "Take it easy this afternoon. Watch a movie with these two idiots, and make sure they feed you." He cupped my face in his palm as he straightened, giving me a stern look.

The contact restored my battered spirit. "Yes, sir."

"I'll see you later tonight, Kitten." His face remained stern, but his eyes softened at our private joke. As he left the room, Austin rose abruptly and stalked out after him without a word.

For the rest of the evening, the three of us watched movies while curled up in a pile on the couch. Caleb made popcorn and ordered pizzas while Cole demonstrated a caring, sensitive side that I hadn't known he possessed—attentively making sure I was comfortable and warm and using his magic hands to rub the tension out of my muscles while we enjoyed the light hearted comedies that Caleb had chosen. Somewhere around three movies in, I fell asleep cuddled between these two solid men who had been pampering me all night.

I wasn't sure how long I'd been asleep when strong arms lifted me and carried me into a bed smelling of pine trees. I mumbled incoherently into the hard chest, wrapping my arms around his waist to cuddle closer.

"I'm so sorry, Kitten," River whispered in my ear.

I rubbed my cheek against his naked skin and found a comfortable spot to rest it. "What for?" Too sleepy for a deep conversation, I hoped it was something simple.

"Earlier..." The tension in his body coiled around me, and

a note of uncertainty in his voice tickled at my senses. I'd never heard the dominating team leader sound unsure.

"Earlier, when I mentioned tying you down... I didn't mean... I don't want you to think..." He trailed off, and I forced wakefulness to lift my head and look at him.

"I know what you meant." I smiled. "You don't need to apologize. I thought I would have been horrified, but I wasn't."

"You weren't?" Disbelief underscored his words.

I shook my head. "I trust you, River. I wasn't horrified, I was intrigued..." I wasn't sure whether it was my answer or the naughty whisper, but he looked stunned for a second before his lips curled into a naughty smile.

He gripped my hair, then pulled my head back for a hard, desperate kiss that left us both panting. Before it could go any further though, he rolled me over and cuddled me from behind.

"Sleep, Kitten," he commanded.

"Yes, sir." I yawned, already halfway back to sleep.

Chapter Twenty Four

Breakfast the next morning was an awkward affair. Everyone seemed to be treating me like I was some fragile fucking butterfly, and it put me in a nasty mood. Yes, I had a traumatic childhood, but it was in the past, and I had been dealing with it in my own way for five years. The fact they were *suddenly* treating me like I was breakable was pissing me off. *I'm no different today than I was yesterday, you dickheads.* Eventually, I lost my patience with them after Caleb *willingly offered* the last pancake.

"Can I borrow someone's car? Mine is still in the school parking lot." I needed a change of scenery because

I was worried I'd bite someone's head off if they kept up this behavior much longer. That reminded me I really needed to move my car to the boys' house so I wouldn't end up in this situation again. Having been travelling to and from school every day in Caleb's Mustang, it just hadn't been a priority so far.

They all seemed to hesitate and looked to River for a decision, except Cole, who answered from where he was washing dishes.

"I'll take you into the city, if you want," he offered. Nice, but the whole point was to get away from the kid gloves for a bit, not trap myself into an awkward car conversation for hours.

"We can take my bike. No talking necessary." He must have read my mind, but that sounded much more appealing.

"Done. Let's go," I accepted, hopping off my stool.

He didn't take my urging, instead studying my clothes. "That won't do."

I looked down at the skinny jeans and close fitting gray sweater I had on.

"What's wrong with this?" I frowned.

"You'll freeze," he retorted. "It's a decent drive, and it's a pretty cold day."

Good point, but I hadn't packed anything much heavier when we'd grabbed my clothes a few weeks earlier. I was going to need to take another trip to my dorm soon.

"Here." Caleb tossed me a leather jacket that he'd grabbed from his room. "It'll be huge on you, but at least not as big as one of Cole's."

"Thanks," I said, smiling gratefully, and slid my arms into the soft leather, which still managed to smell like cinnamon and vanilla. As I was yanking on a pair of low-heeled suede boots, River warned Cole to be careful and the big guy grunted in reply.

The ride into the city was exhilarating on the back of Cole's sleek, black Harley Davidson Breakout. Spending an hour and a half wrapped around his huge, leather-clad frame with the crisp wind in my face did wonders to clear away the cobwebs of my foul mood, and when we arrived I was in considerably higher spirits.

Dismounting the bike after he parked it, I buzzed with energy, and my cheeks hurt from smiling.

"That was incredible! Why have I never done that before?" I was bouncing a little on my toes, and Cole chuckled at my enthusiasm. I paused at the sound, trying to remember whether I had ever heard him laugh before. Over the last few weeks, my initial fear of him had subsided, but I still carried a healthy dose of cautiousness in our interactions. Having seen his lethal potential in our combat sessions, I would have been an idiot not to be a bit wary. In a stark contrast to Mr. Gray though, Cole appeared to take no pleasure from inflicting pain. The way his eyes hardened and jaw clenched whenever we were sparring gave me the impression he was not enjoying it, which reassured me.

"All right, Vixen. What do you want to do with your day?"

I grinned at his play on my name; he was sharper than I'd given him credit for. A kit was a baby fox, while a vixen was an adult female one.

"I don't know; I just needed to get out of the house. After everything I told you guys last night, this morning has been..."

"Suffocating?"

"Exasperating."

He nodded in understanding. "Do you want to just browse in some shops and then go for lunch somewhere?"

"That sounds perfect!" I clapped my hands together while he locked up his bike then pocketed the keys.

We spent the next few hours leisurely wandering through shops. Cole had mentioned he needed to pick up some new boots because he'd worn a hole in his current ones, so I used it as an excuse to browse through the women's section and ended up spending far too long trying on every pretty pair that caught my eye. What could I say? Everyone had their vices; mine happened to be shoes. Cole was a surprisingly good shopping companion too; given that he scowled at the majority of pairs I tried on, I knew the few he nodded at must have been fantastic. I made a mental note of those so I could come back another day and buy them when I had a car to carry them home in.

Chapter Twenty Five

Cole steered me into a little Italian restaurant that looked like it had been there for a hundred years. It was the real deal, with red and white checkered tablecloths and an over-the-top authentic Italian host who gushed over what a cute couple we were while he ushered us into a tight booth in the back of the restaurant. As the host left us with our menus, I glanced over at my huge, imposing, tattooed companion, unsure of his feelings on being called "cute," but his body language was relaxed and he seemed almost happy.

"I love this place," he rumbled, studying me rather than

the menu. "Do you want me to order?"

I raised a brow but glanced at the menu myself. "You don't know what I would like."

"Try me," he challenged.

Why not? I closed my menu then gestured my assent to him, curious to see what he would choose. The waiter hurried back over, having apparently been watching for our closed menus.

"Are we ready to order, Signore e signora?" the waiter inquired.

"Yes, thanks. I'll take the house special, extra large, and my lovely companion will have a large pepperoni with extra cheese," Cole confidently ordered for both of us then gave me a small grin. "It's what you've ordered the last three times we had pizza at home. I do pay attention." A warm fuzzy flickered inside me, and I said nothing in response.

The food was magnificent, and by the time I had only one slice left, I was slumped in my seat and clutching my over full belly. Cole watched me with amusement then generously offered to finish the remainder, which hurt me to accept. Yet I thought if I ate another bite I might burst the button on my jeans.

As he made a big show of slowly devouring my last slice, a small, weasel-like man approached our table, reeking of stale cigarette smoke and body odor.

"Cole, hey! Fancy running into you tonight!" he jabbered nervously, his gaze darting all over the place.

"Harry," Cole muttered in a slightly threatening tone. "What do you want?"

"Oh, hah! Straight to the point! Always like that about you. Never one for chit chat, ha ha. Nope, not you! Gosh, how good is the food in this place, right?" He wrung his hands, his jittery body language contradicting his light chatter. Cole just stared at him.

"Boy, your date sure is pretty! Have you guys been together long?"

At a low rumbling noise from Cole, Harry blanched.

"Right, get to the point. Sorry. Uh, so the boss saw you come in here earlier and sent me over to ask if you can fight tonight. He had the Iceman on the cards, but he got picked up last night on some bullshit drug charge, so we're in need of a replacement..."

Cole continued staring at the little man, and I swore he hadn't blinked once. I was definitely glad to have never been on the receiving end of that look. By the sweat beading on Harry's brow, he was wishing he wasn't right now.

"So, ah, what do you say? Boss says he'd be real happy if you could help him out. He's paying too!" The anxious chatter continued as if he could placate danger with enough syllables.

Eventually, after making the poor man squirm for a

minute, Cole broke his silence. "No."

The foul smelling man paled even further and looked ill at Cole's refusal.

"But, ah, I don't understand. The Boss himself is asking, and, ah, you don't want to say no to him. Right?"

"No, *you* don't want to say no to him. I'm here for a nice day out with my lovely friend, not to fight." His eyes narrowed, and I badly wanted to tell Harry to just cut his losses and leave. The little man looked panicked and almost like he might start hyperventilating soon.

"Don't decline on my account." I blurted out, compelled to try and stop the panic attack happening before us. "I don't mind so long as I can watch."

Harry's narrow features relaxed into a huge smile. "Ah, I see why you're with this one! Excellent taste as well as a pretty face, hey? Don't see many of those around these days. Where did you say you two met again?"

Cole gave me an odd look then turned his death stare back on Harry.

"Who is it against?"

At his grunt, Harry's wild panic vanished, and he rubbed his hands together. "Yes! Ah, it's Odin."

A glimmer of excitement warmed Cole's glacial eyes, and he looked at me hesitantly.

"Hey, don't let me stop you. I have no problems hanging

around and watching. In fact, I'd quite like to see if you're half as good as you think you are." At my tease, the corner of his mouth kicked up.

He looked back at the pungent man standing in front of our table and gave a sharp nod. "Very well. Normal time?" When Harry nodded in answer, Cole continued and said, "Tell your boss I expect additional payment for the short notice. An extra fifty percent will do." The foul smelling man continued nodding so hard I half worried his head might pop off his shoulders, and Cole gave him a shooing gesture to make him leave.

Leaving the restaurant, Cole led the way down the street towards what I assumed would be the location for the fight.

"Wait." I frowned. "How is this going to work? You don't have a change of clothes or gloves or anything. Do they have, like, rental gear or something?" *That sounded less stupid in my head.*

Cole just gave me another odd look, a small smile playing at the corners of his mouth. "Not really that sort of a fight, Vixen. You'll see."

Walking into the dodgy, underground fight club, I could see what he had meant.

The entrance was a shady, unmarked door hidden in

a dirty alleyway, guarded on the inside by a burly security guard who demanded a password from us. Once inside, we descended the badly lit stairs into a basement packed with all sorts of shady characters and an empty caged-in octagon in the center. My excitement spiked, and I bounced on my toes a little. I couldn't wait to see Cole in action. I knew he was good because I'd been training with him for weeks, but I'd yet to see him against a real opponent. Despite the fact that he never seemed to enjoy our sparring matches at home, in the anticipation of this illegal cage match, his eyes were sparkling.

Cole tugged me over to a corner where there were some seats set out on a slightly raised platform and lifted me onto one before looking over at someone I couldn't see and giving them a head nod.

"Okay, you should be fine to watch from here. I'll make this as quick as possible, and then we leave straight away. Yes?" He stared intently into my eyes, and I nodded my understanding.

"Don't move from this spot, Vixen. There are some bad sorts in this room, but you'll be safe here. There are guards watching."

I smiled at his protectiveness, as if I couldn't take care of myself. Now, however, wasn't the time to argue with him.

"I understand, Cole. I won't leave. Good luck!" I gave him a light punch in the shoulder. How embarrassing, I didn't know what had possessed me to do that, and the funny look he gave me seemed to agree with my awkward sentiment.

His name was called out loudly over the speakers, and he gave me another concerned look, as though I was planning on getting into trouble the second his back was turned, so I rolled my eyes at him. He sighed, then whipped off his leather jacket and handed it to me, followed by his tight black T-shirt, and my jaw fell open. In all our training sessions, I had yet to see him shirtless, and I was kind of glad because there was absolutely no way I would have been able to concentrate if I had. Covered in more ink than bare skin, he was a marble-cut work of art, and I shivered in response. Luckily his focus was already on the fight ahead, and he didn't seem to notice my slip in composure. He toed off his motorcycle boots and socks, leaving everything with me, before he prowled over to the cage and climbed in with lethal grace.

The crowd went a bit nuts, confirming my suspicion he was a bit of a regular in this scene, with bets suddenly flying around the room and trashy women screaming his name.

His competitor was announced, and the crowd went equally as crazy, so I wasn't sure who the favorite was between them. Odin turned out to be a well-built man, but still several inches shorter than Cole's six foot five. He appeared better prepared for the match, wearing lightweight silk shorts and strapping tape around his ankles. Dancing around the cage, Odin played it up for the crowd, hopping around energetically and doing flashy flips and shit. My money was definitely on Cole, who stood there in his jeans and bare feet, seemingly bored with the situation.

The announcer bellowed out that the fight was about to begin so all bets must be placed, and there was another quick flurry of money changing hands before all fell quiet.

When the fight began, everyone surged to their feet. The crowd crushed forward, blocking my view of the cage. I tried standing on my toes and peering around them, but frustratingly, in my low-heeled boots I didn't have the height to see past the taller men in the crowd. Even on the raised platform where I stood, I couldn't see anything, and the hisses and cheers of the crowd were driving me nuts not knowing who was winning. Eventually I resorted to standing on top of the rickety folding chair just in time to see Odin get mercilessly taken to the ground. Immediately Cole switched positions in order to grab Odin in a rear naked choke hold. Tapping out frantically as his face turned an ugly shade of purple, Odin lost. The spectators went insane, and I hastily hopped free of my chair when it got bumped.

Things were getting intense with the group in front of me, as clearly they had placed money on the loser and weren't happy about the outcome. One of them shoved another, and a man stumbled into me. Not wishing to be trampled, I tucked Cole's things away and headed for a ladies room down a mostly clear corridor to my left. I'd be back in my spot when Cole was done with his victory lap.

Chapter Twenty Six

Walking the short distance to the bathrooms required some agility, ducking intoxicated and angry or celebrating people. I made it quickly enough then headed down the mostly deserted corridor to the bathrooms. Just as I reached out my hand to push open the ladies room door, a meaty paw landed on my shoulder, spinning me around.

"Well, well. Look what I've found." It was the man from the gun range, Sergei, and he grinned gleefully as though he'd just won the lottery. "Emily, wasn't it? I don't think I've seen your man around here anywhere tonight..." His leer promised all sorts of bad things, and I bit back a snappy retort, remembering the simpering idiot act I had put on when we met.

"Oh, hi!" I gave him my best vacant doe eyes and batted my long lashes. "Sergei, right? What are you doing here?"

He ignored my question, a cruel smile on his face. "You know, places like this aren't safe for little girls like you. Anyone could just *snatch* you right up, and no one would say a word." He crept in closer to me, boxing me against the door. I debated my options, fairly sure I might need to break character and feed this guy his nuts in order to get out of this situation. Right in the nick of time, a bloodied hand snaked between us and yanked me out from under my would-be captor's sweaty gaze.

Sergei looked up at my savior, surprised and a little wary. "Cole. Good fight, my friend. I always know my money is safe on you."

Cole glared his scary death stare as his fingers clamped tight on my hip.

"Sergei." Cole sneered the smaller man's name with distaste. "Can I ask what you think you're doing with my girlfriend?" Crap. River hadn't told him about my prior run in with Sergei.

"*Your* girlfriend?" He grinned like a Cheshire cat. "I thought she was *River's* girlfriend?"

The low rumble from Cole's chest frightened even me, but I stepped in a little closer to him, instinctively drawn to the sound.

"We like to share." He glowered at Sergei without so much as missing a beat. "Now fuck off."

Sergei flicked a nervous look at the still wet blood on the hand clamped possessively over my hip, then gave me a parting leer.

"I'm sure I'll be seeing you around, Emily." Then he scurried back down the hallway as though chased by the sound of Cole's growl.

Evidently I wasn't off the hook yet as Cole turned his angry gaze on me, pinning me to the spot. Yeah, I shouldn't have left the chair.

"I had to move," I defended myself before he could start. "There was a fight breaking out right in front of me, and I didn't want to be trampled!" He gave me another long stare, then shocked the hell out of me by sweeping me up in a huge hug.

"Don't scare me like that again, Vixen. I went to get my shit, and you were gone... There are some seriously dangerous people here tonight," he muttered, not putting me down yet.

"I'm sorry," I squeaked, patting his huge shoulders. "I thought I'd be back before you noticed."

He continued to hug me for a second, his hot, sweaty body

dampening my shirt, then gently lowered me back to the floor.

"Let's get out of here." He grunted, picking up his pile of clothes where he had dropped them, then tugging me further down the hallway and out through a fire escape, which led into a different alleyway. He pulled his leather jacket back on then paused to tie his boots. He must have just stuffed his feet in them before coming to find me downstairs. I inspected his bloodied hands for injuries, but they seemed to just be a little bruised around the knuckles, so the blood must have been from Odin.

"Nice of River to have mentioned you've already run into Sergei," he muttered, narrowing his eyes at me as if expecting an explanation, but I just shrugged.

"He's not the sort of guy you want taking an interest in you," Cole continued. "He's mixed up in this human trafficking job."

"I assumed as much when River used a fake name for me." I dropped the hand I was still holding. Whoops. "Quick thinking on the whole 'we share a girlfriend' thing, though."

He gave me a long look, the corner of his mouth twitching, then wrapped his massive paw around my cold hand and tugged me along behind him.

"We better get back before they send out a search party," he commented, heading towards where we had left his bike earlier in the day. As we walked, he pulled me in closer and tucked me under his massive biceps, his hand resting once more on my hip, and I got another warm fuzzy inside.

"Um, Cole?" I asked, biting my lip and not wanting to ruin the moment. Unfortunately, my bladder had other plans.

"Hmm?" He replied, looking down at me.

"I never got to pee... I doubt I'll survive the drive back to Cascade Falls." Actually, I doubted I would make it far at all.

He gave me a confused frown for a second, then coughed out a gruff laugh. "Sure thing, Vixen. Let's stop for dessert somewhere that has a bathroom."

Chapter Twenty Seven

COLE

What the fuck had I been thinking? It had been three days since the fight against Odin, and I was still kicking myself. I should never have taken Kit to that damn fight club; it was way too dangerous, and now she was on Sergei's radar. I had received a serious talking to from River that night about my *blatant disregard for Kit's safety*, and he was right, even if it was his personal feelings for her talking.

"Cole, buddy. Are you listening to me?" Harry, the stinking little rat of a man, was all up in my face again, and *fuck* if I didn't want to just deck him.

"I'm not your fucking buddy; now move," I snarled at him, pushing his smaller frame out of my way and reaching for the door handle to the office he had been guarding.

"I'm telling you, he doesn't want to be disturbed right now," Harry tried again, this time grabbing my wrist to try and hold me back. I paused, looking down at his sticky hand on my skin as though it was a poisonous frog.

"Don't *ever* touch me, again," I said quietly, with a promise of pain in my voice, and he wisely snatched his offending appendage back. I pushed into the dirty office and immediately saw why Sergei wouldn't have wanted to be disturbed.

A pair of huge tits bounced and slapped the desk while he pumped away furiously behind the naked girl bent over the desk. She was his usual type. Young, skinny, fake tits, and too much makeup, which was currently smeared down her face like some sort of nightmare makeup. I recognized her as one of the dancers here at *The Pussy Palace*, but she used to be a bleached blond. Sergei must have sprung for a trip to the salon, or at least a box of dye, because she was now a flaming redhead, and it pissed me off.

The hairy Ukrainian saw me standing there and kept going. He slammed into her a dozen more times while she rolled her eyes at me and made fake noises of pleasure until he grunted and convulsed like some sort of constipated animal.
Goddamn that is disgusting; I'm fucking glad I skipped lunch today.

Finished, he withdrew from the girl and tossed a baggy of white powder onto the desk in front of her. "Get back to work, Candy."

The girl eagerly grabbed the bag, then stood and collected her tiny scrap of a dress from the floor. "Cole, hey baby," she purred in a voice thick with whatever substances she was already on. "I still have ten minutes before I'm due on stage…"

I eyed her with thinly veiled pity, standing there without a stitch of clothing on her body and another man's sweat coating her skin. "No."

She shrugged and stepped into her ridiculous plastic stripper shoes, not bothering to put her dress back on. "You know where to find me if you change your mind." She winked at me and sauntered out of the office with an absurd sway to her skinny hips.

"You sure?" Sergei leered, snapping off his used condom and flicking it into his waste basket. "She looks smoking with that red hair now, huh? I would have thought you'd be all over that ass."

I hardened my features into my carefully blank mask. Integrating ourselves into this disgusting business was part of our job, and I couldn't risk fucking that up now. "What can I say? My needs are being met just fine already." This undercover work had never bothered me before, but knowing he assumed it was Kit "meeting my needs" made my skin crawl. Not that

I wouldn't want her to—in fact, I doubted I had ever wanted anything so badly in my life—but I despised talking about her like this.

"I'm sure they are... How is Emily doing?" He licked his lips like the lecherous bastard he was, and I fought the urge to knock his teeth out. *Emily.* I couldn't imagine why River had chosen that as Kit's fake name. She looked nothing like an Emily.

"None of your fucking business, Sergei. I just came to pick up my money for the Odin fight. Boss told me it was here." I folded my arms and tried to look at anything but him, given he was still just standing there proudly naked. *Not much to be proud about, though.*

He stared at me for a minute, and I could practically see the gears turning in his slimy head. Bending to collect my packet of money from his floor safe, I was treated to an uninterrupted view of his pasty rear end, and I knew my lip was curling with disgust.

Fuck, he was revolting. When he straightened again, my mask was firmly back in place, but even so, it was an internal battle not to throttle him when he held out the envelope then pulled it back as I reached for it. *Fucker.*

"You know, it strikes me as strange," he commented, tapping my envelope on his hand. "You and River don't seem like the sort of guys who would be happy with their girl sleeping around. You're both too... alpha male. You know?"

"No. I don't. Give me the envelope, Sergei. I have places to be." *Like anywhere but here.* I scowled at him and allowed just a little of my anger leak through.

He looked like he was considering fucking around a bit longer, but something in my expression must have convinced him otherwise because he audibly swallowed and handed over the envelope of money. I jerked my head in lieu of a thank you and turned to leave the dirty office before his voice halted me.

"Hopefully I will run into your pretty girlfriend again soon. You won't always be around to protect her, you know." His taunting words snapped the tenuous hold I had over my anger, and I spun back to him, closing the gap between us in one wide step and grabbing a tight fistful of his junk.

"Do I have your undivided attention right now, Sergei?" I asked, and he responded with a high whimpering noise. I tightened my grip a little tighter, and he howled. "I asked you a question, Sergei. Do I have your undivided attention? I don't want there to be any misunderstanding here."

"Y-yes! Yes! Undivided!" His voice was a pained squeak, which gave me a grim satisfaction.

"Good. Now listen closely. If I find out you've so much as *breathed* in Emily's direction again, I will rip this pathetic excuse of a cock straight off your body and shove it down your throat. And I *will* find out. Are we clear?" I hissed the promise to him, and he nodded frantically. "I'm glad we cleared that up."

I released his crown jewels and stormed out of the club, wiping my hand off on my jeans. It was almost the end of the day already, and I still needed to buy Kit those shoes she had been drooling over. But first, maybe I should sterilize my hand.

Chapter Twenty Eight

KIT

It felt like the day would never get here, but *finally*, we would break into Blood Moon Testing Laboratories. I'd been going insane the last few weeks of planning, desperate to find out what secrets their records room might hold about me or possibly my parents.

We piled into two vehicles, Caleb's sleek black Mustang GT and a white panel van that Wesley used as a comm center for jobs where he needed to be within closer range of the targeted site. The drive out to our location was a tense one, no one speaking except to respond to River, who ran through the plan in detail again and checked that everyone was clear on their jobs.

We parked at a rest stop off the main road, some five miles downhill from the labs, and did a double check of all our gear. Caleb still didn't think my knife fighting was anywhere near up to scratch, so he'd opted not to arm me with any blades, but Austin, grudgingly, had been impressed with my marksmanship, and so they'd equipped me with a slim, black nine millimeter pistol. I had it tucked securely into an underarm holster strapped across my chest, which blended into the rest of my all black attire. The boys were all more heavily armed than me, but if all went according to plan, we should be in and out without running into anyone.

Wesley and Lucy were staying with the van to run comms, and the rest of us set out in silence, trekking through the steep forest with efficiency until we reached the edge of the compound. Enclosed by a high barbed wire fence, the facility didn't invite company. Cole clipped through the wire with ease, allowing all of us to slip through. At River's hand signal, we split up to our assigned tasks. Cole, Austin, and River headed towards the front of the complex to create a diversion, while Caleb and I snuck in the back, where it was closest to the records room on the blueprints.

The moon was full, giving us plenty of light to work with along with the bright flood lights evenly spaced around the exterior of the building. Caleb and I sprinted across the lit area during an opening in the patrol to reach the door selected as our access point.

I pulled out my rolled up leather pouch of lock picks and went to work on the door security. We only had a short amount of time to get in and out. Without more information on the contents in the records room, we needed the maximum amount of time to look through it all.

Within seconds, I had the door open.

"Nice work," Caleb whispered, clearly impressed. Pride at having my hard-learned skill appreciated filled me.

We cracked the door, checking the hallway before venturing farther. Two guards were located down the hall. Our patience paid off when a loud explosion went off toward the front of the compound. The guards took off. Taking advantage of our opening, we raced toward the records room.

Again, I made quick work of the locks. Caleb pulled me inside with him and soundlessly closed the door behind us, even as he pulled out a small flashlight to look around.

I clicked on my own flashlight and gasped at the sight before us. I had expected a small room of paper records; after all, most things were electronic these days. But the room was enormous. Either they had expanded this area since the time those blueprints had been filed or the plans we'd used were just plain wrong, because the room was easily four times the size of what we'd anticipated. It was chock full of file boxes stacked high on shelves and in row after row after row. I had no idea how we were going to find anything that we needed in this.

"Uh guys?" Caleb murmured quietly into his earpiece. "We might have a problem here."

"What is it?" River responded immediately.

"There are way, *way* more files in here than we thought. This would take months to sort through." He echoed my own thoughts.

"Years." I groaned. We were so close to my truth, and now this... It sucked.

"Sending Austin your way, but he might be a few minutes. There are considerably more guards than you would have expected for a science lab." River sounded annoyed, which was likely due to events not playing out exactly as his control-freak personality had planned.

"Let's get hunting." Caleb turned to me. "I'll start on the left, you go right. Let's focus on finding anything dated around, what? Eighteen years ago?"

"Sounds good." I took off to my assigned row and ran my flashlight over the labels on the front of the boxes. The ones I had started with were from the *eighteen hundreds*. Holy crap, this thing was so much bigger than I'd anticipated. I moved farther down the aisle. They were all in chronological order. Skipping the next row, I made my way closer to where Caleb had started, hoping he'd found the more recent files.

"Kit, Caleb, you have guards heading your way." Lucy's voice crackled through our earpieces. "I'll see what havoc I can create by opening some locked doors."

Caleb and I looked at each other. We needed to hurry, and quickly made our way down the next row together.

A loud siren started blaring from somewhere overhead, and the sounds of yelling and heavy boots marching down the corridor grew louder. My senses were all screaming at me that it was only a matter of minutes before we were found in here. I could only hope they wouldn't immediately think to check a records room for intruders.

"Shit," Wesley cursed over the radio. "They've seen you. Our CCTV override didn't catch that there was a camera inside the archive as well as outside. Sorry guys, you need to get out of there now!"

Not willing to give up so easily, I continued hunting, finding a box labeled with a date in June, five years before I was born. Close enough, it'd have to do. I grabbed Caleb's bag and stuffed in as many files as possible. Then the door slammed open.

"Too late. They're on you," Wesley said helpfully.

"Austin should be almost there," River updated us. "We will work on another diversion."

The pounding of boots approached, even as I zipped

Caleb's bag closed. He slung it on his back while I pulled my gun from its holster and spun to confront whoever was coming. It felt like a freight train slammed into me from nowhere. The guard knocked the gun from my grasp, but I launched into an offensive. A punch then a kick took the guard down. A second man grabbed me from behind, pinning my arms to my sides.

Caleb was occupied with three guards himself, so I stomped my boot onto my captor's foot and threw my weight backwards to loosen his grip. The moment it slipped, I slammed my elbow into his gut. Twisting around to face him, I followed up with a swift punch to the face, which sent him flying backward into a stack of file boxes. Caleb was taking a few too many hits as the three guards he fought gained the upper hand. Grabbing my gun, I twisted onto my back and fired a shot through the man closest to me. He dropped instantly, giving Caleb the advantage. He finished off the last two then grabbed my hand and pulled me to my feet.

"Come on; we need to split," he urged, and we raced back out to the corridor, which was in mayhem.

Apparently Lucy's idea of a diversion was to disable the locks on every electronic door in the facility and then set off the sprinklers. Caleb and I exited the archive room but only made it a few feet before a group of eight guards rounded the corner ahead of us. Too many for us to attempt on our own. As one, Caleb and I turned the other way and sprinted. Three more guards cut us off, and we rushed them.

Before we got to them, someone appeared behind them. The man looked maybe a few years older than me but with several weeks' growth on his face and a rough, feral look in his eyes. He shoved one of the guards hard into a wall, and the sickening crunch of his head on impact echoed. The savior punched the second one hard in the chest, his fist sinking right through the flesh. When he pulled his arm back, his hand was slick with blood. The third guard fled, dashing past Caleb and me. The bearded guy calmly plucked a gun from the dead guard's waist and shot the retreating one in the back.

Caleb mirrored my surprise as we remained rooted, watching the man wipe his bloody hand off on the other guard's shirt before he looked at us.

"I take it I have you to thank for this mayhem?" His voice was scratchy as though from disuse, and his eyes were those of a wild animal. I nodded dumbly, and he smiled, extending his non-bloody hand for me to shake. "Well then, thank you. The name's Finn. I'll owe you one sometime."

I accepted his hand hesitantly, but he just gave me a quick squeeze then tipped an imaginary hat toward us before he sauntered off whistling.

We barely got a chance to process what had just happened when the larger group of guards caught up to us and once again we were fighting in earnest. Severely outnumbered, things didn't look good. We were too tightly packed in the narrow corridor. It forced me to draw hard on both my enhanced strength and speed, as well as on every lesson Cole had drilled into me in order to try and get the upper hand. Luckily, for whatever reason, none of the guards we'd encountered yet had attempted to shoot us, or we definitely would not have lasted this long. Even I couldn't dodge bullets... as far as I knew.

Pushing my enhanced strength into my moves gave me an upper hand, and then all of a sudden, a leather belt hooked around my neck. The force cut off my airway, and panic surged through me. I clawed at the belt, but I couldn't get a grip to rip it away.

My vision blurred and blackened around the edges as a high-pitched ringing deafened me. Caleb pointed a gun at my head, and fired. The force cutting off my oxygen ceased, and I slumped to the floor, coughing and spluttering. Caleb pulled me to my feet, and then I realized *Caleb* was actually still fighting. It was Austin who'd saved my bacon.

"Thanks," I managed to gasp, rubbing my throat. He said nothing, but turned to help his brother finish off the last of the guards. With them down, we sprinted for the exit.

Thankfully we met with no further resistance on our dash back to the entry point. Soaking wet, sore, and bruised, we didn't slow until we were deep into the forest. Wesley alerted us we were clear, thank God. Then River ordered us to meet back at the vehicles.

Half an hour into our hike back through the trees, Austin must have been bored because he was first to break the quiet.

"You know, this saving your life thing is becoming a bit of a habit, Christina," he commented lightly. Certain something snide hid around the next corner, I waited. "I'm starting to question whether you actually did half of the jobs credited to The Fox. Seems to me like you can barely walk in a straight line without needing to be rescued."

Yep, there it was. *Asshole.*

"What the hell are you talking about?" I snapped, whipping around to face him. "You've saved my life once, and I said thank you."

"Twice, actually. I'm the one that saved you from the kidnappers. You're welcome." Sarcasm marred his tone, despite his smile.

I swallowed my frustration, refusing to take his bait, and stomped down the hill. Unfortunately, I wasn't looking where I was going and hit a bad rut, pitching head first into a ditch before a pair of strong arms grabbed me by the waist and set me back on my feet.

"See what I mean," Austin snarked. "Now that's three times."

I gritted my teeth. *Stupid Kit, not looking where you're going.*

"Now you say, 'Thank you for saving my life, Austin.'"

My jaw clenched so hard I thought I might break it as I ground out the words, "Thank you for saving my life, Austin."

"Three times," he added smugly.

"Three times," I spat. "Now do you mind letting me go?"

Austin looked down and appeared shocked to see his hands still firmly encircling my biceps. He dropped me like a hot potato then jumped across the ditch to where Caleb waited for us with an amused expression on his face.

Chapter Twenty Nine

Scattered around living room, we each had a stack of the stolen files to read and sort through. It was worse than slow going. To my utter dismay, a good portion of the files I'd grabbed were heavily redacted or referenced other documents that we didn't have. No matter how resolutely I tried to focus on the papers in front of me, I couldn't escape the fact that I'd killed someone tonight. I hadn't even batted an eyelid over doing it either; I had acted on impulse and barely even registered what happened until we were in the car on the way back and I'd begun trembling, my adrenaline surging once more. I didn't say anything. The guys were all experienced in this field, and I didn't want them thinking I couldn't handle myself, especially after the scene with Austin in the woods. I could. I just needed to quietly get through my emotional breakdown first.

Thankfully, Wesley announcing he'd found something pulled me out of my internal guilt trip. Thank God. I rushed over to where he perched at the kitchen island and tried not to snatch the file out of his hands.

"What is it?" River asked, looming over my shoulder.

"This first page is a copy of a letter sent by a Dr. Samuelson to someone by the name of Dupree. It reads:

REGARDING THE RECENT BREAK OUT IN THE WASHINGTON TESTING FACILITY. IT IS NOW CONFIRMED THAT TWENTY-SEVEN TEST SUBJECTS HAVE ESCAPED WITH THE ASSISTANCE OF SEVERAL EMPLOYEES WHO DISAGREED WITH OUR LESS CONVENTIONAL METHODS. OF THOSE TWENTY-SEVEN, TWELVE HAVE ALREADY BEEN DETAINED OR TERMINATED, HOWEVER THE REMAINING FIFTEEN HAVE NOT BEEN FOUND. THIS INCLUDES TEST SUBJECTS 37, 82, AND 113. FINDING AND RECOVERING THESE THREE IS, OF COURSE, OUR PRIMARY OBJECTIVE, AND WE UNDERSTAND THE IMPACT ON OUR EXPERIMENT IF WE WERE TO LOSE THEM. WE HUMBLY ASK FOR AN INCREASED BUDGET ALLOWANCE TO CONTINUE OUR SEARCH AND RECOVER THE SUBJECTS.

I paused, flipping to the next page. "The response simply reads, '*Granted.*'"

I set those two pages aside. The rest of the folder included files on the twenty-seven escaped patients. The first few I skimmed through had a red inked stamp of *DECEASED* across the person's photograph. Some of the patient numbers were in the thousands, which gave me a chill to think about how many people might have died in this experiment.

Quickly flipping through, I searched for the three specifically mentioned in the letter: 37, 82, and 113. I pulled them from the stack but froze at the photo for patient 37.

It's me... Or it would be, if I had been alive some thirty-odd years before, as per the date stamp on the bottom of the image. Her hair was shorter than mine, cut to sit above her shoulders, and her eyes were green as opposed to my ice blue, but other than that it was like looking in a mirror. I scanned all of the information listed, despite the redactions. Patient 37 was a female of indeterminate age, but she entered the program in... *1882?*

That wasn't possible. The photo was in color and dated only thirty years before. The girl looked to be my age, not more than twenty. It must be a typo. Her physical characteristics listed her as being only five foot three and of slight build. In a section labeled "attributes," all of the information had been blacked out, but it looked like a long list.

There wasn't much more of any use in the file. Trying to curb my disappointment, I paged through to find patients 82 and 113. Both were men, but again there seemed to be a discrepancy in the intake date versus the photo date. All three photos were dated the same day, so they must have done an update across all the files on that day. The intake dates were different—patient 82 came into the program in July 1911. Patient 113 arrived October of 1946. Neither of those seemed any more possible than patient 37 being admitted in 1882. Both men looked a similar age, maybe in their early to late twenties.

I returned to staring at patient 37 again, the file clutched tightly in my shaking hands when I heard a curse from Caleb. He'd picked up the patient files I'd discarded and begun looking through them.

"What?" I snapped a little more abruptly than I intended, but the adrenaline overload from the night's activities had me badly on edge. Austin peered over his shoulder at the file and released a grunt of surprise before snatching the page and handing it to me.

"Kitty Kat." Caleb frowned. "Isn't that Mr. Gregoric?"

I studied the picture in my hand, and sure enough, our newest teacher stared back at me from a paper labeled *Test Subject 897*. Once again, dated thirty years before. I stared wide-eyed at Caleb and handed the picture to Lucy, who sucked in a breath.

"I have no idea what to make of this." I groaned, rubbing my face with shaking hands.

"I guess it means you're not the only one that can heal yourself," Wesley commented, earning everyone's attention.

"How do you mean?" I frowned, uncertain of the connection.

Wesley shrugged. "Well it stands to reason if your body can heal injuries, it can probably heal all the associated effects of aging too. After all, growing old is just our body deteriorating."

A very valid point, but by that reasoning, did that mean I would never age? The train of thought hurt my head, and I rubbed my face again, the quivers in my hands now radiating up my arms. Lucy must have noticed because she gave me a nudge.

"Why don't you go for a run or something?" she suggested quietly, giving my hands a pointed look. "I need to head back to school anyway. Someone needs to feed that fucking fox of yours; I keep finding him sitting outside your window."

"Use the gym," River interrupted. "I don't want you outside alone just now."

I couldn't argue with his unspoken reasons. Nor did I want to argue with Lucy. I gave her a quick hug before leaving the others, and I headed down to the basement gym. I needed to burn off my fear, my mad... my whatever the hell I was.

Chapter Thirty

After fifteen minutes of barefoot sprinting on the treadmill, I didn't feel any better. My brain couldn't seem to switch off and kept circling around and around between watching myself shoot that guard, to Finn punching his fist through a man's chest, to Mr. Gregoric's picture in a thirty year old file, and finally, to the girl who could be my twin. If anything, my adrenaline continued to build with no relief, despite having already healed all the injuries I'd acquired during our escape.

A big hand reached over the top of the machine and hit the shut off. The belt slowed me to a walk, and I stared at

Cole's stormy face.

"Let's spar," he suggested gruffly. "I think you need something more mentally challenging than running right now."

Dressed in soft gray sweatpants and a black T-shirt, he appeared to have already showered. Yet his idea sounded like exactly what I needed.

"Wesley noticed while watching the cameras that you got surprised from behind a couple of times," he commented with a thread of anger as I followed him to the mats.

My cheeks burned with embarrassment that my inferior skills had been noticed, but I nodded tightly.

"Let's work on that then." He positioned me with my back facing him then paused. The stance left me uncertain when the attack would come. Without warning, he lunged forward and pinned my arms from behind in his vice-like grip, similar to how one of the guards had done earlier in the night. I reacted with the same move.

We continued this for a while, with Cole correcting my moves to make them more effective, and I pulled my punches so as not to actually injure him. It worked better than the treadmill, but my mind was still racing and the images kept playing on a loop.

Caught up, I failed to concentrate on the lesson Cole was trying to teach, then the next thing I knew I was flat on my back. The air whooshed out of me, and his solid form pinned me.

"Pay attention, Vixen," he ordered as I tried to suck in air. Necessity demanded a snappy retort, but he hovered over me. His face was so close to mine. His tightly coiled body pressed against the length of mine. My gaze darted to his mouth. Before I could second guess the desire, I closed the gap between us and pressed my lips lightly against his. He froze, and I panicked.

Shit, what have I done? Where the hell did that come from? Oh my god, I have totally misread this situation!

Thankfully, he interrupted my mental flagellation and kissed me back fiercely, pressing me into the mat then gripping my face in his huge hands.

I groaned as the energy I'd been trying to burn off surged again, hotter this time. The sudden rush of hormones made my actions more frantic, and I yanked Cole's T-shirt over his head, exposing the beautifully illustrated body I'd only caught a small glimpse of at the cage fight. My wildness seemed to rub off on him. Even as I ran my excited fingers over his torso, exploring the ridges of countless scars, he tore my tank top in two, right down the middle.

I gasped, unaware tearing clothes like that actually worked in real life, and he even paused a moment as though surprised himself.

"Sorry," he muttered, dropping the ruined garment, and I grinned, *oh my God, he is so fucking hot.*

"Don't be." I breathed.

Renewing my fevered exploration of his body, I used a little extra strength to push him roughly, rolling us over until I was on top and giving me a fleeting sense of satisfaction at being in control. His pupils dilated, and the next thing I knew I was in the air, legs still wrapped around his thick waist as he rose in one smooth motion then slammed us against the wall. I didn't even mind losing control again; the fight for the upper hand was driving me *crazy*. He deftly flicked open the clasp on my bra then palmed my breasts in his huge hands. When he rolled my nipples with surprising gentleness, it amped up the wildness rushing through me.

I pushed him back a fraction and dropped my feet to the floor. With eager hands, I pushed his loose sweatpants down and was immediately rewarded with the eye opening sight of his equipment.

Fucking hell!

Sucking in a pleased gasp, I wrapped my hand around his massive cock. I stroked firmly, and he groaned low in his chest. Our teeth clicked slightly as his mouth claimed mine once more, his tongue thrusting in deeply and exploring every bit of my own. It wasn't enough though, and I fumbled with the button and zipper of my jeans before desperately peeling them off. I had barely finished yanking them off my feet before he had seized me once more with his huge calloused hands, gripping the backs of my thighs, pinning me back in place with his hips.

"Oh fuck," I moaned as his hard length ground against my hot, lace covered pussy. He grabbed the edge of my panties as if to rip them too, giving me an amused smirk.

"Cole! Don't you dare," I snapped, meeting his sexy granite gaze. "I don't have enough underwear here as it is, and I like these."

"I could buy you more?" he teased, his hot breath caressing my skin as he kissed a path along my neck, but he left the fabric intact. Instead he nudged it aside and eased two thick fingers into my already soaked core, eliciting another breathy curse from me. *Holy hell, is he trying to kill me?*

"Shit, Vixen..." He groaned, as though equally as lost in the heat as he pulled his fingers away only to flick his thumb over my pulsing clit. I reached for him desperately, pulling his hips closer and lining his cock up with me, clenching my legs tighter around his waist and using my hips to push the broad tip of his shaft just inside.

"Fuck, *fuck*!" he swore, pulling back out and dropping my legs, only to bury his face against my shoulder.

"What?" I asked, not sure what could *possibly* be wrong right now. "What's wrong?"

He released a pained groan, his hard length sandwiched between us while my fingers were holding tight to his muscled sides. "We can't."

"Huh?" I frowned, my brain still lost in a haze of arousal.

"I don't keep condoms in the gym, and since I didn't exactly come down here for this..."

He pulled his face back from my neck, giving me a pained look, and I couldn't prevent a little laugh escaping at the sheer torture on his normally stoic face.

"Why," he asked menacingly, "are you laughing right now?"

I tried to squash a smile as I met his gaze and bit my lip. "I have the implant, and I'm clean. If you are too then..."

He looked dumbfounded, so I took his fingers and guided them over the small rod under the skin of my arm. It took a moment for my words to sink in, and then a feral grin lit up his face. In one smooth movement, he spun me around and planted my palms against the rough wall. This time, he did tear through the fragile lace of my panties, and my hips jerked at the hot contact of his hands. Next time, I was sticking with cotton. Or chain mail.

Cole's lips pressed once more to my neck, sucking and biting as his rock hard length breached my entrance, slowly at first as my muscles stretched to accommodate him, and then he drove into me, tearing a satisfied cry from my throat. He paused, as though he was checking that I was okay, but I wiggled impatiently and he began to move.

Feeling a bit like I was possessed, I bucked against him,

meeting each thrust and whimpering in need until he snaked a hand down and teased my already swollen clit. The added stimulation pushed me over the edge into bliss; my muscles clenched and dragged more gritty curses from Cole, which he silenced by clamping his mouth onto my neck and biting hard as he climaxed himself. The sharp pain of his bite seemed to prolong my own ending, and I quivered, my eyesight darkened at the edges and hot sweat slicking down my spine where his chiseled front was pressed.

After an eternity, I panted back to reality and rested my forehead against the wall, my whole body jelly. Cole's strong grip was the only thing holding me upright. He reluctantly withdrew, turning me to face him, and draped my arms around his neck as he gave me a tender kiss. Butterflies seemed to erupt in a flurry of wings within my stomach at the gentle press and sweep of his lips across mine; it was just such a stark contrast to our frenzied fuck against the wall. We remained like that for a while, my face resting on his broad chest and his head resting on the wall above my shoulder, and I ran my hand down his back, my fingers stroking over the raised lines disguised by his colorful illustrations.

"What happened here?" I whispered, running my index finger back and forth across a thick, ragged one near his shoulder that had an almost matching scar on his front. It was cleverly woven into the scales of a huge black and green dragon, which continued over his shoulder and onto part of his back.

Cole puffed out a sharp breath, his skin tensing under my fingers, and his stubble grazed my neck as he shook his head slightly. "Another day. It's not a pretty story."

I didn't push him, knowing all too well about ugly stories. Spent, I yawned. The void left behind after the overwhelming energy always left me exhausted, and my eyelids were now drooping heavily. Cole must have heard my yawn because he eased away from our cozy embrace, and braced me against the wall. It took him a moment to scout the room for our discarded clothing. My destroyed shirt wouldn't cover anything, but he had the grace to look a little sheepish before offering me his T-shirt for me to wear instead.

"Sorry," he apologized, eyeing the fabric as if a bit surprised by what he'd done.

"Don't be." I grinned. "That was seriously hot."

He barked out a laugh and pulled on his own sweatpants. "Go shower; the rest of us will have to do a debriefing and report to our superiors to explain the casualties tonight."

A chill ran down my spine at the mention of casualties. I had contributed to them.

"What will you tell them...? About me?" I asked hesitantly, suddenly understanding they might be forced to out me for my life of crime.

Cole shook his head reassuringly. "It's up to River, but I'm pretty confident he will leave your involvement out of it."

I let out the nervous breath I'd been holding and then started up the stairs with Cole's hulking form close behind me. Right as we reached the top, he grabbed my hand and tugged me back around to face him, sealing his lips to mine in a searing hot kiss.

"Get some sleep. Take my bed," he said, breaking away and slipping past me into the living room where everyone was still gathered.

Chapter Thirty One

River

How long were these things meant to take? Maybe I should go down there... I clenched my jaw and gritted my teeth, knowing I couldn't. Cole had already beaten me to it, *the bastard.*

Kit had looked really rough before she went down to the gym, and concern for her was clouding my brain to the point that I was barely hearing anything Wesley was saying. I knew she had needed to burn off her spiking adrenaline, but she had been down there for over an hour already. Surely that was enough time? I could only hope Cole was keeping a close eye on her and wouldn't push her too hard right now.

"...assuming it was her first kill." I turned back in to catch the last part of Caleb's sentence and snapped back to reality.

"Repeat that," I ordered, not willing to let my team know how badly I had been off in my own head when I should have been focusing on the mission debrief. Not that we could officially debrief without Cole—*what was taking him so long?*

"I said, Kit might be pretty shaken up at the moment; she shot one of the guards to save me. I doubt she has ever actually killed someone before; her Fox jobs sounded all pretty innocuous, so she might need a bit of time to wrap her head around this." Caleb delivered this information with the calm detachment we had all adopted for discussions around fatalities, but there was a line creasing his forehead and the corners of his mouth looked tight.

"You're worried about how she will be reacting." I needed him to clarify. Despite my superior skill in reading subtle body language, my team was so highly trained in controlling their expressions that sometimes I found myself guessing incorrectly with them.

He hesitated for a moment, flicking a glance at his brother. "Yes."

I nodded in understanding, watching Austin closely. He stared back at me, face carefully neutral, and I got nothing from him. He always had been the hardest to read, even harder than Cole, and ever since Kit had arrived into our lives, he'd seemed like more of a closed book than usual.

"Let her take your bed tonight. We shouldn't take too long on this debrief, so you can have some time with her," I told him, and his tight shoulders relaxed the tiniest bit.

"What, you're all taking turns now, are you?" Austin sneered with a disgusted twist to his mouth, but I caught the quick flicker of hurt in his eyes before he dropped eye contact with me.

"Austin," I began, but Wesley, of all people, cut me off.

"You need to stop, Aus. She's not fucking Peyton, so just calm the hell down." He glanced up from his laptop and must have seen the three of us looking at him in surprise because he blushed and cleared his throat. "I'm just saying, Kit is a nice person and she should be allowed to do whatever she wants. It's not hurting anyone, and God knows it wouldn't be the first time you guys have shared a girl."

"Caleb and I are twins, so it doesn't count," Austin muttered, but he was clearly backing down. It was so rare for Wesley to stand up to him that he, like the rest of us, generally dropped an argument when Wes got involved.

Good for him; I was wondering when that kid would speak up. Wesley was easily my easiest team member to read, having considerably less field experience than the rest of us, and for weeks now I'd watched as he'd grown more and more annoyed at Austin's attitude towards Kit. I might even go so far as to say he had a little bit of a crush on her.

"Irrelevant. What Kit, or any of us, do behind closed doors is no concern of yours, Austin," I told him, taking back control of the conversation. "Unless you're also interested?" My suggestion hit the intended mark as his face flushed in outrage and he glared death at me. "No? Well then, you needn't worry. Caleb and I have already discussed this in private and come to a gentleman's agreement, so we shall leave it at that, yes?"

"How very fucking *British* of you," Austin quipped, "Now can we get back on task, here? This isn't a knitting group."

I gave him a warning look, and he dipped his head in acknowledgement; he knew when he was pushing boundaries with me. "Caleb, please continue with what you were saying earlier regarding the patient you and Kit encountered." I switched my attention to the other twin.

"Ugh, yeah, that was beyond weird. He literally punched his bare fist straight through a man's chest. Like, completely through. In one side and out the other." He shook his head as though he could hardly believe it himself. "Wes, did you see it on the cameras? It was... fucking nuts, and then he just thanked Kit and shook her hand like they had just met at a party or some shit. Told her he would 'be seeing her' and totally ignored me standing there, like I didn't exist."

"No, I didn't see any of that, sorry. Lucy had your camera

views at that point, and she mentioned seeing you guys speaking to someone, but he was standing directly below the camera so she couldn't get a picture of him," Wesley responded, much to my disappointment.

That interaction, the way Caleb described it, was leaving a sick, churning feeling in my gut. It was more than simply knowing there was someone else with enhanced strength, it was the interest he seemed to show in our girl afterwards. The wild, primal part of me that I kept tightly caged was raging, screaming for this stranger's blood. I took a deep, calming breath and tightened the cage. *I am in control, not my emotions.* It was a mantra I had to repeat on a daily basis, sometimes several times daily.

My focus was broken by the sound of footsteps coming up from the basement gym, and my heart skipped like I was a bloody teenager with his first crush. *Jesus man, get a grip.*

I tried to tell myself I was just anxious to make sure Kit was recovering okay from her injuries and adrenaline spike, but that wild part of me felt like it was laughing at the half-assed lie.

"Cole. All okay?" I asked in a deliberately calm tone, maintaining my iron grip on my emotions, but my eyes darted behind the big man to look for Kit.

"Yep. She's gone for a shower," he replied, having caught my glance and raising an eyebrow. *Shit, that bastard is too perceptive.*

"How's she doing?" Caleb asked, not even trying to hide his concern any more.

Cole didn't respond for a minute while he poured himself a glass of water in the kitchen then came back to join us, flopping himself down into an empty armchair. "Good."

"Good work out?" I inquired, dreading his response as I took in his lack of shirt and the sheen of sweat coating his illustrated chest.

"Great work out," he smirked back at me, with so much more amusement than I had seen from my best mate in *years.*

"Bugger," I cursed. *The bastard.* I knew I should have gone down to check on her instead of him. Still, I could never be jealous of Cole's happiness, and for some reason I genuinely didn't feel threatened by whatever had just gone on in the gym. I was confident in the connection I had with *my Kitten.*

"Looks like you might need to discuss that *gentleman's agreement* with Cole too, Alpha." Austin snickered, clearly enjoying the extra drama despite his insistence that this wasn't a knitting circle. I ground my teeth together to stop from snapping at him for calling me by my call-sign. I hated those stupid call-signs, but they were assigned by the director of Omega Group himself and we were not permitted to change them.

I suspected the main reason I disliked mine, *Alpha*, was

that the wild part of me responded to it so much, and it made me feel out of control. Not that I would admit that to my team, though. They all didn't seem to mind their own, and not long after we had formed as a team, we had all incorporated them into tattoos.

Cole seemed to be watching me as I thought about it. The huge black and green dragon curled over his shoulder and onto his chest represented his call-sign, *Drake*. Caleb, the *Viper*, had a black and gray, deadly-looking snake curled around his calf from ankle to knee. Austin's *Bengal* was hiding between his other ink on his back; even Wesley had his *Crow* inked on his side. My own wolf, my *Alpha*, was thankfully on my back, so I didn't need to constantly see it. I desperately wished I had used a less talented artist because *fuck* if those eyes didn't look real.

I sighed heavily and rubbed a hand across my tired eyes. The lids were beginning to feel like sandpaper because I kept putting myself on night shifts for our investigation with the human trafficking ring. It was a reckless move, and not one I would allow any of my team to make. Too little sleep can lead to stupid mistakes, so I enforced a strict schedule to avoid them pulling too many nights in a row. A rule I found myself breaking far too often lately. I knew why too; it was the lure of coming home knowing Kit had been in my bed all night.

Fuck, I'm in trouble; what is this girl doing to me?

"All right. Let's debrief the mission quickly, and then Cole and I can speak about the personal developments of the night. I have no doubt Caleb is eager to get to bed." I gave him a knowing look, and he winked back at me. *Cheeky bugger.*

"Hang on, I just need my phone charger." Austin hopped to his feet. "If I see the *princess,* I will tell her about the new room assignment."

"Be nice!" I yelled after him then turned to deal with Cole. "Mate, not now. We can discuss it later."

Chapter Thirty Two

KIT

Stepping out of the shower into the steamy bathroom, I kicked myself that, in my haste, I hadn't grabbed any fresh clothes. Wrapped in a fluffy, white towel, I cracked the door open, popping my head out and checking that the coast was clear before darting down to the hall closet where I'd stored my bag of clothes. I pulled out a T-shirt and clean panties, then shut the door and found a scowling Austin on the other side of it, making me jump and let out a girly scream.

"Christina," he taunted, and the evil glint in his eye told me he knew he'd been sneaking up on me. Asshole.

"What?" I snapped, grabbing my towel a bit tighter to ensure I wasn't flashing anything. His eyes narrowed, and he sniffed in my direction, a frown creasing his beautiful face. "What do you want, Austin?" I repeated, uncomfortable standing here with him while wearing nothing but a towel.

"Caleb sent me to tell you to sleep in his room tonight. We'll all be in debriefing for hours yet to explain this fuck-up of a mission." He wore an irritated look, as though it was all my fault he'd had to kill people tonight, and it was. I nodded tightly, sure that if I spoke, I'd say something bitchy.

"Oh, ah, that's okay. Cole said to take his room." I waited for him to leave, but he continued glaring at me.

"Why?" he challenged.

"Why... what?" Not entirely sure what he was asking, I played dumb.

"Why did Cole tell you to take his room? We're all home tonight, and he physically can't sleep if anyone else is in the room." He narrowed his eyes, and inexplicably I found myself not wanting to admit to him what had just gone down in the gym.

"No reason..." I croaked, and he gave me a triumphant look.

"Well then, take Caleb's room." He paused a moment longer, his gaze lingering on my neck. "I guess you don't heal everything, then." He smirked then brushed past me to return to the living room. After his weird remark, I lifted a hand to my neck. Oh, Cole's vicious bite. Sure enough, I could feel the indent of teeth and a raised, puffy bruise. I couldn't help grinning at the reminder.

After gathering my dirty clothes from the bathroom, I retreated to Caleb's room to get ready for bed. At the last minute, I swapped my sleepshirt for the T-shirt Cole had loaned me. His was soft and baggy and smelled like him, like campfire embers.

It was almost dawn by the time I crawled into Caleb's cloud-like bed, and I fell asleep almost before my head had even reached the pillow. I woke from a nightmare to a room flooded with bright sunlight.

Caleb must have come to bed after their debrief because he curled tightly around me, his face against my shoulder. He patted my face with his free hand as he shushed me. My nightmare must have woken him, too.

"Shhhhhh Kitty Kat, back to sleep," he mumbled, and I had to stifle a giggle.

"Caleb," I whispered as he continued stroking my face. "Caleb!" I prodded him when he didn't respond to my first call.

"What?" he mumbled as he lifted his head, looking confused and sleep-tousled.

"You were patting my face," I answered, smiling at his confusion.

He raised an eyebrow, unapologetic. "You were having a nightmare. It seemed right."

I chuckled at his logic and snuggled in closer, as the air outside the blankets was freezing. He tucked his face back into the crook of my neck, breathing deeply, and then paused.

"Why does your hair smell like my brother?"

"Oops, I guess that's who owned the tasty-smelling shampoo. Mine had run out." *Damn. Of course it was Austin's one that I would use.*

Caleb snickered quietly. "Oh, he's going to kill you when he finds out! That stuff costs him megabucks. And is this Cole's T-shirt?" He slid his warm hand under the garment in question, clasping my waist.

"Um, I think Austin already knows." Maybe that explained his weird sniffing. "And Cole's T-shirt is comfy..." I didn't want to admit he had torn mine in half.

"Mm hmm?" He murmured, his lips against the bite mark on my neck. "Sure that's the only reason?" The tip of his tongue traced the edges of the bruise gently, and I shivered in pleasure. Damn obvious erogenous zones.

"Shh, Caleb. Back to sleep," I huffed, snuggling tighter and shutting down the conversation. He chuckled, but tightened his grip on me and within minutes was breathing deeply. To my disappointment, sleep was harder-won for myself as my brain started churning over the events of the night once more.

One face kept flashing in my mind, over and over. The girl who looked like me. *Who was she?*

Chapter Thirty Three

I woke slowly, refreshed, content, and alone in the cloud bed. Caleb must have woken before me, then turned on a heater. The room was toasty warm. I spent a few minutes just lying in the bed and enjoying the luxury. Caleb's thoughtfulness never failed to make me feel good. Fucking hell, how had I suddenly gone from zero romance to three impossibly hard to resist men all inexplicably interested in me? Everything about our situation had the potential to go really sour, even though I had the feeling they all knew what was going on. Good things like this never lasted, not with me. Maybe I should make the most of it while I could. Life turned on a dime— mine did anyway. So why borrow more trouble?

Ugh, speaking of trouble.

The events of the night before came flooding back, and I groaned, burying my face in the pillow but unable to hide from my own thoughts. Reluctantly, I peeled back the blankets and climbed out of bed. Quickly darting out into the cold hallway, I grabbed fresh clothes from the closet before getting dressed.

In the kitchen, only Cole sat at the counter, finishing off a cup of coffee and reading something on his phone.

"Where is everyone?" I asked, grabbing my own giant cup from the cabinet. It was one that had appeared shortly after I started staying here and was about three times the size of the normal mugs, so I knew without a doubt it was for me. The words "Kit's Koffee Kup" printed on the side of it helped.

"Here and there," he replied, locking his screen before setting his empty cup in the sink. "I have to head out now, too, but River is around the house this afternoon."

"Huh? What time is it?" I took a long sip of the fresh coffee then moaned in pleasure. So good.

Cole watched me for a moment with a heated expression. I was starting to appreciate that his eyes, so capable of such intense coldness, were also capable of the opposite, and right now they set me on fire.

"Three." He responded, prowling closer and boxing me in

with his palms on the counter to either side of me.

I spluttered a little on my coffee. Shit, I had slept for going on ten hours! My mouth gaped open stupidly, and Cole took the opportunity to seal his lips to mine in a blisteringly hot kiss, then pulled away. With a sultry smirk, he dragged his thumb over the mark on my neck.

"I have to head out. Stay out of trouble, and I'll catch you later, Vixen." The nickname sent tingles through me, and I struggled not to drool watching him walk away.

I was still standing there when River entered and swiped the cup out of my hand, helping himself to my coffee. *My coffee*. That was a sure fire way to snap me out of a daze.

"Woah, what the hell are you doing?" I snatched my cup back after he had already pilfered several mouthfuls. "You're likely to lose a hand pulling a crazy stunt like that!"

He grinned before stealing a kiss, tasting like stolen coffee.

"Tastes better when it's yours, love." He winked, and I wondered if we were still talking about the coffee. I blushed and cleared my throat, hunting for a change of subject.

"What's the plan today? Apparently it's already afternoon, but I'm not sure I believe that..."

He laughed, pulling out some food from the fridge, and I tried to remember if I'd ever seen him so jovial before. It was a good look on him too, his easy smile lifting the small scar near his lip, which I couldn't stop staring at, and setting his golden eyes dancing.

"Cole mentioned you were in need of some more clothes, so I thought I'd run you back to your dorm room?" I spat coffee, remembering why I needed new clothes. Panties in particular. Bastards.

"Sounds good," I muttered, eyeing the sandwich River assembled. He had already put in three different types of cheese that I could see, and my stomach growled loudly. Some holy deity must have been smiling down on me because after he pressed on the top of the sandwich, he handed the *whole thing* to me.

"Fuck, I think I love you." I groaned, eyeing up the cheese-filled masterpiece. River made an odd noise, and I frowned at him. "I'm talking to the sandwich, you narcissist."

"Sure you were, love." He chuckled, taking advantage of my full hands to swipe another sip of my coffee, the dick.

"Hurry up and eat that, and we can go," he told me, taking another deliberate sip, and I abandoned all manners to stuff the rest of the sandwich in my mouth and snatch my cup back.

"Such a lady." He sighed, then grabbed his keys off the hook near the door. "Come on then, let's go."

Grumbling at his implication that I wasn't a lady, I downed the remaining coffee before jogging after him into the garage, which I'd yet to explore.

River clicked his key fob, and a sleek, gunmetal gray

Aston Martin Vantage made a sexy beep as it unlocked. My eyes grew bigger as I stared at the gorgeous beast and gave River my very best puppy-dog look.

"Can I drive? Please? *Please?*" I was bouncing on my toes and whining like a two-year-old, but I didn't care. I bet that machine was a dream to drive.

"Not a chance in hell." He chuckled at me before sliding into the driver's seat while I pouted my way around to the passenger side.

I sank into the butter-soft leather seats and inhaled the new car smell. I needed to work my charms a little harder to get the keys to this someday. The sight of River's sexy, grinning face behind the wheel of this incredible machine made my last pair of clean underwear damp.

We pulled out of the garage in a rumble and glided out onto the road, River navigated the tight corners with ease as I studied him. I knew so little about the man, and I'd all but moved in with him and the other members of the team. What I knew? He was the team leader to a group of secret operatives, drove a quarter-million dollar car, wore thousand dollar suit pants and custom made shirts with sleeves rolled up to the elbows. Beyond that, I knew nothing else.

"What?" he asked, noticing my attention on him.

"I know nothing about you," I blurted out. "I've completely thrown caution to the wind, given you guys my deepest, darkest secrets, trusted you with information that could get me killed, and yet none of you have told me anything about yourselves. Except Wesley."

"Wesley?" he asked, surprised. I didn't blame him; the youngest team member was also the most introverted.

"Yeah, he told me about his brother and how he'd ended up with Omega Group." I continued to take the opportunity while he watched the road to study his face. His permanent three-day growth of stubble was trimmed neatly, barely hiding the faint white scar on his upper lip. He flicked another glance over at me, catching me staring—again.

"Well, what do you want to know, love?" His tone was amused.

"Uh, how about... how did you join Omega?"

"Far less of a noble story than Wesley's, I'm afraid," he remarked dryly. "My parents were older when they had me—an accident I suspect, as they were never very affectionate towards me. When I was six my father decided I required too much hard work and had me enrolled in military school here in the States. I completed my schooling at the top of my class then enlisted. Two years later, I was approached by Omega Group, and the rest, as they say, is history."

"And the expensive car? The designer suits? Are they all just a part of your 'cover'?"

The corner of his mouth lifted in a half grin. "No, Kitten,

they're not my 'cover.' My parents died while I was in the army; they were very wealthy people, and I had no other living relatives. I simply happen to like the feeling of wearing suits and driving nice cars."

I had to snort a little at his description of this luxurious machine as "nice."

"As if you're one to judge," he teased me. "Don't think I haven't noticed your penchant for designer shoes."

I huffed but changed the subject. "How did you come to work with these boys?"

"Cole and I have been best friends since we were kids. He had some shit happen when he was about twelve or so, which landed him in the same military school as me. When we graduated and I joined the army, he went on to do his semi-pro fighting career. After Omega approached me, they also approached him. Apparently they had been keeping tabs on us since some aptitude tests while we were in school. The twins joined around three years ago, right after school, and Wesley a year later. We were formed as an official team not long after Wesley passed recruitment but had been doing jobs with the twins since they joined. We don't simply work together; we're family. It's what makes us one of the best teams at Omega."

I considered what he'd said, then my curiosity ran away with my mouth. "What happened to Cole to land him in military school?"

River shook his head firmly, "That's not my story to tell. I'm sure you'll find some way of making him talk, though."

I squirmed under his knowing look.

Then he continued, "And I'm sure Caleb will tell you national secrets if you ask nicely, so if you want their story, I would speak to him and not Austin." This last suggestion was made with a healthy dose of amusement, and I whacked him in the arm.

"Yeah, yeah, hilarious. I think it's pretty obvious Austin hates me." I pretended to sulk, but my feelings were actually a bit hurt by his continued hostility toward me. I had genuinely thought that if he got to know me, we would be okay, but it just seemed like nothing I did had any effect on his dislike for me. I'd never been so inexplicably hated before, and it was getting under my skin.

"He doesn't hate you," River placated. "You just remind him of someone."

"Let me guess, I'll have to ask him myself if I want more information?" The question was rhetorical, and he shrugged less than helpfully as he pulled into the visitor parking bay in front of my CFA dorm.

I was slower than him to unbuckle my safety belt, and he was already opening my door for me before I even reached for the handle. Who said chivalry was dead?

Once I was out of the car, he placed his hand on my lower

back as we walked into the old brick building.

"Speaking of my team," he said, continuing our conversation as we walked, "I should probably warn you that as a rule we don't keep any secrets from each other."

I tensed at his words and almost tripped on the low step up into the building, catching myself just in time to avoid face-planting into the marble floor.

"Ummmm." I was at a loss for words. Was this the part where he called me a slut and told me I was no longer welcome in their house? God damn it, why did I have to be attracted to more than one of them? Now look at what I'd done. Would it really have been that difficult not to act on impulse? Of course the answer to that was *yes*. Not acting on my desire for these men would have been like trying to hold a wild horse with dental floss. Impossible.

"Hey." River tilted my face up to look at him. I realized I'd been lost to my inner monologue for longer than what was generally polite. "I'm just telling you in the interest of full disclosure so you don't think we're gossiping behind your back. That's all."

"That's it?" I was dumbstruck. "You're not... kicking me out of the clubhouse?"

A fierce look crossed his face, and he slipped his fingers into my hair, holding my head tightly. "You're not going *anywhere*," he stated and lowered his mouth to mine, nudging my lips apart and taking his time stroking my tongue with his. When we eventually separated, our breathing was ragged and my cheeks were flushed.

"I'm glad we cleared that up." I exhaled, and he snorted a laugh, intertwining his fingers with mine and tugging me along the corridor to my room.

Stepping into my room seemed weird; it had been only a month since I was last here, but it seemed like a lifetime. I looked around at the familiar surroundings. The cheap, disposable-type cellphone sitting on my bed didn't belong to me.

"River." I pointed him towards it, and he moved in for a closer look.

"I take it this isn't yours?" he clarified, already knowing the answer. He picked it up, turning it over in his hands, before pocketing it. "Grab your stuff; we can check the phone out when we get home."

With a smile for the implication that their home was now my home too, I stuffed a suitcase full of clothes and shoes, sure to grab warmer things.

Finished, I looked over at River, who frowned at my spartan bedroom with its total lack of any personality. What can I say? Even though I'd lived here almost five years, it had always felt temporary, so I'd never truly moved in.

"Done?" he asked when he caught me looking at him. I

nodded, and he picked up my bag for me. "Let's go; we can get Wes to have a look at this phone for us."

Chapter Thirty Four

River called the team on our drive back to the house, but we still had to wait several hours for them all to get back from whatever they were off doing. Luckily, Wesley was already home when we got there, so he went to work on examining the phone while I paced the living room.

Eventually he declared there was not much to tell; it was a prepaid burner phone, bought in cash and totally untraceable. There was only one number, labeled "CALL ME," stored in the contacts, so it didn't take a rocket scientist to work out what it was there for. River insisted we wait for the rest of the team before making the call, but the waiting was driving me insane. I tried calling Lucy, but she didn't answer. Wesley said she hadn't gone home until early in the morning after I went to sleep, so she was probably still asleep, but she would be pissed to miss this development.

I attempted to distract myself by looking through the test subject files again, but if anything, it only served to make me more anxious, seeing the ageless face of Mr. Gregoric and the woman who could be my twin. Just when I felt like my head might explode, Caleb's car pulled into the garage, closely followed by the rumble of Cole's motorbike. Caleb must have been out on a job with his brother because they entered in from the garage together dressed identically, with their hair slicked back the same way and sporting matching eyebrow piercings.

The effect was eerie and a little overwhelming, but I could still pick them apart based on the way they looked at me. Caleb dropped onto the couch beside me, then pulled me onto his lap for a hug.

"I didn't know you had a piercing," I commented dumbly, fingering the eyebrow jewelry. How had I not noticed before?

He grinned and winked lasciviously. "What makes you think that's the only one?"

"That's enough," Austin snapped. "I'm sure River didn't call us off the job just so you two could eye fuck each other."

"I didn't," River answered, his serious expression firmly in place as he held up the burner phone. "This was left on Kit's bed at CFA. It has one number saved under 'CALL ME,' so I think it's a fairly safe assumption that it might be related to last night's mission."

The team went silent as they absorbed the information.

"I take it Wesley has already checked it over?" Caleb spoke first. "Well then, it sounds like we need to make a call."

River did a quick sweep around the room to ensure everyone was in agreement, then handed the phone to me. "Put it on speaker, then dial the number."

I slid out of Caleb's lap and tapped the call button, not knowing what—or who—I expected on the other end.

"Oh good!" the friendly, weathered voice of an older woman with a British accent answered. "You found the phone. I knew you would."

"Um..." I frowned at the phone. Her cheery tone threw me completely.

"Now, Christina dear, I really must tell you I was most upset to see the mess you made of my little testing facility last night." The grandmotherly voice continued; the woman was a *nutcase*.

"I'm... sorry?" I responded, baffled at how one was supposed to respond to a crazy person.

She clucked her tongue. "Never mind; what's done is

done. No use crying over spilled milk, now is there, dear?"

"Who the fuck are you?" I blurted out, my shock subsiding and my filter gone.

"Language!" she snapped sharply. "That is no way to speak to your elders. However, you're right; I was terribly rude not to introduce myself, especially seeing as I know so much about you." I glanced at River, but he motioned for me to keep going.

"Okay... so who the hell are you?"

An exasperated sigh greeted my demand. "My name, dear girl, is Claudette Dupree. You may call me Madam Dupree."

"Sure thing, *Dupree*," I sneered back at her, raising an eyebrow to the boys and tapping the documents on the coffee table containing the letter written to Dupree regarding the escaped patients. "So what the fuck do you want? Obviously something, or you would have left a fucking bomb instead of a shitty phone."

Okay, now I was deliberately swearing to piss her off. I could almost hear her teeth grinding over the phone.

"I wanted to offer you a trade. Obviously you're searching for information on your mother and her time here with us; I can offer you that information," she told me in a slick, oily voice.

"My mother?" I blurted the words, surprised but not totally blindsided. It was a fairly logical assumption based on the similarity between subject 37 and myself.

"You thought I didn't know you were Bridget's daughter? The resemblance is uncanny; I even thought for a moment you were her when I saw you on the cameras." The woman scoffed a little at the idea, and I had to bite back the thousand questions clamoring for answers. The last thing I needed was to show she had the upper hand. *Holy crap my mother has a name!*

"Let's cut to the chase shall we?" she continued briskly. "We both want answers. I'm offering you the answers you want, if in exchange, you willingly participate in a few tests at my facility."

Cole and River shook their heads immediately, but I ignored them. This was my call. And I wanted as much information as I could get.

"What sort of tests?" I asked, and the hesitance in my voice wasn't an act. The guys around me wore differing levels of panic. Even Austin looked grim and gave me a death stare along with a sharp headshake.

"Oh, nothing too invasive." Dupree laughed. "I'm just interested to see what traits Bridget might have passed on to you. It would mostly just be questions. An interview you might say."

River's beautiful green-gold left eye was twitching, and his jaw looked like it was clenched hard enough to break something. I strongly suspected he might have a brain aneurism if I kept ignoring them. I needed to wrap the conversation up.

"I'll think about it," I said, and his teeth made a loud grinding noise.

"You have twenty four hours," she responded, apparently scenting weakness and demanding control. "Call back on this number and let me know your choice. But Christina, dear, I recommend making the *right* choice." The line disconnected.

The phone was snatched out of my grip before I could even open my mouth to speak, and I glared hard at Caleb who was holding it in his fist.

"What the fuck do you mean, *you'll think about it?*" he demanded. "The answer is no. There is no *thinking about it* required here!"

"Over my dead fucking body," Cole swore.

"For once, I'm with these dickheads. You can't accept that shit, Christina." *Since when did Austin give a shit what happened to me?*

"Woah, *woah!*" I yelled over their stubborn declarations. "Just back the hell up! If you're not capable of talking this through with me rationally, then we won't talk at all and I will decide for myself."

"There will be no decision, Vixen," Cole roared menacingly. "You didn't see what we saw in those labs."

"Ah, I beg your pardon?" Yep, looked like my high horse

had come out to play. "I saw a man punch *his fist* through another man's chest! I'm sure it wasn't worse than that."

"Trust me, Kitten, it was," River said quietly. "We saw some of the test subjects, and I promise you, they were not there for 'interviews.' We didn't want to say anything last night—you had enough on your plate with the pictures in the files—but it was bad. Really bad."

"They're right," Wesley piped up, the traitor. "It's why Lucy started opening all the doors. We only caught a tiny bit on camera, but it was enough to say you can't willingly go there."

I studied their stubborn faces; not one of them seemed willing to consider any sort of compromise, and my temper flared. "I'm not an idiot, I know it's probably a trap. I just think that we can--"

"No. We are not even entertaining this as a possibility. This is way outside of the assignment we came here to do, and I am sorry, Kit, but I am putting my foot down." River's tone held no room for negotiation.

"Well. Thank you all for your opinions." I seethed, and inside I was a boiling mess of anger. "I will take them under advisement while I consider the best course of action *for me*. Now if you will excuse me, I am going to go and think of some way I might meet Dupree halfway on her offer." I stood and started out of the room, then hesitated. I didn't really have my own space in their house.

"Take my room," Cole rumbled. "I'll leave you alone."

Not responding, I continued to his room and closed the door firmly. Lying on his bed, I stared at the ceiling as though it held the answers I needed.

At some point, a tentative knock on the door jarred me from my thoughts. The door opened just a tiny crack to allow the sound through.

"Kit? It's me... ah I mean Wesley." I rolled my eyes—as if I didn't know his voice. "I just wanted to check if you're coming out for dinner? You must be hungry..."

"No!" I yelled back. The *last* thing I wanted to do was sit around and play nice with a bunch of misogynistic assholes. *How dare they tell me what I can and can't do?* I wasn't stupid enough to just waltz into the bad guys lair thinking we would have tea, but they wouldn't even discuss how we could have used this opportunity.

I heard Wesley murmur something unintelligible, and then he knocked again a short while later.

"Hey, Kit? It's just me again... Wesley... I figured you would still get hungry at some point, so I made you a sandwich. I'll just um... leave it here." There was a pause, and I heard the plate tap against the door as he set it down. "So um... night!"

I retrieved the sandwich and smiled at how thoughtful he was. The sandwich was crammed with three types of cheese and had been zapped in the microwave to melt it all. *Delicious.*

Hours later, I still hadn't come up with a solution. If what the boys stated was true, and I couldn't see why they'd lie, then nothing Dupree said could be trusted. Which meant I would need to come up with a foolproof plan to ensure my own safety and have some sort of extraction plan in place in case shit hit the fan in a big way.

I changed into one of Cole's massive shirts with the intention of sleeping. After more lying there staring at the ceiling for an eternity, I gave up and began pacing again. The boys' reluctance to give specifics on what they'd seen left my mind going wild. I could imagine all sorts of horrible things. When you grew up the way I had, you could imagine evil a lot more easily than good.

Shuddering at the thoughts, I still wasn't ready to give up. We'd come the closest I ever had to figuring out what made me different, and I'd be damned before I let the opportunity slip by simply because I was scared. I'd bounced back from a lot in my life; I had to have faith that my luck would continue.

Just as I was about to wear a hole in the carpet, Cole stormed into the room and scooped me up before tossing me onto the bed.

"For fucks sake, Vixen, get some sleep," he commanded, stripping down to his boxers and climbing in beside me. I wanted to protest, but he clamped an arm over me. It was obviously what I needed because in seconds, the sleep eluding me swept over me like a wave and dragged me under.

Chapter Thirty Five

I woke the next morning alone but resolute. Somehow while I'd slept, my subconscious had come up with a brilliant plan, and I bounced out to the kitchen, excited to tell the guys my idea.

As I entered the room, a heated argument cut off abruptly, and all the guys avoided looking at me. Not even Wesley would make eye contact with me, and I got a sinking feeling. I wished I had been paying more attention coming down the hallway so I might have heard what this was about, but I had been too caught up in my amazing plan to listen.

"Hey guys..." I greeted them, suspicion threading through me. Hard to miss that I was the topic of the argument. "What's going on?"

Seemingly as one, all of them turned to Austin, who jutted out his jaw stubbornly.

"Ask him," Caleb ordered while pulling out my coffee mug and filling it for me. *Such a nice boy*. Austin narrowed his eyes at his twin then met my gaze unapologetically.

"I did nothing wrong," he glowered. "We all voted and agreed. I simply acted on it."

"We also agreed to speak with Kit when she woke up, seeing as she wasn't in the vote," Cole barked, his neck muscles seeming to strain.

Austin shrugged. "I didn't want to give her the opportunity to flit around here, batting her eyelashes at you guys, looking like *this*"—he waved a hand towards me, and suddenly I was aware of wearing only Cole's massive T-shirt and tiny boyshort undies—"and changing your minds," he finished, folding his heavily inked arms. He was wearing a T-shirt, and I'd never seen him in anything less than long sleeves before. "I took necessary preemptive action to ensure the safety of our group. An action that we all, as a team, agreed on last night."

Wait a minute, what the hell...? "What did you do?"

He didn't give me an answer, the tension in his jaw suggesting he had no intention of giving me one either.

Caleb handed me the mug of coffee and said, "My fuckstain of a brother took matters into his own hands and declined Dupree's offer for you." Anger underscored his words, but it didn't compare to the rage curdling in my gut. They took a *vote*? They decided my future? And Austin had acted on it

"You did *what*?" Please tell me I'd heard them wrong.

"You heard," the asshole spoke. "It was a stupid offer and was only going to get more people killed. We all voted, and it was unanimous to decline the trade." He seemed smug and confident in the fact that they outnumbered me.

"Give me the phone," I snapped, holding out my hand.

Austin had the grace to look a tiny bit guilty. "I destroyed it after sending the message. It's standard protocol not to keep anything that might lead the enemy to your base of operations."

The ringing in my ears amplified, and I slammed the coffee cup onto the marble counter. I'd pictured Austin's face, and my beautiful cup shattered with a deafening crack, spewing coffee everywhere. It wasn't just my cup breaking, but the marble countertop that cracked beneath my fist.

Still furious, I took one look around the stunned men then pivoted on my heel and stalked out of the house.

"Kit!" River, the first to recover, barked after me. "Where are you going? It's not safe to be alone right now."

I didn't bother answering and headed outside to the

garden where I plonked my butt on one of the outdoor couches overlooking the empty pool. I wasn't a total moron; of course I knew it wasn't safe to be wandering around aimlessly, but I needed some breathing room to process the latest hairpin turn in the train wreck of my life.

It was freezing outside, and dressed as I was in just a T-shirt and panties, it wasn't long before my teeth were chattering. Still I refused to go back inside and face the guys. How could they do that to me? More, how could I have lost it in there like I did? What if it had been one of them and not the countertop?

An image of Finn punching his fist right into a man's chest flashed across my mind's eye.

What the hell was happening to me? More and more these days I seemed to be acting on impulse, and it scared me.

A heavy warmth dropped around my shoulders, and I whipped my head up to find Wesley awkwardly tucking a comforter around my trembling shoulders.

"Hey," I whispered, giving him a grateful smile. He smiled back and sat beside me, saying nothing and simply staring out at the empty pool with me.

"Are you okay?" he eventually asked, watching me from the side of his glasses, and I shook my head.

"No." There was no point in lying. "How could he do that? It wasn't his call to make—it wasn't any of your calls." Though

I was still angry, the cold seemed to have taken the edge off, but I was close to tears.

"I know," Wesley murmured. "He—we? We decided because we care. He did what he thought was best, because he cares."

Who was he trying to fool? "Cares? About you guys, sure. Austin couldn't care less if I got killed in this mess."

"That's not true," Wesley argued, though he lacked any real force in his tone. "He's saved your life, what, twice already?"

"Three times," I muttered, remembering the ditch. Ugh, such a dick. "Did you all really vote on this behind my back?"

He shifted uncomfortably, an answer without words. Great. They were just as guilty as Austin. Okay, probably not *as* guilty but my anger didn't see well in shades of gray.

"You don't understand, Kit. The shit they were doing to those other 'test subjects'... we can't let you volunteer for that." A shudder ran through him. He believed what he said.

"It was *my* call to make," I said. I'd been the one trapped in the foster home from hell. I'd survived that nightmare. I had these abilities. It was *my* damn life. "That crazy bitch knows who I am. She knows *what* I am. You have no idea what it's like to not know *what* you are." Tears burned my eyes, but I refused to shed them.

He shifted closer, easing under the edge of the blanket and giving me a hug.

"I'm sorry." His whisper carried every element of sincerity. "We will find the information another way, I promise."

I set my head to his shoulder and hugged him back, grateful for the comfort he offered. His body seemed perfectly built to fit mine, and he squeezed me with just the perfect amount of pressure, making it impossible to stay mad at him. Fucker.

We stayed like that for a while, not speaking, just hugging, until the cold penetrated the thick blanket and I began shivering again.

"Come on," Wesley said, standing and offering me a hand. "You can hang out in my room today if you want. I've got a ton of work to do on my computer, and the others know not to disturb me."

I took his hand and kissed him on the cheek in gratitude. "Thanks, Wes."

He blushed scarlet and awkwardly cleared his throat before heading back inside. I hesitated a moment, watching as he made his way back to the house, and noticed for the first time what a great ass he had.

Jesus Kit, all this stress is making you loopy. Quit thinking about Wesley's ass when you have bigger fish to fry.

Chapter Thirty Six

After I dressed in warmer clothes, I hid in Wesley's room for a few hours. He worked at his desk, quietly muttering under his breath to himself as he tapped away on his keyboard. I stretched out on my stomach across his bed with a stack of our stolen files in front of me, slowly pouring through them again, hoping to discover something that might make sense.

At one point, Caleb came in with a fresh mug of coffee for me, and I just glared at him.

"Hey, Kitty Kat... peace offering?" he cajoled, holding out the mug to me, but my temper flared and I opened my mouth to tell him *exactly* what I thought of his peace offering.

"Caleb, maybe now isn't the best time?" Wesley interjected, smoothly rescuing the mug of coffee and ushering my friend out of the door to the hallway.

"But—" Caleb started to object.

"Look. Kit's feeling pretty hurt and betrayed right now, by *all of us*, so just... give her some space. I don't think anything nice was about to come out of her mouth by the look she was giving you just then." Wesley was speaking quietly, but the slightly open door allowed me to hear what he was saying. I couldn't hear Caleb's reply though, so he must have moved farther down the hall. Wesley returned inside, closing the door behind him.

"Thanks," I muttered, and he just nodded, turning back to his work.

My eyes were just starting to blur over from looking at the files too long when my phone vibrated with an incoming video chat from Lucy. I smiled; my best friend always seemed to know when I needed to hear from her.

"Hey, girl," I greeted her warmly as the video feed clicked in. The image showing, though, was not what I expected. I sucked in a sharp breath. It was Lucy, but she was gagged and bound to a chair, a dark, heavy-set figure standing behind her with his huge gloved hand wrapped around her throat. Her eyes were wide and pleading as she looked toward whoever held her phone, and there was already a rapidly darkening bruise along the side of her delicate face. Her eyebrow was split open, and blood was trickling past her eye. Wesley turned toward me at the sound of my gasp and must have registered the shock on my face because he yelled for the others.

"Christina." The voice, which was definitely not Lucy, jarred me as it echoed over the speaker. "I tried to play nice. I tried to give you the opportunity to turn yourself in peacefully, but you rudely declined my offer. This, dear girl, is the price of insolence." Dupree's grandmotherly voice was gone and replaced with the cold ranting of a madwoman.

The boys crushed in around me to see the screen, and someone cursed.

"Now watch carefully, Christina. This is what happens when people displease me," Dupree continued cruelly, and a second dark figure threw a brutal fist into Lucy's stomach, causing her to cough and gag for air. "If you do not present yourself *alone* to my testing facility in twenty-four hours, I will go after the loved ones of your precious little boyfriends there." The shadow man hit Lucy again, this time in the face, the crunch of her nose audible.

"I'll be seeing you soon, dear." I could almost hear the dangerous edge of a smile in Dupree's cold voice. A moment before she ended the call, the big man moved from behind Lucy in order to aid in her beating, but in the space where he had stood I recognized something. I knew where they were.

I dropped my phone and scrambled off Wesley's bed, flying down the hallway with the shouts of my name echoing behind me. I snatched River's keys off the hook where he kept them, because I still hadn't picked up my damn car from school, and pushed a little extra speed as I raced into the garage. Once there, I slipped into his sleek car. Tapping the steering wheel impatiently, I glared at the slow moving garage door opening. Just as it opened enough to let me escape, the passenger door flew open and Caleb landed inside. He barely got the door closed again before I accelerated down the driveway.

"Kit. Talk to me," he panted, buckling his seat belt.

"I know where they are." I chewed each word out through gritted teeth. "When that fucker moved, right at the end, I saw a blue unicorn spray painted on the wall behind him."

"I don't get it." Why would he? He'd never been there.

"It's a stupid picture that some kid used a few years back to mark good locations for parties. There are all sorts of abandoned or private locations in the area with them, but only one of them is blue."

He nodded but didn't question me further as I raced River's baby around the tight corners of the mountain roads at a breakneck speed. His knuckles went white on the door handle, but I couldn't slow down, I *wouldn't* slow down. Not when my sister was in trouble.

Chapter Thirty Seven

Screaming to a stop in front of the abandoned auto shop, I burst out of the car without even turning off the engine. The easiest way in was around the back, but I didn't have time to waste, so I kicked in the front door and broke it off its hinges. The shattered door hit the ground and revealed Lucy still tied to a chair in the middle of the floor with the two massive goons beating the shit out of her.

At my abrupt entrance, one of them took off towards the back door, but Caleb gave chase, leaving me to deal with the other. The asshole actually started to laugh at me, and I lunged at him with a solid kick. He crashed into the wall and crumpled into a heap. I gave it a beat, made sure he stayed down, before I went to Lucy.

Rushing over, I slid to a stop on the floor next to her. I tore the ropes from her wrists and ankles before gently setting her on the floor and removing the tight gag from her mouth. Her delicate, pixie face was almost unrecognizable in a mass of fresh bruises, swelling, and gashes. Her body probably wasn't much better. There was a sickening, wet rattle in her breathing, which suggested she might have broken ribs. God, what if one was piercing her lungs?

"Lucy!" I fluttered my hands over her face, wanting to check her out but not wanting to hurt her. "Jesus, fuck, Lucy. I'm s-so sorry." Tears streamed down my face. "Luce, p-please be okay. I'm so so s-sorry."

She didn't move, and my heart shredded. How the hell did I drag her into this mess? Why hadn't I kept her out of it? If she died, it would be entirely my fault. Why did I keep pushing for more information? Why couldn't I have just looked the other way at those stupid goddamn files?

Get your shit together, Kit! Lucy needed help, real help. Forcing my breathing to slow down, I glanced around the room. I needed a phone, and mine was at the house.

A rush of motion near the door had me leaping to my feet, ready to defend my broken friend against a new threat.

It was the rest of the team who poured in, and I dropped back to Lucy's side. Wesley took her other side, checking her over with practiced skill.

Austin checked the goon I had kicked into the wall and declared him dead. Good. He deserved worse.

Wesley's motions grew more frantic. "We need to get her to a hospital. Cole, help me get her into River's car; it's the fastest. We don't have time to wait for an ambulance. Let's move."

Cole gently lifted her tiny body in his massive arms before striding out to the car and carefully placing her across the back seat. Wesley climbed in with her, sitting in the foot well and holding his fingers to the pulse in her wrist. I ran around the car and slid into the passenger side as River took the wheel and smoothly accelerated out of the parking lot.

The drive to the hospital was tense, and no one spoke except for Wesley giving us updates on Lucy's vitals every few minutes. River's hands were clenched tight on the steering wheel, his knuckles white, while I stared ahead, tears flowing silently down my face as I willed the vehicle to go faster.

We were still too far from the hospital when the wet rattle of Lucy's labored breathing stopped, and Wesley began to swear.

"River, you need to get us there *now!*" His scream echoed the wrenching in my heart, and I twisted in the seat to watch as he tried to resuscitate my best friend.

River tossed me his phone. "Call ahead; let them know we're coming."

Of course. It made sense to alert the hospital. I called and managed to answer all of the nurse's questions in a mostly clear voice. She assured me that they would be waiting, and a minute later when we screeched to a halt in front of the emergency room doors, I was relieved to find she was right and a team of doctors waited with a gurney ready.

River helped them carefully lift Lucy onto the bed, and Wesley rattled off everything he had observed while another nurse took over the resuscitation. They were a blur of motion, wheeling her into the hospital and towards an operating theatre as Wesley ran alongside, continuing his report. I stood in the doorway, frozen, watching them get farther and farther away.

I was shaking, and I knew on some level that I was in shock, but I couldn't move. It was like my muscles had shut down and I was just an observer, looking out from behind watery eyes.

River wrapped his strong arms around me, then led me over to the waiting area. He murmured words in my ear that were no doubt meant to be comforting. When he pressed me into a chair, I obeyed, too busy drowning in a lake of guilt to argue.

He continued talking to me, but his words had no meaning. His lips moved, but all I heard was a sharp ringing in my ears. The intensity on his face suggested he wanted to tell me something important, but I didn't care. My best friend—my sister might be dying because of me.

At some stage, the rest of the team arrived. Caleb swept me into a tight hug, kissing my hair and rocking me back and forth. For some reason, his actions snapped me out of my daze, and the paralysis caging me burned away under my anger.

Breaking free of his hold, I shoved him away then glared daggers at all of them. He stupidly reached for me again, and I swatted his hand away from me, hissing a little in anger.

"Do not fucking touch me," I spat, sparing none of them my wrath as I glared at each in disgust. "This is *your fault*! If you hadn't turned down that psycho bitch's offer, *none of this would have happened*!" I recognized how unreasonable I was being, but the fury kept building in me, and I needed to blame someone other than myself. They had made a unilateral decision about me without me there, and then Austin had run with it.

"Kit." River layered a command in how he said my name and demanded my attention. "Now is not the time. You need to calm down before you burn out."

I glanced at my hands, which were shaking so hard I must have looked like I was having a seizure. My terror was causing a massive adrenaline overload, and I was probably minutes away from a blackout. There were too many witnesses at the hospital, so I headed back outside. The Aston wasn't in the ambulance bay any longer. River must have moved it into one of the parking slips nearby.

River followed me, but none of the others. They probably thought he was the best one to deal with me. Maybe they were right.

I didn't care.

Dropping to a crouch, I slid my hand under the cuff of his slacks where he kept a small, but sharp knife. Freeing it, I took the blade and cut a deep gash in my forearm from elbow to wrist.

"Fuck," River gasped. "Kit."

Hot blood gushed from the wound, but the skin was already knitting back together as good as new. The rush of healing should have balanced me out, but the buzz, while decreased, wasn't gone.

So I repeated the action, only I cut deeper this time and it hurt like hell. Healing flooded to my arm, and the skin sealed closed. Still, the wildness coursing in my veins seemed to throb. I might need a third injury; maybe I could dig the blade in deep through muscle. Head spinning, I tried to steady my breathing. I'd never healed so quickly or had so much energy surging through me.

I staggered, losing my balance. River didn't let me fall, though. He pulled me close even as he slipped the blade out of my hand. I let him hold me while I caught my breath. Steadier, I pushed away from him and wiped the blood off my arm onto my T-shirt.

"Talk to me, Kitten," River begged, not letting me get too far away before he cupped my face in his hands. "What the fuck was that?"

Meeting his gaze, I shrugged. "You told me to sort myself out. I didn't think this was the right time for a thirty-mile sprint or a quick fuck in the car, so I gave the energy something to heal instead. I'm fine now."

My voice sounded as flat and numb as I felt, despite the roller coaster of guilt and blame in my gut. Tugging my face away, I turned to head back inside. I needed to wash my hands, and hopefully the staff would think the blood was Lucy's.

Lucy. My heart squeezed.

River moved with me, a hand on my lower back. I was too exhausted to tell him not to touch me, so I said nothing. Once back inside, I chose a chair in the corner of the waiting room and curled into a ball with my head against my knees. No one spoke, but they also didn't leave. After an eternity, I must have fallen asleep because a gentle hand shaking my shoulder woke me.

"Miss Davenport?" The nurse asked in a careful but

friendly voice. "The gentlemen over there told me you are Miss Jones' next of kin?"

"I... yes, yes I am. How is she? Is she okay?" Shaking off the fog, I rushed to my feet. The nurse's relaxed smile offered me the first real measure of hope since I'd answered the video call earlier.

"She's in critical but stable condition. We have her in a medically induced coma until the swelling in her brain goes down, but her vitals are good." She patted me on the arm. "Do you want to see her? It'll have to be quick though."

Did I want to see her? I nodded eagerly and hurried to follow her to the Intensive Care Unit where Lucy rested in a private room.

Lucy looked so tiny and frail covered in bandages and with her right arm in a thick cast. She had a breathing tube in, and her face was a patchwork of different bruises. The machines around her beeped steadily.

"Why don't you sit with her for a few minutes? A lot of people think you can still hear your loved ones talking to you through a coma." She gave me one last pat on the arm. "I'll be back in ten minutes."

I sank into the chair beside Lucy's bed and stared at her. I had no words to say, and even if I did, I doubted she would want to hear my voice. It was my fault this had happened to her and no amount of apologies would change it. So instead I sat there, crying silently and praying she would be okay.

Chapter Thirty Eight

The boys were waiting for me in the waiting room, then they ushered me out of the ER and back to the cars. I had no idea what to say to them, and they apparently didn't know what to say to me.

I got in the car because they told me to. When I didn't buckle my seat belt, Cole reached over and did it for me. I had no idea why. Why should I care about keeping myself safe in the event of a car crash when Lucy had almost died tonight? Caleb sat beside me, holding my hand while I stared out the window at the world rushing past.

I had so many questions for Lucy's doctors that I wasn't

able to vocalize. How long would she be in the coma? Would she have any aftereffects of the brain trauma? What if she could never speak again? What if she could never work her magic on the computers?

That didn't even take into account the damage to her right wrist and hand. How would that affect her gadget creation? Fuck me, she lived for those inventions. Had knowing me cost her everything? She'd never forgive me.

I'd never forgive myself.

At some point I realized we'd arrived home because Caleb had my door open and unbuckled my seat belt. Then he tugged me out of the car and guided me inside. He didn't slow until we reached Wesley's bathroom.

While he messed with the tub, I stared out the picture window. How long had we been at the hospital? Then Caleb stood between me and the window, and his mouth moved.

What the hell did he want from me?

I looked past him to the bright blue butterfly flapping around the windowsill. It reminded me of Lucy's awesome new hairdo since summer break. How she managed to get that color past our school headmaster was beyond me, but she always did have a way with people. *Does*. She *does* have a way with people. Fuck, she was not gone. She had to be fine. That was what the nurse said. Wasn't it? A tear rolled down my face.

Fabric briefly obscured my view as Caleb began stripping me out of my clothes. The butterfly disappeared, and then Caleb lifted me into the hot, foamy water.

My limited attention shifted to the softly moving bubbles. Caleb crouched beside the bath, an expression of anguish on his face. What did he have to be so upset about? It wasn't like he even knew Lucy. Not really. Ugh, he continued talking, and it distracted me from my inspection of the bubbles.

"Get out," I croaked.

"Kitty Kat! Hey! I was—"

"Get. Out," I repeated, forcefully. Lucy was my fault, but the boys weren't without blame.

Hurt creased his features, but I didn't care. They'd betrayed me by going behind my back on a choice that was mine and mine alone. Eventually he stood and left. The warm bath must have thawed me some because I could hear the quiet exchange between Caleb and one of the other guys just outside the bathroom door. A moment later it opened again, admitting Wesley.

"Kit, um... Caleb thought maybe it's best not to leave you alone, but I understand why you maybe don't want to see any of us..." His mouth twisted downward, and he shuffled his feet. "Would you be okay with me hanging out with you for a bit? We don't have to talk."

I dragged my gaze from the bubbles to his face and stared

for a long time. I didn't get them. None of them. Wesley least of all.

"Aren't you worried?" I asked suddenly.

He flushed, his face crimson. "About ahh..?" He couldn't seem to finish the question and settled for pointing at me in the bathtub.

I didn't give a damn if he saw me naked. "About your family. Grant and your mother."

Strangely, he looked relieved rather than concerned. Venturing into the bathroom, he closed the door behind him. Finally, he settled into the same spot he'd sat in when I bathed the last time.

"Um, no?" He sounded confused. "Why would I be?"

"That bitch threatened them. She said if I don't turn myself in that she will go after your loved ones. You said your little brother was in a wheelchair... what if...?" My voice hitched, and the tears threatened again. It was bad enough I had Lucy on my conscience. I couldn't fathom it happening to other innocents.

"Oh that." Wesley nodded, but he still didn't sound concerned. "No, I'm not worried. She was bluffing. We all got new surnames and histories when we joined Omega Group. There is no way of connecting our families back to us. Even if she had somehow worked it out, which I promise you she hasn't, I have all sorts of alerts and cameras set up so I know they're safe."

"What about the others?" No one could be totally safe.

"Um, well, I guess they won't mind me saying too much under the circumstances..." he spoke to himself thoughtfully. "River, I think he already told you, has no remaining family. The twins lost their parents and older brother in a plane crash when they were little. They grew up with an aunt, but there is definitely no love lost there. Cole..." He paused, his mouth twisting slightly. "Cole lost his mother when he was twelve. As for loved ones, they're all here in this house."

I considered his words. Despite Wesley's objections, I still didn't believe Dupree had been bluffing. Wesley's little brother seemed like the most obvious target, but it could be anyone. I found it unlikely that the other four men in the house had literally no one else they cared about.

"Come on," Wesley said, rising and grabbing a massive towel. "Your water is probably getting cold, and you're running out of bubbles."

He held the towel out and politely averted his gaze, his cheeks flaming. My bubble cover was sparse at best. Standing, I took the towel from him and wrapped it around me before stepping out of the tub. Someone had brought in a change of clothes for me at some point. Probably a good idea since all my other clothes had been drenched in blood.

"You can, um, sleep in my bed if you want? I know you're

still pretty pissed at everyone... I can go sleep on the couch or something." His awkwardness made it impossible to stay mad at him.

I was too tired to be angry. "Don't; your bed is big enough. We can share."

Chapter Thirty Nine

Wesley wasn't in his room when I left the bathroom. I should probably get food, but I wasn't remotely hungry and I didn't want to go out to the kitchen. Picking a side of the bed, I slid under the covers. With the lights off, I was trapped in a dark room with only myself for company.

The door cracked open, and a broad frame in shadow padded in and came to crouch beside the bed.

"Hey, Kitty Kat," Caleb whispered cautiously, probably expecting me to snap at him again.

"Hey," I answered.

"Wesley just had to make a couple of calls, so I thought you might want some company until you fall asleep?"

I nodded, scooted toward the middle of the bed to make some space, then lifted the blankets in silent invitation for him to join me. His sigh of relief was just barely audible as he crawled in and encased me in his arms.

"I know it's not enough, but I'm so sorry. You know I love Lucy, too." He breathed the words against my hair. Guilt stabbed at me for my behavior that day.

I snuggled tighter against him. "I'm sorry for being a bitch. It wasn't your fault." It really wasn't; it was mine. And there was no way in hell I was going to let anyone else suffer on my behalf, ever again.

I drifted to sleep in his tight embrace, only waking when he slipped away and Wesley climbed into the other side of the bed. When Wesley stayed on his side of the bed, I scooted over to invade his personal space.

He welcomed me with one of his hugs.

"Thank you for being you," I whispered into his chest, and he just hugged me tighter in response.

"Get some sleep, Kit," he told me quietly. "It's almost five in the morning."

I nodded against him, concentrating on my breathing and slowing it down to a pace suited to someone asleep, forcing my muscles to relax. It wasn't long before Wesley really went to sleep and I was able to slide out of the bed without waking him.

As silently as possible, I crept out to the hallway. The house was dark and silent. Retrieving my bag from the closet, I changed my clothes there in the hallway. Dressed, I made my way to the kitchen. Caleb's mustang was parked in the driveway. That would save me from having to open the garage and risk waking the guys.

He kept his keys in a bowl near the door, so I retrieved them and slid out into the night.

Once in his car, I released the emergency brake and allowed the vehicle to roll further down the driveway before starting the engine. When I'd made it through the first five minutes on the road with no one following me, I let myself relax.

I'd escaped undetected but I couldn't shake the sickening feeling that something bad was about to happen. It had been gnawing at me since the moment I stepped out of the bath and had finally got bad enough that I needed to act. I could only assume someone was going after Lucy again, and I needed to go back there and keep her safe.

Chapter Forty

The drive flew by, and I was running on autopilot. I didn't speed, not when the last thing I wanted to risk was getting pulled over. Before I knew it, I was back in the hospital parking lot, then rushing down the quiet hallway towards Lucy's room. I had no idea what this feeling was that was pushing me forwards but I just needed to make sure she was okay. She was the one person I loved more than anything in this world.

Miraculously, no one stopped me and I pushed through the door to her room seconds later. She was exactly as I had left her. Unconscious and hooked up to a million beeping machines. I heaved a sigh of relief, prematurely, as two huge shadows stepped into my line of sight from where they had been hidden.

"I wouldn't, if I were you," one of them warned as I stepped back into a defensive stance, "not if you want your friend to live." The other figure took one step closer to Lucy's comatose body and cocked his gun, pointing it at her.

"Please," I whispered, staring wide eyed at the gun pointed at my best friend's head, "don't hurt her. It's me Dupree is after."

"We know." The man speaking was just slightly behind me so I couldn't get a clear look at him, but the cold press of metal against my spine said he had a gun on me too. "The boss is going to be real pleased with this turn of events."

His friend chuckled and the sound scratched across my nerves like nails on a chalkboard. The speaker prodded me with his gun.

"You and me, we're going to walk out of here real casual like and get into a car. My buddy here, he's going to stay and keep an eye on your friend. Just to make sure you cooperate. Understood?" I nodded frantically. Anything to get them away from Lucy.

"How do I know you won't kill her after I'm gone?" I asked in a shaking voice.

"You don't," he gloated, "but if you don't come with me,

we will kill her. Right here, in front of you. Is that what you want?"

I shook my head and he prodded me again with his gun. "Well then, let's move."

Doing as I was told, I walked with him out to the parking lot. I didn't dare try and raise an alarm or fight him. My safety wasn't worth Lucy's life. Surely I could find a way to free myself later once I knew she was okay.

Once we reached a nondescript looking van I felt the familiar jab of pain in the side of my neck as the man behind me plunged a syringe into my flesh.

I woke alone in a tiny concrete room and lying on the single piece of furniture—a cot. The door was a steel mesh, with holes probably barely big enough for a small hand to fit through. The cell opposite mine appeared identical.

Clearly, Dupree's wish had come true. She had me at her mercy. I could only hope that now she would leave Lucy and the guys alone. I would never forgive myself if any of the guys had to suffer the same heartbreak if Dupree made good on her threat.

I tucked my knees up and leaned my back against the concrete wall, waiting for the drug induced headache to subside. It wouldn't surprise me if it were hours before Dupree showed her face. If she showed it at all. In the movies, the bad guys left their captives to sweat it out in solitude before confronting them.

I passed the time counting the squares in the mesh door, and sure enough, it was hours before I heard any kind of movement. When I did, I sat up at attention, as it sounded like something heavy was being dragged down the steep staircase and along the narrow corridor.

Several guards came into sight, but they ignored my cage in favor of the one opposite. They tossed a body inside, locked the door, then clomped away down the corridor without a word to me. That worked; I didn't want *their* attention.

Once they were gone, I rose and peered through the door to study the man in the other cell. My stomach lurched when I recognized the tattoos on one of the limp arms.

"*Fuck*. Austin, you fucking dickhead, what the *fuck* are you doing here?"

When he twitched suddenly, rolling over and spitting out a mouthful of blood, I jerked back a step.

"Nice to see you too, Princess." He groaned, dragging himself up to his hands and knees with agonizing slowness.

"What are you doing here? I left to keep you all safe, you goddamn fucking moron!" I wanted to bang my fists against the cell until the door shattered.

"No shit." He glared at me, one eye blooming a beautiful

shade of purple. "I think it's fairly obvious I followed your stupid ass when I saw you sneaking out. Figured you were likely to pull an idiotic move like this and, oh look, I was right. Always nice to be predictable, sweetheart."

At a loss for the right retort, I screamed in frustration and slammed my hand against the cage door.

"Good comeback." The infuriating man laughed, then winced.

At the top of the stairs, the door opened again. Austin collapsed back against the floor, and I waited to see what fresh hell approached.

Chapter Forty One

The footsteps grew closer, slow and measured. Definitely not the guards. I checked Austin, but he was slumped as though the guards had just dumped him there. I steeled myself in preparation for who might be coming, but nothing could have prepared me for... Simon?

"Well, well. Aren't you a sight for sore eyes." His familiar face leered at me, and my stomach lurched again as though I might be sick.

"Simon." Why was he there? "What the hell...?" Shock held me prisoner. Simon might have gotten weird, but he'd been my friend… Lucy's friend.

He ignored my question and cast a disgusted look at Austin's still form. "Friend of yours?" Not waiting for my response, he continued. "We caught him creeping around the perimeter fence not long after you had so wisely turned yourself in. After your little stunt the other night, our security has been considerably heavier, as I'm sure you can appreciate."

Smirking, he banged the cage door with his boot, as if trying to wake Austin up, but Austin didn't even twitch. "It looks like the guards might have dropped your friend a couple of times while escorting him in here." He clicked his tongue making a mockery of his concern.

"Si, what the fuck?" I repeated my earlier sentiment. "What are you doing here? Why are you keeping Austin when you already have me?"

He turned back to me, a cruel smile twisted across his face, and I barely recognized my childhood friend in the face of this monster.

"Why am *I* here?" He echoed my question with an edge of crazy in his voice. "Well, that is quite a story…" He trailed off, staring intently at my face then dragging his lecherous gaze down my body. The action left me feeling slimy, and I shuddered. The movement seemed to snap him out if his daze, and his cold gaze returned to my face as he continued speaking.

"After... after you left, the foster home I was placed in didn't want me. They sent me back to social services after only a month in their house. *Too damaged,* they said. I heard my social worker talking about placing me in a group home, but there was no way in hell I was going back to one of those places, so I snuck out when no one was watching me. Went and checked into a homeless shelter and told them I was eighteen, just small for my age. I lived on the streets and between shelters for years, picking up odd jobs where I could in order to live..." His eyes had a foggy, faraway look as he spoke, as if he was lost to the memory.

"Anyway, one day I saw a flyer posted in one of the shelters. Blood Moon Research Facility was looking for volunteers in a new drug trial, and the money they were offering was *unbelievable.* Their only criteria was that they were looking for reasonably healthy people under twenty-five. Loads of us applied; normal people wouldn't turn down that much money, let alone homeless people.

"They gave everyone a blood test when we arrived, and then only thirty or so were asked to stay. I was one of them." He actually sounded proud of the fact. "Once the rejects left, we were lead into a room filled with hospital beds and strapped down. They started hooking people up to IV lines, filling them with some drug, but it started working before they got many hooked up, and the ones who were first just..."

screamed in agony. I had never heard anything like it before. People started freaking out, demanding to leave, but the doors were locked and they weren't letting us go anywhere.

Bile burned in the back of my throat.

"One of the doctors must have taken pity on us, the ones still waiting and watching other grown men howl in pain and piss themselves. He explained that the drug they were trying to develop was supposed to enhance the normal human body to be able to achieve extra human abilities, all sorts of stuff he listed, but what caught my attention was healing." He clucked his tongue, his gaze zeroing in on mine.

"They were trying to give people the healing ability that *you* already had. Well, I knew I had a bargaining chip that could save my ass from ending up in the epileptic, foaming mess that some of the 'volunteers' were turning into, so I asked to speak with his superior. When they refused, I told the doctors in the room my story, all about a little girl I used to know who could heal from anything. *Anything*. And I tell you what, Kit, they ushered me out of that nightmare room and down to a plush-looking office faster than you could turn your head." He laughed, proud of how betraying me, saved him. "When I got there, a fine looking older lady demanded I tell her again, but I wanted some assurance first because I'm not stupid, you see? So we struck a deal, me and her, that I would be exempt from the drug testing but I wouldn't be free until I could deliver you." His grin split his face. "And here. You. Are."

"You sold me out?" I couldn't imagine anything worse, yet he was proud of giving me up. "What the fuck, Si? We were best friends!"

"*No!*" he screamed, slapping his hand against the cage door. "No. You and Lucy were best friends; I was *in love with you*! And then you left and never looked back." He hissed the last words at me, spit flying from his mouth.

"Did you know what she did to Lucy? This bitch that you're in league with? Did you know Lucy almost died yesterday?"

He laughed, a madness in him I'd never seen before. "Know what she did? Who do you think told her about your desperate need to protect the underdog?"

The bile in my throat made it hard to swallow. "You sick fuck. How could you do that to her? She was like a sister to you!"

"*Like* a sister. She was *like a sister,* and yet you both managed to waltz off into your perfect new lives without so much as a backward glance for poor little Simon, who was *like a brother* to you." He sneered the words with hatred, his face turning red with rage. "You didn't give a damn about me, but you would always do anything to keep little Lucy safe. Even turning yourself in here for unimaginably painful experimentation." He grinned manically again, his mood swings giving me whiplash. "So, lucky for me, this sack of shit generously volunteered to guarantee your peaceful cooperation here." He kicked Austin's cage door again.

"What makes you think I care what you do to him? He's not exactly my biggest fan," I bluffed, still trying to wrap my brain around this psychopath who'd invaded my friend's body.

He considered my words for a minute, then whipped a Taser out and shot a buzzing jolt of electricity into Austin's still form. I screamed as Austin convulsed, but he didn't let out a sound, as though he were still unconscious.

At my cry, Simon's eyes lit up. "Oh you don't care? How about now?" He switched his Taser for a gun and pointed it at Austin's back.

"Stop! Okay, I get it. Please, leave him alone." I was out of ideas but desperate not to get Austin hurt any worse than he already was.

Simon smirked in satisfaction, but thankfully puts his gun away.

"I'm glad we cleared that up," he said with the same cold, reptilian smile.

"I don't get it, Simon. Why is this Dupree bitch so hell bent on getting her hands on me? By all accounts, she has had hundreds of test subjects, if not thousands. Surely some of those must have been successful or else she would have given up by now?" I was confused as hell, but also determined to keep his attention on me and away from Austin. Despite what an asshole Austin had been, he was still Caleb's twin and a member of the team.

"Of course there have been successes," he sneered. "But none since the little coup that your mother staged. All of the successful test subjects were either lost or terminated during recovery after that. When they ran out of the samples already collected, they were back to square one until they could find new, viable genetic material to... *harvest*. Don't get me wrong, the speed, strength... and all the other abilities, there have been a few successes with them recently—but not the healing. And it's the healing that is the goal."

"What's the endgame? I don't believe for a second this psychotic bitch is attempting to cure cancer or end world poverty, so what's she really trying to do? Huh?" I was still frantically trying to think of a plan to get Austin out, but so far nothing was coming to me. Knowledge was power though, so the longer I could keep Simon yapping in his stereotypical villianesque rant, the more likely he might give something important away.

"She's doing what any smart person would do. Ensuring her own immortality." His eyes glowed at the concept. Did he think he was going to get a slice of the crazy pie?

"That's absurd. I can heal injuries and have a little extra strength and speed. It doesn't make me immortal. You've seen for yourself the damage people can do to me. One day, it'll be too much and I won't recover, just like anyone else." I snorted at him, the nutcase, but he only burst out laughing, clutching his sides. Eventually he sobered and wiped the tears from the corners of his eyes.

"Oh wow. You have no idea what you are, do you?" He was still bubbling out small giggles, so I decided to try my luck.

"Why don't you tell me what *you think* I am?" I coaxed, and he stared at me for a long moment, considering my question.

"No," he finally said. "No, I think this is more satisfying that you're in the dark. I bet that really gets under your skin, doesn't it? That I know something about you and won't tell?"

I went for the nonchalant shrug, whether I could pull it off or not. I might be desperate for the info, but I wouldn't beg.

"So now, what, you're going to talk me into a coma and then harvest me for tissue?" I kept it sarcastic, even as a cold shiver ran down my spine.

All trace of humor left his face, and his stare turned scarily intense. "Not quite," he murmured. "But close. You see, the coup your mother staged taught Madam Dupree a thing or two about ensuring her test subjects are sufficiently.... *broken* before commencing testing. Because without the will to live, what's the point in escaping?"

"You know torture won't work on me," I reminded him. "Anything you might do to me has already been done, and I survived. So I'll survive again."

My bravado was wasted as his creepy crocodile smile crept back over his face. "You're right; physical torture alone won't break you... but it's a good thing I know you well enough to push those psychological buttons in just the right way, hmm?"

Reality set in, and it was as though someone had doused me in cold water. Surely he didn't mean to repeat Mr. Gray's abuse... He wouldn't. When six guards came trooping toward my cell door, I braced myself for a fight, but he pointed the gun at Austin again and clucked his tongue.

"You know the rules." It was a sick reminder. "You don't fight back, and your friends don't get hurt." Simon faced me, as did all the guards, so none saw Austin turn his head and look at me questioningly. I gave him a barely perceptible headshake. There was no sense in both of us suffering, and while Simon thought Austin was unconscious, he might be safer.

The guards entered my holding cell. One particularly stupid goon got dangerously close to me, and I had to force myself to remain still and not snap his neck. I considered my options, but with Simon still holding a gun on Austin and six guards to get through, the odds were stacked heavily against me.

They crowded in, shoving me toward the tiny cot. My composure threatened to crack as the past rushed up to greet me, but I forced myself to cooperate. It was hell. The guards used solid looking metal cuffs to shackle my wrists and ankles. Once I was locked to the cot, they leered down at me. My respiration increased; how far down the dark hole had Simon gone?

"That's enough!" he snapped. "You're done here. I can handle the rest myself." Even though he attempted to imbue the words with authority, the guards were barely tolerating him.

"You sure about that squirt?" one guard said over his shoulder. "She might be too much woman for you, even shackled up."

Simon screamed, swinging the gun toward them. "Get. Out."

Finally, one by one, they skulked out.

The respite was painfully brief because Simon took their place in my cell. A heavy blanket of panic began to descend, and my heart hammered as though it were a hummingbird trapped in my chest.

So many dark, cruel memories rose up to swamp me.

For his part, Simon continued to grin as he removed a long, wicked knife from his belt. With patience I would never have credited him with, he began cutting away my clothes. More than once, he drew blood with the knife until I was naked and bloody before him.

My vision grayed, my breaths came in short and shallow, I barely noticed Simon tugging off my boots or tossing them aside. He had me right where he wanted me. Hopelessness threatened as he stood back and admired his work. His own breathing grew shallower, and his pupils dilated. Miserable fuck was turned on.

I desperately tried to shut down, mentally picturing the steel wall I had prepared for situations like this. But it had been years, and today my mental walls felt as strong as rice paper and barely contained the horror and revulsion threatening to drown me.

Simon leaned so close I could smell his sour breath on my skin. He pressed the sharp knife against my throat as he slid his free hand down to my sex. He grabbed at me, his fingers biting and painful. At the invasion, my tenuous hold on my panic attack snapped, and my vision blackened. Passing out didn't seem so bad.

Simon's sick chuckle echoed against my ear. "I'm going to leave you to marinate a little in this delicious fear." He hummed before taking a long sniff, then licking his tongue along my cheek to my ear.

Gross.

"Don't go anywhere, Foxy; I'll be back soon with a couple of your old favorite toys." He cackled at his own joke. "You always were a fan of that metal tipped whip, weren't you, darling?"

I was past the point of being able to respond, lost in my

panic attack. It wasn't Simon, but Mr. Gray who spoke to me. Staring at him, I had to blink to try and filter through memory and reality. They melted together.

Snap out of this. I'm stronger than he is. I've survived this before. It won't matter what he does—I'll survive. Yet the phantom crack of the whip played over and over in my ears along with the agonized screams of the child I'd been when I first went into that room.

The child they'd killed with their torture. The woman I was had been born there.

I couldn't be that horrified child again. She was a ghost.

Chapter Forty One

AUSTIN

As soon as that slimy, freckled dickhead strutted away down the corridor, whistling of all fucking things, I was on my feet and at the door to my cell. I couldn't see everything from my position on the floor, faking unconsciousness, but I'd seen more than enough. I would rip his nuts off and shove them down his throat.

I pulled a couple of long pins from the hem of my jeans, which got missed in the sloppy pat down they'd given before my asskicking started. Studying the lock, I found no keyhole on the inside. That meant I needed to pick it from the outside.

It only took a second of trying before I realized there was no way in hell my giant fucking mitts were fitting through the tiny squares in the mesh to be able to reach the lock. *Shit.*

In the cell opposite me, Christina seemed to have woken up slightly from her blackout but flinched at unseen blows and whimpered, begging her memories to stop.

Of course our best hope of escape would be with the Princess, who was right now in the middle of a psychotic breakdown.

Fuck.

Why the hell had I decided to follow her from the house? I could have just as easily woken the boys and left them to deal with their idiotic little girlfriend, but no, Austin the stupid fuck just had to try and save her stupid, sexy ass.

God fucking damn it.

"Christina!" I hissed across, not sure if there were any guards within earshot. When none came to investigate, I tried again. "Christina!" I barked this time, but still she didn't respond.

What was it with this chick and needing to be saved constantly? Talk about pathetic. I didn't know how my brother could stand her, let alone Cole and River. Even Wesley seemed to actually enjoy her company, which made me think they'd all been drinking the same Kool-Aid or all suffered some sort of group aneurysm or something.

"Hey!" I yelled this time. "Princess, I need your help with escaping here!" Still nothing... *Jesus fucking Christ*. I wouldn't put it past the little drama queen to be doing this to me on purpose. Okay, I didn't actually believe that. I wasn't that conceited, but it might just piss her off enough to snap her out of the panic attack.

"I swear to fucking god, Princess, if you are faking your panic attack deliberately to make me worry, then you are the most selfish, conceited, stuck up little bitch that I have ever had the displeasure of knowing!" I yelled again. Hope spiked when her flinching and whimpering seemed to die down a little. She mouthed something, but I couldn't hear her.

"Speak up, you spoiled brat; I can't hear you," I sneered at her. Could she even hear me, or was she still lost wherever it was she'd gone?

She mouthed something again, and it was a weak, raspy word. But I heard it.

"Asshole."

"Yeah, Princess, it's me. Asshole."

She squeezed her eyes tighter shut, huge, wet tears running down her cheeks, and she started to toss her head, as though fighting someone off. Dammit, I needed to keep her focused or she'd go right back into that panic attack.

"Hey, stay with me Christina! Stop ignoring me, you

fucking airhead!" Okay, I was scraping the barrel on insults here, but I was pretty sure she wouldn't remember any of it later. Pissing her off seemed to be the most effective method of getting through to her.

She mumbled something new, but her eyes cracked open just the tiniest bit. Progress.

"What did you say? I don't speak pathetic," I jeered at her.

"I said," she rasped, "stop calling me Christina, you *fuck*!" The more she spoke, the wider her eyes became. She blinked several times, maybe clearing away the ghosts. I laughed; she was coming back—pale and trembling—but coming back.

"Okay, keep talking to me, *Christina*." A tiny spark of relief flared, but she wasn't near her usual feisty self yet. "You do understand you're giving those fuckers exactly what they want?"

She frowned. "Huh?"

"Yes, great comeback you ditz. That *freak* said he's doing this to break you. Is that what you want? To be *broken*?"

"What? No... I...." Her trembling subsided, but she was still foggy. I needed to push a little more. Hopefully she wouldn't kill me later.

"Maybe this is what you *deserve*. If you're too *weak* to even get yourself out of your own memory trap, then you're too *weak* to be a part of our team. I told Cal that you were a waste of time from day one, and it looks like I was right."

I used a deliberate sneer of disgust in my tone and prayed it came out believable. "All you do is put other people in danger trying to save you from your own idiocy. I bet right now the guys are planning some sort of jailbreak for you, and they're likely to get hurt, just like me, all because *Princess Christina* is too fucking *weak* to get herself out."

She stilled completely, then her eyes snapped open. She focused on me, glaring daggers. The intense rush of relief at seeing her usual fire almost made me stagger, and I leaned against the cell door to stay on my feet.

Come on baby girl, time to kick some ass.

Chapter Forty Three

KIT

The fog cleared from my head, the memories growing fainter as reality grew sharper and all I could hear was Austin's dickish voice yapping on and on about how weak I was.

The fucking asshole. How dare he call me weak? He had no idea the shit I have lived through. Ugh, I had seriously had enough of putting up with his attitude. The second I got out of this cell, I was punching him straight in the smug, chiseled face.

"I'm seriously going to kick your fucking ass, Austin," I hissed at him, narrowing my eyes.

"I'd be more worried if you weren't handcuffed to a bed right now, Princess." Despite his sneer, I could swear there was a playful smile ghosting across his lips. He had a point though.

"Any bright ideas on how to sort this mess out?" he asked, and I could have screamed at the sarcasm.

"Actually, Captain Cynical, I do." The handcuffs holding me were strong, made of steel most likely. The one on my left wrist was just a tiny bit looser than the rest, so I knew it was my best option. I sucked in a deep breath, then using the edge of the bed frame for leverage, I dislocated my thumb and slid my hand out of the bracelet in a move I had practiced countless times since leaving foster care. Once clear, I gritted my teeth and pushed it back into place, the pain relief instant.

"Holy shit," dickhead muttered in what might have been admiration. Still, I ignored him and considered the other shackles. They were too tight for the same trick to work, and I didn't have my lock picks.

"Do you have anything—" I started to ask but stopped when a thin steel pin landed on the floor near my free hand. "Perfect. Thanks." I frowned, unused to Austin being so accommodating, but he just shrugged. I used the pin to release my limbs, and once free, I rubbed the blood back into them. I stretched out my tense muscles then checked out the lock on the door.

"I already tried," Austin admitted. "Couldn't fit my hand

through the mesh."

It was my turn to smirk as I easily slipped my smaller hand through the mesh, reaching around and picking the lock on the cell door using his steel pin. The door clanged open. Triumphant, I glanced at Austin.

"All right, so you're not completely useless," he reluctantly admitted. "Are you going to get me out of here too? Or just stand there admiring me?"

"You want to try that again? Seems to me like you need me. Poor, *weak*, little me. Now, would you like to ask me nicely?" Probably wasn't the time for this, but he owed me for all the crap he'd thrown at me.

His jaw clenched, and his lip twitched in a snarl but he grit out, "Please, *Christina*, will you get me the fuck out of here?"

"Pretty please with rainbow unicorns on top?" I prompted.

This time I swore I could actually hear his teeth crack as he responded. "Pretty please with rainbow unicorns on top, *you fucking nutcase*," he muttered the last under his breath, and I let it slide before unlocking his cell door for him. I expected some sort of thanks for freeing him, but instead he whipped off his T-shirt, showing me a whole lot more ink. Holy crap, was it actually physically possible to have that many abs? I thought there had to be a legal limit or something, but it looked like I was wrong because damn... He coughed awkwardly and thrust his shirt out to me. Why the hell did I want his shirt...?

Oh, I was naked.

Completely naked. *Fucking Simon.*

Crap. I dragged the fabric over my head and turned my face back towards my cell, allowing myself some privacy. From the corner of my eye, I spotted my boots. Thankfully they had been excluded from Simon's cutting exercise. I took a minute to tug them on, trying to shake the lingering feeling of Simon's hands. An instant rush of calm washed over me with the scent of honey and oatmeal and a touch of man sweat. What the actual fuck was going on? Was I *smelling Austin's shirt* right now? I must have been more messed up from that trip down memory lane than I thought.

Trying not to think too hard about my possible brain damage, I remained grateful Austin was so tall because his shirt hung like a dress on me, mercifully covering my bare ass. There wasn't much I could do about the heat staining my cheeks, and right now, it didn't matter. We needed to get out of there. Ready, I led the way down the hallway in the direction I'd been escorted in from. Austin, for once, refrained from making smart remarks as he followed me closely up the narrow staircase and along the short passageway at the top until we reached a locked door, and we both groaned in frustration. It was an electronic lock, meaning we couldn't just pick it. The only way we were getting out was with a swipe card.

Austin quickly jogged back down to the cells and checked the other direction, but it was a dead end. We needed to wait until someone came down here in order to make our escape.

"We shouldn't need to wait long," Austin said, his gaze on the door. "That skinny prick sounded all too excited to get back with that whip, so I doubt he'll be gone much longer."

I didn't respond. The last thing I wanted to do was think about Simon or the whip right now.

We positioned ourselves on either side of the door and waited.

Chapter Forty-Four

As annoying as it was to admit, Austin was right. We only waited a few minutes before I spotted a uniformed guard sauntering down the hallway on the other side of the door, his cap pulled low on his face. I signaled to my unlikely companion, and he gave me a tight nod of acknowledgement. The guard looked bored, which hopefully would play well into his lack of awareness until it was too late.

At the door, he scanned his swipe card, and the door lock whirred then beeped green before sliding smoothly open. He stepped through, and Austin launched a swift fist to his head. Pulling his punch right at the last second, his knuckles glanced off the side of the guard's face instead.

"Shit, sorry bro." He winced as Caleb, dressed as a guard, clutched his face. Despite the situation, I laughed. It was ridiculously good to see Caleb again. He grabbed me into a huge hug, lifting me off the ground.

"Kitty Kat!" he exclaimed, twirling me around and burying his face in my neck. "Holy crap, you had us so worried! If you ever pull a stunt like this again, I'll-"

"You'll what?" Austin interrupted, as though amused at fun-loving Caleb's attempt to threaten me.

"I don't know yet," he murmured in response, pulling back to stare into my eyes. "But you won't like it." I ducked my gaze. I already hated what had happened here. I didn't need the threat.

"If you're done with this Hallmark moment," Austin commented dryly, "you might want to put Christina down. I have seen quite enough of her naked ass for one day."

Caleb frowned and slid his hands down my back until he reached naked skin where Austin's shirt had risen up, then he froze, a murderous look transforming his face.

"Kit... why are you naked under Austin's T-shirt...?" His voice was deathly quiet, and tension thrummed through his arms where they were still wrapped around me.

"Uhhhhh..." I stalled, not really ready to recount the whole ordeal yet.

"Why don't we get the fuck out of the funhouse and save the story time, bro?" Austin's save surprised me, but I'd take it.

Caleb took another long, scary look at me, his face like thunder, but he didn't push the subject. Instead, he gently set me on my feet and tugged my borrowed T-shirt back down.

"Right." He nodded, turning back to his twin. "We should get out of here. River called in backup, but we have no way of knowing how soon they will be here and I'd rather not wait around. It looks like they already showed you a bit of love, brother?" He indicated the myriad of bruises decorating Austin's exposed skin. Austin just grunted in response, leading the way back down the hall.

We barely made it past the first corner when the heavy thump of security boots echoed down the hall ahead of us. Caleb ushered us all into a supply closet to avoid confrontation. It was a tight squeeze, and I was trapped between the twins in the dark, my front pressed against Caleb with Austin at my back. We waited in silence, listening to the sound of boots clomp closer, and then as they faded again, Caleb chuckled quietly in my ear.

"You make such attractive sandwich meat."

Austin growled a warning, and an entirely inappropriate flush rushed through me at Caleb's dirty insinuation. Thankfully the hall sounded clear of guards, so we cracked the door and checked.

"Clear," I whispered and hurried out of the suddenly tense closet.

I was in such a rush to get out of the fucked-up place, I didn't check the next corner before plowing around it and right into the first group of guards that had handcuffed me earlier.

A pathetic squeak of fright escaped. Shit, they recognized me.

"Well, well, well. We were just discussing paying you a little visit, and here you are, like magic." One of them, with a piggish upturned nose, leered.

"Excuse us for a second, sweet thing, while we take care of your friends here. Then we can *take care of you*." This from a second guard, and I shuddered in revulsion.

Strangely enough, they completely ignored me in their rush to tackle Caleb and Austin.

I was all too happy to stand back and watch the twins efficiently dispatch the idiotic guards. As I admired their flowing, elegant technique, a sharp pain smacked into my side, followed by the loud crack of a whip.

The world seemed to move in slow motion as I grasped my burning side and pulled my hand away to find it slick with blood. Well, that was a first; I couldn't remember ever having been shot before.

"What the…" I spun around a little unsteadily to find a

woman not much older than myself advancing down the hall with a gun trained on me. She fired again, but this time I had my wits about me and dodged using my superior speed. The act pulled my existing injury painfully.

It was already trying to heal closed—with the bullet in there—as I lunged for my attacker. I slapped the weapon from her hand, then thrust a fist at her head. Yet she moved almost as fast as me, and my fist met thin air. Off-balance, I stumbled. She regained her footing and lashed out, slicing four deep gashes in my other side with… *claws?*

Using the wall for leverage, I shoved away to create some distance. Her hands were indeed morphing back and forth between normal human fingers and crazy, vicious looking half-animal claws. Another product of the insane experiments here? Other than the unnatural situation happening with her hands, she looked normal.

I didn't know what was happening to her or why she was here, but she'd attacked me and I had a fight on my hands. My side was healing, but I was hurting. She easily had my strength, if not more, and her speed was nothing to scoff at either. She was the toughest opponent I'd ever faced.

I managed to land a lucky hit to her face, breaking her nose. The distraction gave me time to get away from the wall and more room to maneuver.

My assailant growled like an enraged animal and

charged me, striking wildly. Her nose wasn't healing though, and blood continued to spray from the injury. Maybe Simon hadn't been lying.

Thankfully, rage made her sloppy, and I avoided the flurry of her blows. Using the same move I'd trained so hard with Cole, I flipped her off her feet and onto her stomach. Without hesitation, I was on her, snaking an arm around her neck and applying just enough pressure to render her unconscious without killing her. I wasn't a natural born killer.

Once her body went limp, I relaxed my hold but remained still for a moment, feeling every damaged inch of my body. I'd lost a lot of blood, but I was barely able to catch my breath before two sets of strong hands hauled me up and began frantically checking me over.

"I'm fine." I groaned as one of the twins pressed just a little too hard on what must be a fractured rib. "Just give me a few minutes to heal. It seems to be working a whole lot faster these days." As I said it, the bullet from my side slid free from my flesh, as though of its own accord, and clinked lightly against the hard floor.

Flashes of concern washed over Caleb's chiseled face and, surprisingly enough, Austin's as well. Yet when he caught me looking, he went stony. Why the hell did I care what the dickhead thought?

"Let's get out of here before anything else goes wrong." He

scowled. "Christina seems to be a magnet for disaster."

I snorted. "Well that is just..." Actually pretty accurate; I did seem to attract disasters. "...rude." I finished lamely, and he gave me a smug look. *Bastard*.

I flipped him my middle finger, showing my maturity, but like them, I was eager as hell to get out of here.

Chapter Forty Five

We made it to the front entrance without running into anyone else, thankfully. Caleb kept scouting ahead, but his body language relaxed visibly when we hit the front.

"Looks like the cavalry is arriving." He shoved the door wider for us to see several armored trucks pulling up to the gates.

We dashed across the open space to the gates as teams of heavily armed agents piled from the trucks and took out the gates. They rushed past us toward the building. When one group paused to possibly detain us, Caleb flashed an

Omega Group ID badge to a helmeted man, and he waved us through to where Wesley's van had just pulled up.

"Thank fuck for that!" Caleb exclaimed. "I was not looking forward to trooping back down to the rest stop again."

The other guys piled out of the van, and Cole snatched me up into a tight hug, pressing on my still injured side, and I cried out sharply in pain. He released me so fast I staggered and nearly landed on my ass.

His sharp, dangerous eyes raked over me, taking in the tears, gashes in Austin's T-shirt, and the blood now running down my thighs. He went to lift the shirt to check my wounds, but as soon as his hand slid underneath, he had to have noticed I was naked. When he went still, his frigid eyes turned murderous.

"Later," I promised him and shook my head firmly. I was not reliving my nightmare out here.

His mouth tightened, and he considered me for a moment before barking at Wesley, "Wes! Do you have spare clothes in the van?"

"Uh, yeah? I think so?" he responded, digging around in the back of the van and then popping out with a zip-up hoody and sweatpants, which he tossed over to us. Cole caught them without taking his eyes off me, then held the pants out for me to step into, which I did gratefully, pushing them over my boots. Once I had them on and had tightened up the drawstring, Cole handed the hoody to River to hold up and shield me from other eyes before he carefully peeled Austin's ruined T-shirt off me and tossed it aside. I shivered in the cold air and crossed my arms across my naked chest, but allowed him to inspect my bloodied torso. Caleb wordlessly handed him a bottle of water, which Cole used to wash some of the blood from my skin, exposing the almost healed gunshot wound and the still fresh gashes from that crazy bitch's mutated claw-hands.

"Why aren't these healing?" Cole asked gruffly, contradicting the soft caress of his fingers around the gaping cuts.

I shrugged, already noticing the rest of my bruises were virtually gone. "No idea, but some chick did it with her claws." They all stared at me like I'd taken one too many knocks to the head, and I made an exasperated noise.

"I'm serious. The woman that shot me—somehow, and I don't know how, she transformed her hands into, like, mutated werewolf claws. It was the weirdest shit. So maybe it has something to do with whatever gave her that ability?" I shivered again, and River took the hint to wrap Wesley's hoody around me. Turning me to face him, he zipped it closed, then pulled me close for a hug, careful of my injured side.

"We will be discussing your insubordination when we get home, Kitten," he murmured in my ear, then held my gaze long enough for me to see all the hurt and worry in his eyes.

I'd meant well, but I'd fucked up coming here. So, I nodded and whispered, "Yes, sir."

Our emotionally charged moment was broken by the loud whirring of a helicopter taking off from the roof of the laboratories, and we all craned our necks as if we could see who was inside.

It wasn't long until Austin stalked back over to us from where he had been speaking with one of the black armored men who looked to be in charge of things.

"It was the bitch and that skinny dick," he snarled, but I'd already known it would have been. "Plus, a couple of her scientists and test subjects. Seems they had the heli camouflaged somehow so the recon team hadn't picked up on it until it was too late. The rest of her staff have been detained, and the patients will be getting medical assistance shortly."

I shuddered at the mention of Dupree's patients and at how close I had come to being one of them.

"We need to get Kit seen to," River announced. "If those gashes aren't healing, then they need stitches."

Austin looked surprise, but he'd missed our earlier discussion.

"I'm pretty sure they are healing. Just really, really slowly." I fingered the edges of the wounds through the fabric of Wesley's hoody, but the skin itched and pulled as it knit together. "Let's just get out of here so I can shower." I was desperate to wash the feeling of Simon's hands off me.

River gave a sharp nod and waved everyone into motion. Without asking, I followed the twins to Caleb's Mustang. To my surprise, Austin climbed into the backseat with me. I gave him a look, tilting my head as though to ask what the hell he was doing, but he just met my gaze with a steady stare, giving absolutely nothing away on his handsome face.

I was way too tired to pick a fight, so I just shrugged and got comfortable against the door, closing my eyes. As I drifted on the edge of sleep, a strong, calloused hand lifted one of mine and threaded our fingers together. But I must have been imagining it because it was only Austin in the back seat with me, and such a tender gesture of comfort would never come from him.

Chapter Forty Six

It couldn't have been two minutes since I'd closed my eyes, when I found myself being lifted out of the car. I cuddled into the strong arms and broad chest. The scent of pine trees surrounded me. Pine trees and safety. I didn't try to open my eyes as he carried me into the house. I didn't think I could even if I wanted to.

River deposited me on his huge bed and carefully lifted the hoody to check my side. He ran his fingertips over the tender skin and sucked in a sharp breath. It was almost healed, and I didn't need to look. Judging by the level of discomfort, I suspected it was just in the nasty, red-purple-scarred phase.

"I need to shower," I murmured in a voice thick with sleep.

"Love, you're exhausted. Just sleep," River urged, but I shook my head firmly, cracking my eyes open.

"No. I *need* to shower." I couldn't bring the lingering feeling of Simon's hands into River's bed with me. What I really wanted was to peel my entire skin off like a lizard and start fresh, but given that wasn't a realistic option, a shower would suffice.

River sighed and scooped me back up. He carried me into the bathroom and sat me beside the sink while he turned the water on to warm up, then came back to me with a concerned frown marring his handsome face.

"I'll be fine, Alpha." I smiled weakly, and his eyes widened.

"Why did you just call me that?" His tone was weird, but I was too tired to read any further into it.

"I have no idea." I shrugged. "Just trying out nicknames for you, and it was the first thing that popped into my head. Now get out; I need to scrub off a layer of skin."

He stared at me for a moment longer, then kissed my cheek softly. "Cole will stay with you while we debrief. Just yell out if you need him, okay?" I nodded, then shooed him from the bathroom so I could take my shower.

Once scrubbed to the point of almost bleeding, and with fingertips shriveled to prune status, I finally got out and dressed in the freshly laundered men's sweatpants and t-shirt that had been left on the basin for me. Back in River's bedroom, I could see Cole's shape stretched out along the bed, dead still as though he were asleep. It was already daylight outside, but the heavy curtains blocked all but a few strips of light from the room. It gave me just enough light to see his eyes open a crack.

I slipped in and snuggled into his warm body, but he went rigid trying to avoid my injuries.

"It's fine; I'm almost healed," I assured him. "It was only those scratches from the, ah, claws."

"Yeah, you mentioned that earlier. What the shit? Some chick had claws?"

I considered the memory of her grotesquely mutated fingers. "I know, it sounds... insane. But I don't put much past Dupree and her mad scientists anymore."

He hummed in thought. "Why do you think it took so much longer to heal? Aus said you got shot as well and it healed in under half an hour?"

"Yeah," I said around a yawn. Why *had* those gashes been so slow to heal when, by all accounts, my healing was now quicker than ever?

"It had to be something to do with her claws. Maybe they had some sort of... poison? Venom? I don't know..."

He hummed. "What did they look like? Like... proper animal paws or something in between?"

"In between. Like a bad eighties werewolf or something, except the tips kind of looked like they'd been dipped in some sort of metal." It was super weird to be thinking about a person's metal-tipped, mutated hands.

"Let's speak with Wes about it later," Cole decided, then tucked my head under his chin. "Get some sleep, Vixen. You'll need your strength for the reprimand you'll be getting in the morning."

I groaned with dread—and he chuckled, the bastard—but floated into a blissfully dreamless sleep.

River sliding into bed next to me woke me later. He planted his freezing cold feet against mine, and I yelped. Chuckling, River slid his equally cold hands over my waist and tugged me out of Cole's embrace.

"River," Cole muttered, cracking one eye open. "The fuck are you doing, man? You're like a goddamn ice cube; I can feel you from here."

"I know," he replied smoothly, and I could almost hear the smile in his voice. "It's why I need this hot little thing to warm me up."

I grumbled under my breath, but his hands were starting to warm up where he touched me, so I let it slide. Cole must not have had any good arguments because he went quiet for a moment.

"How'd debrief go?" he asked finally, rolling to us. His head was on my pillow, and their warmth bracketed me.

River made a noise of frustration. "It didn't. Director himself wants to debrief with us so is apparently going to be in touch tomorrow. In the meantime, we're all to stay put."

Cole made another masculine-sounding hum in his throat as he lifted a hand to lightly stroke my face. His eyes weren't fully closed as I'd thought earlier; instead, they were open a fraction so he could watch me. The soft brush of his fingers relaxed me.

"How are the boys?" Cole continued his conversation with River, giving me more appreciation for his place as second-in-command.

"Aus is pretty bruised up, but nothing seems broken. He'll be a hell of a sight for a few days, though, based on how dark some of those marks are already. Wesley wanted me to fetch him if Kit still hadn't healed those cuts, and Caleb is sulking that he has to sleep alone tonight." River's chest vibrated with laughter, and even Cole cracked a smile.

"Poor kid." He grinned, then leaned in and kissed me tenderly on the mouth, lingering far longer than I would have expected given I was still encased in his friend's arms. Though stunned by the bold move, I returned the kiss and then gasped as River pressed soft kisses to the back of my neck.

"Go to sleep, you two," River commanded as Cole broke away from our kiss and winked at me.

"Yes, sir," we respond in unison, and River made an irritated noise. Now wasn't the time to push him, so I took River's hand from my waist, then threaded my fingers through his and hugged it to my chest. Cole took advantage of the gap and rested his hand over my waist so that I slipped once more into a blissful, dreamless sleep, feeling safer lying between them than I can ever remember.

Chapter Forty Seven

I woke alone but well-rested, lying in River's massive bed, surrounded by the smell of pine trees and bonfire embers. I smiled to myself. How had I gotten so incredibly lucky to have met these guys? Even though I knew deep down they wouldn't have let me go to Dupree without a fight, the fact that they'd come for me still seemed a bit surreal. The fact that they cared enough for me to risk their own safety and jobs... was unexpected and a little overwhelming. Yet I couldn't escape the sensation of rightness.

My sleepy bliss was doused like a bucket of water on a

campfire as my fingers skipped over the still puckered flesh of my side and the horrible events of the past day and a half came pouring back to me. My breathing accelerated, and I desperately tried to get a grip as my ears started ringing with the beginning of a panic attack.

Breathe, Kit. You can have a major freak out later. First things first: call the hospital and check on Lucy. Second... fuck, I didn't even know where to go from there. May as well work on the first thing then, and I used the landline phone on the nightstand to call the hospital.

"Oh, Miss Davenport," the nurse said when I finally got through to the right department. "Yes, I was the one who spoke with you when your friend came in. How are you doing? You were pretty shaken up, dear."

"Me? I'm fine." If we weren't counting the last twelve hours of madness, that was. "How is Lucy? Do you have an update for me?"

"Oh, gosh! I'm so sorry; I left you a voicemail, but you must not have heard it yet," she exclaimed, and a stab of fear sliced through my gut. I had no idea where my phone had ended up, but I hadn't seen it since Lucy was hurt.

"No, I haven't. What is it? Did something—" My words cut off with a strangled gasp, and I took a breath. "Did something happen? Is she not okay?" I swallowed hard, and a tear slipped down my face.

"No, honey, oh no, I am so sorry; my brain is just fried today. Lucy is doing great! I left you a message to say she had pulled through really well and is out of the woods. We are just keeping her sedated a little longer to give her body a chance to recover, but she should be awake tomorrow if you'd like to come and see her?" The nurse's words took a minute to soak through my terrified mind, but when they did, I was overcome with relief.

"That's great," I sobbed out, all of my emotion crashing me into hiccupping tears. "Thank you s-so m-much."

"Oh, it's my pleasure, Christina. I have to go, but I'll see you tomorrow." The warmth in her voice made me cry even harder as I disconnected the call and wiped my face on the hem of my borrowed t-shirt.

Dizzy with relief, I hopped in the shower once more because I still felt disgusting, despite the extended loofah session the night before

Dressed in clothes I'd stolen from River—boxer shorts and a crisp, white dress shirt—I headed out to the kitchen while towel drying my long hair. I couldn't help the broad grin on my face because *Lucy is going to be fine!*

When I reached the open-plan living space, I paused mid-step when I found my guys, er, I mean *the* guys, all sitting around looking decidedly rigid and uncomfortable, their faces like sheets of steel. A tall, distinguished gentleman with perfectly styled silver hair and a custom-tailored suit was the only person standing, and he faced them all as though in the middle of a lecture.

Recovering from my surprise quickly, I wandered across the room, giving a challenging glare to our guest as I headed into the kitchen to make a coffee. My favorite mug was broken and so was the marble countertop. I had to make do with a pathetic, normal-sized mug with a picture of Grumpy Cat on it. I tapped my fingers on the counter while my coffee brewed, deliberately ignoring the thick silence from the men. *They can wait, this is about me anyway.*

When it was ready, I poured myself a mug then carried it out to the living room. The others watched me with varying expressions of panic. I hummed my way past the silver-haired gentleman and skipped the empty couch space in favor of Caleb's lap, which earned me a strangled noise of shock from him. Once I'd wriggled around to get comfortable, I tucked my cold toes under Cole's thigh, then tilted my chin up with a stubborn glare at the sharply dressed man.

River coughed, garnering my attention, and he gave me a pointed look. "Kit, this is the Director of Omega Group, Mr. Pierre," River introduced the man, who was now scowling at me.

"Hey, dude," I greeted him casually, and he released a long-suffering sigh, just as River's eyes widened.

"Nice of you to finally join us, Kit," Director Pierre remarked dryly, "I don't suppose you planned on offering anyone else a coffee when you made your own?"

I snorted a laugh, almost choking on the coffee in question and nodding to the empty cups on the coffee table. "Uh no, they've clearly already had one. Besides, you only drink tea, you weirdo."

He smothered a smile and frowns of confusion appeared on the guys' faces at our interaction.

"Oh gosh, sorry, where are my manners today?" I rolled my eyes, "Guys, Director Pierre is also my dad, Jonathan Davenport. Good old secret identities, hey, Daddy-O?"

He cringed. "Don't call me that, Kit. It's creepy."

The guys were a mixture of confusion and panic, though Caleb seemed the most panicked since it was his lap I'd chosen to sit in while wearing nothing but River's shirt and boxer shorts. I could mess with them a bit more, but I'd already done enough damage over the last day or so.

"Wait..." River frowned. "What...?"

"Alpha Team was just in the process of telling me how they happened to stumble across a highly illegal human genetics laboratory in the middle of nowhere. Your presence here suggests there may be a few holes in their story though." Jonathon gave them a stern look of reprimand before focusing on me. "I should have guessed you'd be neck deep in this, Kit.

River, we'll be having a discussion about why you thought it was appropriate to harbor a fugitive within your team and omit key details in your reports."

Jaw clenching, River nodded once.

"As for you," Jonathan gave me his serious Dad face. "You remember our deal: no more thieving, and I expect to see you in the class of new Omega recruits after you graduate." There was a barely disguised gleam of triumph in his eyes, and I groaned painfully, dropping my head onto Caleb's tense shoulder.

"Hold up," Austin, of all people, spoke up. "You mean to say you've known the identity of The Fox all along? So why assign so many agents to finding her? Was this some sort of test?"

Austin's angry frown eased when Jonathan pinned him with an authoritarian gaze before responding. "That's exactly what it was. A test. And congratulations, Mr. King, your team passed where so many others have failed. You should be very proud of yourselves; you've taken a potentially very dangerous criminal off the streets." This last part was delivered with just a small dose of glee. My dad, the smug bastard.

"Such a gracious winner." I scowled at him, sulking just a little. "I suspect you cheated though. It seems too coincidental that they knew which client I would accept so they could plant that tracker."

"I did nothing of the sort." His eyebrows almost hit his hairline as he gave me an outraged look. "You know perfectly well that I have always kept our deal and never given away any inside information. But fair is fair, Kit. My team caught you, so you will be joining Omega in six weeks. As per our agreement, you may continue your vendetta, albeit under my watch. God knows I didn't expect you to evade capture this long, though."

I really had nothing else to say. He was a man of his word; if he'd really wanted to cheat, I would have been caught years ago when we first struck our deal. He knew from almost day one what Lucy and I had been up to. After all, he didn't become the director of a secret agency by not being observant. We'd had plenty of fights about it in those early days until we had reached our arrangement; I was allowed to continue working through my anger and trauma by hitting those assholes in the wallet, but if I ever got sloppy enough to be caught by an Omega spy, then I would have to join the agency and do things by the book.

At least Lucy will be coming with me! All for one and one for all. Unless this mysterious plan she mentioned really does work out.

"Speaking of," he continued, "where's your demonic partner in crime? It's not like you two to be separated."

"She…" I didn't even know where to begin. "She got hurt, during all of this. But I just spoke to the hospital, and they said she's going to be okay and we can visit tomorrow." I was smiling at the good news, but tears started rolling down my face again at the guilt associated. It was still my fault she had ended up getting hurt in the first place.

Jonathan gave me a stern look, then handed me his cotton handkerchief from his suit pocket. "Give me the name of her doctor, and I will check in with him. Also, let Jill and Frank know what's going on." Of course, I needed to contact Lucy's guardians. I couldn't believe I hadn't done it already. *Stupid, Kit.*

"Mr. Morgan, a word in private please," Jonathan commanded, turning his attention back to River and wiping all traces of kindness from his weathered face. River rose and led my adopted father outside. The tension in the room dropped measurably.

"Why were we all so worked up?" I asked playfully, wiping my face on the soft handkerchief and pretending like I had *not* just been crying in front of them all. "Jonathan's a big pussycat." I wiggled again in Caleb's lap, and he puffed out a pent-up breath.

"Are you seriously trying to kill me, Kitty Kat?" he muttered, picking me up and depositing me onto Cole's lap before standing to not so subtly fix his pants. "I'm going for a cold shower before the director gets back. The last thing I need is Director-fucking-Pierre questioning my intentions toward his daughter." He stalked out of the room in a huff, and I tried not to laugh.

"That was cruel," Austin commented with an unexpected hint of admiration. "Caleb idolizes Director Pierre. He looked so torn between his hero worship and your provocative outfit I thought his batteries were malfunctioning."

Wesley snickered at the robot joke, and I rolled my eyes.

"Hardly provocative," I grumbled, looking down at my borrowed shirt and realizing that my wet hair had turned the white shirt translucent, and it was clinging to my breasts in a rather, er, provocative way. Whoops. Explained the exasperated look Jonathan gave me. Oh well, he had definitely caught me in worse situations over the years; this was nothing in comparison.

"I think it's a particularly good look on you, Vixen," Cole murmured in my ear, his huge hands sliding under the fabric to meet my bare skin.

"Ugh, can you two lay off while we're in the room?" Austin scoffed. "Watching this is making my head hurt, and I'm sure you're making Wes uncomfortable."

I stole a look over to the shy man in the armchair, and he flushed beet red.

"I'm fine, Aus. Shut the fuck up," he mumbled, avoiding eye contact, and I snorted a laugh.

"See, asshole, Wes is fine. And your head hurts because of

how many times you got hit yesterday," I retaliated, and Cole vibrated with a silent laugh as Austin scowled at me with his bruised face.

Our verbal sparring was interrupted by the re-entry of the bosses, and Jonathan gave me a pointed look. He shook his head at where Cole's hands rested under my shirt, and I smiled back at him unapologetically.

"Right, well, it looks like you boys will have your *hands full* then." Jonathan directed the comment to River, obviously continuing a conversation from outside, but gave Cole a decidedly father-like frown. "Kit, Mr. Morgan has requested you remain under his team's protection until you register with the new recruit class. I expect you won't cause them too much trouble?"

"Of course I will," I assured him. "You should know better. I intend to keep searching for information on my mother. Dupree got away too, so I would guess she'll still be gunning for me."

"Hmm, I figured as much. Well, in that case, you're probably in the best hands...." He nodded but his mind seemed elsewhere. "Right, well then. One last order of business for you, kiddo. A couple of hours ago, Cobra Team detained a woman attempting to leave the country under false identification, and we have reason to believe this is your *Dupree.*"

My jaw almost hit the floor, all traces of earlier joking

gone. "What? Where? You're just telling me this *now?*" I scrambled out of Cole's lap and onto my feet. "Where is she? I want to see her."

"I figured as much." Jonathan scowled. "Normally I wouldn't dream of letting you—in fact I wouldn't have even told you until later—but evidently she wants to see you too. Cobra Team just called while I was speaking with River, saying she is refusing to speak to anyone except 'Miss Davenport.'"

"And you're just going to give her what she wants?" Cole's voice was deathly quiet, and I didn't need to look at him to know he had his killer face on.

Jonathan arched an eyebrow at him, then turned back to me. "Go get dressed; I have a helicopter waiting at the Cascade Falls air strip. Maybe we can find out why this woman felt the need to target you, hmm?"

Chapter Forty Eight

As it turned out, the helicopter that Jonathan had waiting was actually a Black Hawk, which worked out well seeing as none of the boys were willing to be left behind and it had enough seats to accommodate us.

We landed at what looked to be a navy base on the coast near Vancouver, and I prodded Jonathan in the side to get his attention over the roaring propellers.

"This is a government site." I pointed out the obvious. "I thought you said it was your team that caught her?"

"They did." His voice crackled over the radio. "But

this was the most secure location close to where they found her, so the Navy is kindly allowing us the use of their space." I nodded in understanding as the propellers slowed and we were allowed to unbuckle our harnesses.

Scooting across the seat, I wobbled a little bit when I stepped out of the chopper, but luckily Austin was there to steady me with his strong hands on my waist. *What the hell is going on? He must have taken more blows to the head than we realized.*

"Thanks..." I said, but he had already turned away from me to follow Jonathan across the tarmac. I shrugged to myself and followed as well, waiting while each of them scanned their Omega Group IDs with a uniformed guard. Jonathan motioned me forward, and I was presented with a visitor's pass on a lanyard.

"Okay, kiddo. When we get in there, if you don't feel comfortable being in the same room as this woman, you don't have to be. Okay?" Jonathan was frowning as though concerned for my delicate sensibilities, but my soul was screaming out for Dupree's blood.

"I'll be fine." I smiled with all the innocence of an angel, not wanting to alert them to my violent thoughts. We all followed another uniformed guard down a long corridor until we reached several closed doors with heavy-duty looking locks.

The guard opened the first one for us, and we walked into

a viewing room with a huge window on one side showing the next room. I assumed it was one-way glass, like in cop movies. Despite my guardian being the head of a secret intelligence agency, I had actually never set foot onto any of his company properties so was basing my knowledge solely on TV and movies.

The window displayed a smaller room that was devoid of any furniture except a metal chair, which looked bolted to the concrete floor. Sitting in the chair was an elegant looking woman, somewhere in her seventies, wearing a ridiculously out of place tweed suit and heels. Her hands were out of sight behind her back, but I imagined they were handcuffed.

"So, is this her?" Jonathan asked after giving me a moment to take it all in. I glanced around me to find all five guys had created a sort of semi-circle around me, as though standing guard.

"I wouldn't have a clue," I told my guardian bluntly. "I never saw her, only spoke to her on the phone. Simon wasn't with her when she was found?"

Jonathan grimaced. "Cobra Team reported there were several others who did get away, as their primary objective was to secure the woman. So, he could have been one of them."

"Has she said anything at all?" River asked with an air of authority in his voice, the same one he used when giving commands to the boys.

"Nothing." This answer came from the uniformed guard who was still in the room with us. "From what I understand, when she was first brought in she asked to speak to Miss Davenport here and then clammed up. Not a word since."

"Well then," I said, rolling my shoulders. "Let's see what she has to say for herself."

I waited impatiently, bouncing a little on my toes, as the guard unlocked the door to the next room for me and swung it open. A huge hand nudged me gently in the small of my back when I paused, and I glanced up to see Cole had followed me.

"Don't worry, Vixen. I'm here with you." He breathed the words into my ear, barely audible. "Just don't let her get to you."

I gave him a tiny head nod and straightened up my shoulders. I stepped further into the room under the glacial gaze of the woman in the chair.

"Well, well." She chuckled, eyeing me up like a hungry shark. "The security footage really did you no justice, Christina dear. The resemblance to your mother is just... uncanny." I scowled at her, saying nothing in response. *Don't let her get to you, Kit. Don't.*

"Tell me, dear, how is your little friend getting on? The one with that god-awful blue hair. Such a shame it had to come to that; I do so despise resorting to violence." She clucked her tongue as though *I* had forced *her* to try and kill my best friend. Something snapped in my brain, and before I realized what I was doing, my fist had already connected solidly with her face. Her nose erupted in a spray of blood, and there was a sickening crunch under my knuckles as her nose shattered and I got a grim sense of satisfaction.

Cole's much larger hand wrapped around my wrist from where he had been standing behind me, but instead of reprimanding me for losing my cool, he simply adjusted my fist so my thumb was on the outside. "Never forget, thumb goes on the outside or you risk breaking it," he murmured with a small smile, and I smirked back, ignoring the wailing cries coming from Dupree.

I stepped back and took a couple of calming breaths, just in case I killed her, then turned back to the sobbing, bloodied woman handcuffed to the chair.

"Don't you *ever* touch my friends again, or *I will fucking end you*," I promised her in a low voice and was rewarded with a flicker of fear in her reptilian eyes.

"You probably don't want to kill me until you hear what I have to say," she goaded, regaining a bit of her confidence, and I gestured to her to elaborate. "Aren't you wanting to know why I have been chewing through hundreds of thousands of *volunteers* in my experiments? Don't you want to know what I was trying to achieve?"

"I already know. You think you can give yourself

immortality; Simon gloated all about it back in your labs." I looked at her in pity and disgust; the woman was clearly delusional. An idea that was reinforced when she began to cackle hysterically.

My fists clenched hard, and I ground my teeth, desperately trying not to smack the laughter off her face. Cole must have seen my struggle because he laid a calming hand on my spine. "Calm down, Vixen," he whispered. "You can do this."

I took a couple more breaths, blocking out Dupree's continued cackling. *I can do this. She has information I need, so I can't kill her. Yet.*

"Judging by your reaction, I take it he was misinformed," I said in my very best calm, coaxing voice. "Why don't you enlighten me? After all, you've got to know you'll never escape here. Don't you want to fill us in so the secrets don't die with you?"

"Of course I want to tell you, you *stupid* girl. Why else would I have asked you to come here?" The blood was now running freely down her creased face, and as she spoke, flecks of it flew through the air. "I know I won't make it out alive, so I may as well drop a grenade before I go. So here it is, *Christina*. You're not human. Your mother wasn't human, and neither was your father." An involuntary gasp slipped through my tight lips, and Dupree's eyes lit up in satisfaction. "Oh yes, I knew your father too. He was another one of my *volunteers* for quite some time."

"Okay." I humored her because she was clearly insane. I mean, I knew I was a bit *extra*, but surely that was just from a bit of genetic manipulation. Like that extra juicy sweet corn they grow out of modified crops. But "not human" was a bit of a stretch. "So, if I'm *not human*, then what does that make me?"

"I never could get a specific name out of Bridget for what freaks like you and her are called, but suffice to say you're of the supernatural variety." She did a little half shrug with one shoulder, as much as her restraints would allow. "Even after all the years Blood Moon had your mother, we still couldn't place her into an exact species."

"*Species?*" I sneered. "You mean like..." I trailed off, frowning. I had no idea what she meant.

"I *mean* that as far as we could tell, she wasn't a shapeshifter, or a witch, or fae, or any other of your garden variety supernaturals. She was something *other,* which was what made her so very valuable." Dupree's eyes gleamed as she stared at me, as though she honestly thought she'd make it out alive and recapture me for testing.

"Hold the motherfucking phone. Are you seriously trying to tell me that these *magical creatures* actually exist?" I scoffed and cast a glance at Cole. His face was a blank slate though, which just confused me further.

"Well, not so much now as there used to be, but I assure

you, *dear*, they are very much real." She smirked at me with bloody teeth from where her nose was still dripping freely. "And it's not as big of a secret as you might think. Would you like me to tell you a story, Christina?"

I honestly wanted nothing more than to walk away at that point, but curiosity wouldn't let me refuse. "Sure, I had nowhere to be today anyway. Tell me your story." Despite the forced casualness to my words, my body was thrumming with tension. Enough that I was almost shaking with it. *Surely it couldn't be any more insane than "you're not human" and "magic is real"?*

"Very well." Dupree's grin was the stuff of nightmares. "I'll make this brief as I am quite sure you have all sorts of fun plans for my death that you're itching to enact." *Shit, how did she guess.* "Around four hundred and eighty-odd years ago, magic was everywhere. Supernaturals outnumbered humans, and they made no secret of their power. They were the master race, and they knew it. After all, how could an ordinary human compete with beings that could change their form at will, or cast fireballs, or read minds?"

"So, what happened? And why does history not remember any of this?" My curiosity pushed the words out of my mouth faster than I could grab hold of them. *Stupid, Kit. Stop playing her game!*

"Greed happened. A small group of powerful humans

became tired of being inferior and somehow coerced a young but *very* powerful witch into helping them. Their goal was to siphon off the magic from a select group that they had held captive and redistribute it into themselves. Their plan actually worked, too. At least at first. Unfortunately, their witch, Tasha, didn't fully understand what she was doing and ended up causing a sort of magical plague. The power drain didn't just stop at the intended victims; it kept spreading until almost the entire supernatural population had been drained of all their magic."

"And the humans? What happened to them; did they get all of this power?" Despite my better judgment, her story was dragging me in.

"They did," she confirmed, "but the human body wasn't designed to hold magic, and they all spontaneously combusted within a week of the plague outbreak. In an attempt to cover her tracks from the millions of supernaturals calling for her blood, Tasha then cast a sort of erasing spell. The memory of all things magical was eradicated from history, and the only ones who kept the knowledge were the scarce few who'd avoided the plague."

"Okay, I don't get it," I said, rubbing my face with a tired hand. "What does this fairytale have to do with me or with your barbaric experiments at the labs?"

She gave me a pitying look, like I was a simpleton. "Oh, my

dear, trust me. This is no fairytale. Why, just ask your father when you meet him. He himself is one of the few shapeshifters who survived the plague, so he can give you a firsthand account. But to answer your question about my experiments, Blood Moon was a facility set up by my great-grandmother in an attempt to find a cure for the magical drain. All that power can't have just disappeared, so there must be a way to utilize it, don't you think?"

"So why experiment on humans? You just said the human body wasn't designed to hold magic, so what is the point?" I demanded, growing increasingly frustrated with this insanity.

"Who said they're all human?" she challenged. "I mean, they could be. I have no way of really knowing. But the law of averages suggests that a solid percentage of the people I test on would be carrying the potential to be *other*. The only problem was, nothing that was tried ever worked. It seemed like the magic was gone for good—until Bridget. Loads of *others* can heal themselves, but *she* could heal *others*."

She stared at me then, like that was the grenade she had been waiting to launch, but I still wasn't following. *Maybe I have taken too many knocks to the head lately.*

"Oh, for God's sake, I have to spell it out, do I?" She sighed. "During her time with us at Blood Moon, a young man was injured quite gravely during an experiment. He was left in the medical bay, assumed dead, and Bridget was sent to clean up the mess. We liked our long-term residents to help with the cleaning, you see. Anyway, within minutes of her entering the room, the young man was not only healed of all his wounds, but tests later revealed he was a wolf shifter. Before Bridget, he was showing to be nothing more exceptional than any normal human." She paused, and it took a moment for the information to sink through my brain, but when it did, I couldn't help a small gasp from escaping. "Ah see, now you get it. Bridget not only healed his physical wounds, she healed his metaphysical ones too."

"So, why the continued experiments? Surely that was the answer you were looking for? I saw the files; they said you held her captive for over a hundred years…" My head was spinning with all this impossible information, and I could hardly believe I was buying into it. But I was.

"Frustratingly, she refused to cooperate. Much like you in that regard. No matter how many people died in front of her, she never healed them. Oh sure, she put on a big show about it, sobbing and crying, putting her hands on them and pretending to try, but nothing ever came of it and they all died, one by one. Only on one other occasion did she actually heal another patient, and he too regained his genetic heritage as a supernatural, so we knew it hadn't been a fluke." Her casual disregard for all those poor people's lives made my stomach churn, and my hands tightened into fists at my sides. *Fuck, I wanted to hit her again.*

A warm hand ran down my arm and grasped my wrist, startling me. I had totally forgotten Cole was in the room with me, let alone the boys and Jonathan watching through the glass. I gave Cole a grateful smile, as he had just saved me from resorting to more violence.

"Okay, so why tell me all of this now? What can you possibly stand to gain from this?" I demanded with a heavy dose of suspicion.

"You didn't think I was the *only* one trying to capitalize on this opportunity for power, did you?" She barked out a laugh. "Don't be so naïve. When power is up for grabs, all sorts of snakes will come out of the sewers. My personal mission might be over, but at least I can make it harder for my competition. As they say, knowledge is power, and you, *my dear*, are now armed just a little better. Well then, that all said and done, I do feel I need to apologize. I know you or your glowering boyfriend there probably have a painful death planned for me, but I really prefer to be the mistress of my own fate." She stared hard at me, clenching her jaw tightly and grinding her back teeth so hard I thought they might break.

"Shit! Stop!" Cole roared, diving past me and grasping Dupree's head in his huge hands as the door to the room burst open and River rushed in, the other boys close behind him.

"What the fuck…?" I asked as I saw Cole desperately

clawing at Dupree's face, trying to pull her jaws open. She continued staring past him at me, and I saw a thin line of white foam leak out from between her bloodied lips.

"Fucking cyanide capsules," River cursed as the elderly woman began convulsing in her restraints, the foam now pouring from her mouth and her eyes rolling back in her head.

Chapter Forty Nine

After Dupree was taken away in a body bag, I found myself shaking slightly but wrapped in Caleb's warm embrace as we stood in the corridor outside the interrogation room. Jonathan and River had gone to deal with whatever was required when a prisoner died in custody and had told us to wait for them to come back. I imagined Jonathan probably wanted to talk about all of the craziness that Dupree had just spouted before killing herself, but I couldn't imagine what he would say. The whole thing was fucking insane.

"Are you okay?" Caleb asked me, and I noticed my

fingernails were digging hard into his sides in a reflection of my thoughts.

"Shit, sorry, Cal. I was thinking about what just went down... It was all pretty cuckoo, huh?" I leaned back just a bit so I could see his face.

"I don't really know what to think, Kit. I mean... we've all seen the way you can heal yourself. If that's not magic, then what is it?" he asked with a frown. I was saved from replying, though, as Jonathan and River returned to where our little group was gathered in the hall.

"Right then, kiddo. Are you okay? I know it can be a bit shocking to see someone die, but you handled yourself really well." Jonathan gruffly patted me on the arm, and I gave him a weak smile.

"Yeah, I'm fine. Not actually the first person I've seen die, but that story can wait. I'm just feeling a bit overwhelmed by what she said in there." I rubbed my arms, still feeling chilled. Caleb had released me from his embrace when Jonathan had approached, but I really could have done with his warmth. *You're not cold, Kit. It's just shock or something. Pull it together.*

Jonathan made an odd noise and looked uncomfortable. "Let's go talk about this somewhere more private. The last thing we need is for the government catching wind of all of this."

I couldn't argue with that logic, and it seemed neither

could the boys, as no one spoke while we followed my guardian back to his helicopter. Once inside, I opened my mouth to speak, but he silenced me with a stern headshake.

As it turned out, "somewhere more private" didn't happen until we were all the way back at the house in Cascade Falls that the boys had been living in. Everywhere along the way it seemed there were too many ears, so by the time we were finally allowed to speak about it, I had completely run dry on what to say. What *could* I say?

"Okay, since you look like you've temporarily lost track of your thoughts, how about I start?" Jonathan suggested once we were all seated in the living room, and I nodded. "So, she told a pretty wild story back there. My one question to you, kiddo, is do you believe her?"

I stared back at him blankly, not comprehending the question he was asking. "What do you mean? She was talking about fairytales, for fuck's sake."

"It's a simple question, Kit. *Do you believe her?* What is your gut telling you?" His stare was getting intense, and I got the impression this was so much more than a simple question, but he was my guardian, my pseudo-dad, I had no reason not to trust his intentions. *Did I?*

"Yes," I whispered. "Yes, I believe her." I heard a few murmurings from the boys, but none of them *seemed* to be disagreeing.

"Right then." He clapped his hands together sharply, standing up from where he had perched on the coffee table. "Now we can move on and come up with a plan to help you find these parents of yours. It sounded to me like Dupree thought they were still alive, yes?"

"Woah! What?" I looked around at the guys, "Just like that? We are just accepting that magic is real and Kit's potentially not human? And we are *all* just okay with that?" I was met with some small smiles and open expressions, not exactly what I had been expecting. In reality, I had been picturing a scene from *Beauty and the Beast* when I admitted I believed Dupree's ramblings. The one where Maurice gets hauled off to the loony bin for telling the townsfolk that a beast had his daughter.

"Austin?" I challenged. "You have no issue with this?"

He just shrugged back at me, not flinching away from my eye contact. "Nope. Makes sense to me."

"Kitty Kat..." Caleb said gently. "Given your abilities, it really does make sense."

"Maybe not *everything* she said," Wesley chimed in, tugging on his hair.

"Oh, finally, I knew you would be the voice of reason, Wes." I smiled at him, and he blushed, ducking my gaze.

"Ah, no. No, I just meant that I doubt her version of events was necessarily the truth. I don't doubt the core information, though. I always suspected you were a little magical." His face flamed even hotter as he spoke.

"Wes has a point. I think the first thing we should do is find one of these surviving *others* and get their side of the story," Cole commented and received nods back from the other boys.

Jesus, if this is all true, then maybe I have the same ability as my mom. I could heal Lucy...

"Kit." River stood from his seat and came over to where I was sitting flabbergasted on the couch. Kneeling on the carpet in front of me, he took my hands in his and pinned me in place with his stunning golden eyes. "Kitten. We are in this with you one hundred percent. From here on out, I want you to understand that you can tell us anything, no matter how crazy it sounds in your head. Even if it's something as small as a fish tank spontaneously exploding at school."

I flicked a surprised glance at Austin, and he just shrugged.

"Yes, Austin told us about that, and I imagine there have been other weird things going on? So, from now on, let's just be open with each other, okay? We all only want what's best for you and will never do anything to put you in danger."

I looked around at everyone in the room, including Jonathan. "All of you?" The skepticism was thick in my question, but they all nodded and murmured their assent, even Austin.

"Okay, good." Jonathan interrupted our emotional

moment with a booming voice. "So, it sounds to me like you all have some work to do finding someone who survived the plague. Mr. Morgan, I expect to be kept in the loop at all times. Kit, can I have a word on my way out?"

I scrambled to my feet with a helping hand from River, then followed my guardian out of the house to where his chauffeur was still waiting in the driveway.

"I'm sorry to be leaving at a time like this, kiddo, but something urgent just came up. You'll be okay, though, won't you? I'm going to give Alpha Team an extended leave of absence to help you on this, and I will be speaking with your school about you taking the remainder of your classes via correspondence. I would just feel a lot better if you were protected around the clock." He was frowning at me as he spoke, and I smiled at his concern.

"I'll be fine, Jonathan. I will call you if I need anything, though." I reached up and gave him a quick hug, which was a little out of character for the two of us.

"Kit..." he added, right before getting into his car. "I know you're probably thinking about healing Lucy when you work out how to do it. I just want to urge you to think it through before you do anything rash. Remember what that woman said, that your mother healing those boys made them supernatural? Just consider whether that is really a choice you can take away from Lucy." I gaped at him, a little lost for words. I *hadn't* considered that.

"Anyway, I know you'll do the right thing. Love you, kiddo!" He smiled as he slid into his seat and pulled the door closed.

"Love you too," I murmured, watching his car pull away and trying to shake the weird feeling of unease at his abrupt departure in the middle of everything. When had this urgent thing suddenly come up? He had been in the same room with us the whole time and didn't take any calls... *Ugh, my brain hurts.*

Just as I was turning to head back inside, I heard the crunch of gravel under someone's shoes.

"Mr. Gregoric?" I called, not totally sure if it was him as his face was mostly in shadow. Our helicopter trip had used all of the daylight, so I was relying on the lights from the house to see.

"Kit. Nice to see you in one piece." He stepped closer and grinned at me with those overly sharp teeth of his.

"That's a pretty strange thing to say," I pointed out, taking a tiny step back from him. "What are you doing here, anyway? This is beyond inappropriate, you know."

"Of course," he said, pulling a folded piece of paper from the pocket of his ratty-looking sweatpants. "I just came to give you this."

I took it from him and unfolded it. "What is this?" I asked, holding it up. It looked like an address but with no name or explanation.

"An address." He grinned. "Now that you have heard Claudette's version of events, you might be interested in hearing a different side. Go there. Tell them N sent you."

"Hang on, you're 'N'? How do you know what Dupree told us? Who the fuck are you anyway?" The words were pouring out of me faster than the thoughts were coming, but he was walking away from me and towards the trees on the edge of the property.

"Wish I could stay and chat, but I have places to be! Good luck, Kit!" He saluted me and stepped behind one of the massive tree trunks, disappearing from sight.

"Hey! Come back!" I sped after him, but when I reached the place he had been standing, there was no sign of him. "More fucking weird shit; this just gets better and better," I muttered, trudging back up to the house holding the folded paper.

The light from the living room where the boys waited was pouring across the lawn, lighting it up just enough to see a bushy red fox dart across. I could have sworn it was the same fox that had been hanging around CFA, but I was no expert; foxes all looked the same, didn't they?

I had so many unanswered questions. A shout of masculine laughter echoed from within the house, and I smiled.

I also had a *team* of guys who had my back.

I'd accomplished a great deal with a whole lot less. Pivoting, I headed back inside.

Time to get to work.

TO BE CONTINUED

THE DRAGON'S WING
KIT DAVENPORT BOOK 2

I should have known my quest for vengeance would eventually be my downfall. I should have been more careful, more paranoid--but I'm glad I wasn't. Who knew that getting caught for my crimes would lead to so much happiness?

But joy can be fleeting...

It turns out, this battle is only just beginning. With ultimate power on the line, my faceless enemies will stop at nothing to capture me, dead or alive. I need to master my abilities, fast, or this could be the end for someone I care far too deeply about.

I'm Kit Davenport and this is going to be a bumpy flight.

About the Author

Oh, hello there! I see you would like to know more about me... Well here goes:

My illustrious literary career began in high school, with an epic tale about a kick ass heroine and her swoon worthy boyfriends, but was put on ice for a number of years while adult life happened. I moved across the ditch from my native New Zealand and met my now husband, we had a fur baby and then a real baby, we opened two bars and a restaurant, and then life came full circle and by a series of unfortunate events I uncovered a 'book' I had written as a fourteen year old. It was... atrocious. But it inspired me to begin again! And do it better this time... or at least I hope so...

With the skeptical support of my darling husband, our cherubic baby and a possessed cat, Kit Davenport came to life.

For more rambling, contact me directly! Here are all the fun places I can be stalked:

Facebook: shorturl.at/qstN6

Readers Group: shorturl.at/npv01

Twitter: shorturl.at/prvO3

Pinterest: shorturl.at/qI135

Instagram: shorturl.at/exzN6

Stay up to date with Tate James by signing up for her mailing list:

http://eepurl.com/dfFR5v

Website: https://www.tatejamesauthor.com

That's all for now! 😊

Ps. Thank you so much for buying/reading The Vixen's Lead. If you made it this far, it'd mean the world if you left a review on amazon! Peace, love and mungbeans xxx

Lightning Source UK Ltd.
Milton Keynes UK
UKHW040715070722
405457UK00011B/459